It Took A Rumor

Carter Ashby

Copyright © 2016 Carter Ashby

All rights reserved.

This is a work of fiction. Names, characters, businesses, places, events and incidents are either the products of the author's imagination or used in a fictitious manner. Any resemblance to actual persons, living or dead, or actual events is purely coincidental.

Digital Edition. Personal use rights only. No part of this publication may be sold, copied, distributed, reproduced or transmitted in any form or by any means mechanical or digital, including photocopying and recording, or by any information storage and retrieval system without the prior written permission of the publisher.

Cover Design by Pink Ink Design

http://www.pinkinkdesigns.com

Connect with the author

www.carterashby.com

ISBN: 153085363X

ISBN-13: 978-1530853632

To all my fellow writers. I gained a lot of encouragement and insight from you all on this one. Thank you!

Table of Contents

Prologue: Once upon a time... 1
Part 1: All the Secrets 7
Part 2: A Busy Sunday 95
Part 3: Tangled Webs 143
Part 4: Dire Consequences 185
Part 5: The Fall of Gideon Deathridge 225
Part 6: Everyone's Endings 297
Epilogue 349
Acknowledgments 359
About The Author 361

Prologue:
Once upon a time...

It was all over town that Ivy Turner was sleeping with one of the Deathridge brothers, only no one knew which one.

Myra Tidwell, the town social blogger, immediately set out to find answers. Armed with her iPhone, she typically used the location feature on Facebook and her connections with local business owners to track down her targets—in this case, Ivy herself. Myra drove a habanero orange VW bug, and frequently dressed in contrast with society's expectations for a woman her age. Today, that meant wearing a vintage midi-skirt swirled with floral patterns in turquoise and orange, a deep blue blouse, and an orange scarf. Her hair, long ago gone white, was pinned up in a twist, and her cunning eyes were hidden behind large, round sunglasses. On her lips she wore a smirk and a bright red lipstick.

The gossip industry was good.

She swerved her car into the parking lot of the local Walgreens, pulled up the camera function on her phone, and strutted in on heels the likes of which most women half her age couldn't pull off.

Ivy happened to be standing in the check-out aisle buying condoms. With a thrill of voyeuristic delight surging through her blood, Myra held up her phone. "Looks like you got a taste of something you like and are going back for more? Fair Grove is dying to know, Ivy…which Deathridge brother did you sample?"

Gossip was a harmless pursuit. Myra felt no compunction about subjecting the young woman to her first round of it. The girl was twenty-six, after all. How she'd remained under the radar this long was a mystery. Just look at her, in her uptight business clothes with her hair pulled back, too good to dress like the rancher that she was. Well, she apparently wasn't too good to sleep with one.

"Uh…um…uh…" was Ivy's response. Then she looked down at the condoms and shoved them behind her back. "These aren't for me. I swear."

Myra grinned and took her stammering as confirmation of the rumor's accuracy. Unfortunately, she wasn't able to get any further information out of the stunned young woman. A shame. But Myra's motto had always been, "If you don't tell me the truth, I'll just make something up."

Myra's next stop was the local watering hole, a rundown tavern where the farmers often had their drinks at the end of a long work day. Boone Deathridge, the youngest at twenty-five and the closest to Ivy's age, stood at the bar flirting with two women. He wore his muddy work boots, jeans, and a sleeveless tee. It didn't much matter what he wore, his baby face held all the allure of a piece of candy from a stranger in a creepy van. Myra adjusted the waistline of her skirt and approached him, iPhone set to record. "What's your response to the rumors? Were you the one slept with Ivy Turner last night?"

Boone grinned. "Did you see her walking today? 'Cause if you did, then it wasn't me."

It Took A Rumor

Myra shuffled backward, just slightly put off by his insinuation. Her profession notwithstanding, at the age of sixty-five, Myra considered herself a refined Southern lady. So what if she published salacious local gossip on the internet for a living? Gossip had a longstanding history in their town, and Myra walked with her head held high.

She moved on to Cody Deathridge who was sitting at a table with two other farmers, deep in discussion about…well…farming. "Cody, would you like to make a statement on the Ivy Turner scandal?"

Cody stood to his full height of well over six feet. He wore the trademark dark Deathridge looks well. His bright blue eyes set him apart from his brothers, and his slow, quiet demeanor earned him a reputation as the stand-up, solid citizen of the crew. "I do have a statement," he said, his low, raspy voice sexy enough to curl Myra's toes in spite of the age difference. "It ain't right her suddenly being treated like she done something wrong just because of some baseless rumors. And you oughtta be ashamed of yourself, Miss Myra." He tipped his cowboy hat and sat back down without another glance in her direction.

Myra sniffed and shuffled her way to the pool table in the back where the eldest two brothers were playing a game. Dallas was widely considered the playboy of the bunch, though he played the reputation down. He was easily the sexiest Deathridge, with dark hair and eyes, and a smile that would melt your panties right off. The tattoos covering his bare arms added to his bad-boy appeal. From what Myra could tell, he was the favorite in the "Which one did Ivy sleep with" poll. "Dallas? Care to confess?" Myra asked.

"Now you know you're the only woman for me, Miss Myra."

Myra wasn't above blushing. Actually she couldn't help it. But dignity demanded she keep pushing forward, so she turned to Jake.

The eldest Deathridge was more handsome than sexy. While the other three were broad shouldered and powerfully built, Jake had the same build as his father—long, lean, and rangy. He wore a dark brown Stetson and an air of authority that came from being the oldest and the sole heir to the property, though Myra could easily remember him as a boy egging houses on Halloween just like all the others. Still, Jake was a no-nonsense kind of guy, and the least likely suspect. However, Myra knew from years of experience in the gossip industry that it was often the least likely suspect who turned out guilty. "And you, Jake? Have you been having an affair with little Ivy Turner?"

Jake frowned and drew himself upright. "Are you recording this? Are you actually recording this? I do not give my permission for you to publish this on your blog."

Needless to say, Myra went home with no more knowledge on the subject than she'd started out with.

However, you wouldn't know that to watch her video blog the next morning.

Part 1: All the Secrets

Myra's Blog

...Obviously, there's something behind this rumor, and my feeling is that Ivy is most definitely guilty of sleeping with at least one of the brothers. And oh my, that certainly was a large box of...protection. Looks like whichever brother it was is likely to be seeing lots more of Ivy Turner.

But why should this be a big scandal? Well, let me give you a little history on the Turners and the Deathridges.

Gideon Deathridge has been refusing to sell his property to Jared Turner nigh on ten years now. If Jared wants to use his property on the other side of the Deathridge land, he has to march his cows down several miles of public highway. For reasons unbeknownst to myself or my sources, Gideon stubbornly refuses to cooperate with his neighbor. But I posit this query: Wouldn't he have to cooperate if that neighbor were his in-law?

So that's the question. Is Jared Turner attempting to perpetrate a good, old-fashioned mercenary marriage? Or has little Ivy Turner become the Juliet in the greatest love story of all time? What do you think? Leave your comments below, and don't forget to vote in our poll...

The video on Ivy's computer screen automatically started playing again. She sat there subjecting herself to repeated viewings of it. Obviously this was a form of self-flagellation, or maybe she was simply caught up in the entertainment value of her own life drama.

How had it come to this? A lifetime of model behavior flushed by Myra the Mouth. "Damn it," Ivy muttered as the video started its fourth replay.

"It'll blow over, sweetie. You gotta stop torturing yourself." Edna Ellis was the office manager at Turner Cattle Company the past twenty years, and the only remaining matriarchal influence in Ivy's life. Ivy briefly recalled her mother being friends with Clara Deathridge back when she was a young child, but in recent years, they must have drifted apart. For the most part, Penny Turner spent her time with ranch hands. Ergo, Ivy spent her time with ranch hands.

"I just can't believe this is happening. I can't believe people are so quick to believe something like this," Ivy said. She wanted to slam something closed, to symbolically shut Myra out of her life. But she was on the desktop computer in her workplace, so all she could do was click out of the browser. She made sure to click extra hard, though.

It wasn't enough that her good name was being dragged through the mud, that people she'd known since she was knee-high-to-a-grasshopper were looking at her like she'd suddenly morphed into a diseased whore…no, the worst part of it all was that the rumor happened to be

It Took A Rumor

true. But how had it gotten out? She'd been so very, very careful not to tell anyone. And it was hardly an affair. They'd had one momentary lapse in judgment. One illicit moment. Not even a very long moment, though one she'd regret until her dying day. Or at least she should. She should most definitely not be replaying it in her mind before bed every night.

"Just out of curiosity…" Edna started.

"Edna, don't you dare."

Edna laughed her husky smoker's laugh. "I'm only fooling. Everyone who knows you knows you're incapable of doing something like this. Trust me. It'll blow over."

How disappointed would Edna be if she knew the truth? Ivy was plenty disappointed in herself. She'd gone to all the trouble to get an advanced business degree, dress like a city girl, and even get herself a city boyfriend for a few years, and all for what? To throw herself at a filthy cowboy in a field in the middle of the day for no reason. Or at least no *good* reason. Her raging hormones and his damn charming appeal were not reasons to give up all semblance of civility and start doing it like animals in the great outdoors.

Ivy dropped her forehead onto her palms and groaned. How had they been caught? The whole thing had happened a week ago. Why were the rumors just now circulating? And why hadn't anyone identified which brother she'd been with? She knew *he* would never tell.

Those boys wouldn't dare do anything to upset their father, and that made Ivy—along with women who couldn't cook, clean, or bear children—strictly off limits. So where had this rumor come from?

"I'm going out for lunch, hun. The usual?" Edna asked.

"Yes, please," Ivy said. The screen door slammed shut behind Edna. Ivy got up to crank the air conditioner, a window unit with a near-deafening drone that had been driving her crazy ever since she took her mom's place here at the office a year ago.

Five minutes after Edna's departure, the front door opened again. Ivy saw the movement out of the corner of her eye. Hot air displaced the cold, which automatically put the new arrival on Ivy's shit list. She'd lost control of her reputation, couldn't she at least have control over her climate?

Ivy took in a deep breath, stood, and prepared to offer a professional greeting to whoever had just walked in. But as soon as the door closed fully and she saw who it was, her words died in her throat, replaced by a cold, creeping dread.

Gideon Deathridge. The patriarch himself.

He was tall, like his sons. He was a gritty, hard sort of man in his sixties. His sun-toughened skin was craggy, and his jaw was covered in silvery stubble. He squinted his eyes at you, whether or not there was sun. Ivy remembered being terrified of him as a child. Even then

It Took A Rumor

he'd had something of a grim reaper quality, like he was judging your very soul.

"Mr. Deathridge," Ivy said, forcing her voice low and steady. *There, that wasn't so hard. Just keep the voice low and steady. Of course you also have to breathe. Breathe, Ivy.* The next step was to extend her hand for a professional shake, keeping it steady the entire time. This took a great deal of willpower, but she managed it. Unfortunately, the old man merely looked at it in disgust. She dropped it back to her side. "My father isn't in right now, but—"

"I came to see you. I wanna know what game you're playing, and with which one of my boys you're playing it."

Low and steady. "Mr. Deathridge, I have no idea how these rumors began circulating, but I assure you they are baseless."

"That so? You think I ain't been wondering how long it was gonna take for your old man to sell you out? Only thing I don't know is if you're the type to let him do it. Are you, Ivy? Would you marry a man just to help your father's business?"

"No!" she said, a little louder than she'd meant to. "I absolutely would not marry for that reason. And I'm not in love with any of your sons." That much was true, at least. A flash in the pan was what that moment had been. No build up. No come down. Just one hot, crazy moment.

"But you're sleeping with one of them."

She swallowed. *Speak! Speak, damn you!*

Deathridge saw the hesitation, and his eyes narrowed.

Ivy threw her shoulders back and her chin up. "Mr. Deathridge, this is the 21st century. People don't need reasons to sleep with each other. They just do it and move on. If...If, Mr. Deathridge...If I was having sex with one of your sons, I give you my word that it would have nothing to do with business."

His eyes narrowed as they bored into hers. The moment stretched. A trickle of sweat dripped down the center of Ivy's back, the air conditioner roared in the background, and somewhere in the distance, Ivy was certain, a lone hawk screamed into the vast and vacant sky.

At last Deathridge stepped back. "Your mother was a good woman," he said. "A fine woman. And I don't think she'd have raised a liar. So I'll take your word, and I won't bother with this no more. But if I find out my trust is misplaced, young woman, don't think for one instant you or your money-grubbing father are getting so much as a square foot of my property. I'll disown whichever one of those boys you've got your hooks in long before I'd let you all ruin my ranch."

He turned on his booted heel and marched out the door. Another rush of hot, summer air blew in. It felt like a promise from hell, and at the moment, it was nothing compared to the fire in her own gut. To be accused of basically being a whore and then to have her momma's memory exploited—it was simply inexcusable. Insulting and undeserved. Hadn't she done good in the community? Hadn't she been a model citizen and an example to young women throughout the town? The old bastard had a lot of nerve talking to her like that.

Time resumed its normal march and Ivy spun around, looking for something to hit or throw. Her search took too long, and by the time she wrapped her fingers around the stapler, she'd calmed down.

"Damn Myra," she muttered, sitting back down to her computer to do some work. She resisted the urge to punish herself by watching the video any more.

The Deathridge dinner table was a quiet place, that night. Only the clinking of forks on China, ice on glass, and knives on forks in an arrhythmic symphony that normally did Clara's heart good—it meant her boys were eating well—but tonight did little to alleviate the disturbed curiosity plaguing her soul. Gideon sat at the head of the rectangular, raw wood table. Clara, sat at the other end, a forced smile on her plump, cheerful face. And in between, their four grown sons. Jake directly to Gideon's right, Dallas to his left.

Gideon cast frequent scowls at each of his sons. Clara made several attempts to start conversation, but they always resulted in monosyllables from her men. She figured this had something to do with little Ivy Turner. Of course, Ivy wasn't so little anymore. Clara could remember a time when she was a chubby, curly-haired toddler running between her momma and Clara as the two women knitted and chatted. There'd been times that Clara had been deeply envious of Penny Turner, having a sweet little girl she could buy pretty dresses for and teach how to cook and bake and sew. Boys were a gift from God, but one didn't receive much affection from them, especially when their father disdained affection in men and expected his boys to behave as tough as him.

Ivy had turned twenty-six. Had a college degree in business management. And until recently, quite a positive reputation around town. Clara felt bad for her. She wasn't convinced there was any truth to the rumors. If there was, she was certain her youngest, Boone, was to blame. In

It Took A Rumor

fact, she might have voted in Myra Tidwell's online poll, though she certainly wouldn't confess to it.

Clara glanced at Boone. He was halfway through his steak, eating with gusto the same as his brothers. Surely a guilty conscience would lead to a loss of appetite. Then again, maybe not with these particular men.

Suddenly, Gideon slammed his fists on the table. "All right," he growled. "Which one of you's is it?"

Clara flinched and all four boys looked at their father. "Which one of us is what?" asked Dallas, the smart-ass of the crew.

"You know damn well what I'm talking about. Which one of you boys is screwing around with Ivy?"

Clara might have intervened in an attempt at making peace, but she was too busy watching facial expressions and trying to determine if the rumor was true...and if so, which one of her boys was the guilty party. Jake and Cody both frowned at their father. Boone smirked. Dallas laughed. "I wish I was screwing around with Ivy," Dallas said. "That girl has the best ass in town."

"Great rack, too," Boone said.

Cody cleared his throat. "I don't think it's right, talking about her like this. She's always been a real upstanding woman, and now there's some rumors and we're all treating her like she's some whore. It ain't right."

"Ha," Dallas said. "That proves it. You're fucking her, aren't you?"

"Language," Jake muttered involuntarily. Being the oldest, he'd early on learned to parrot his mother's rebukes. Clara wasn't sure he even knew he'd said it. He was busy frowning down at his plate.

"Jake, honey?" she asked. "What do you think?"

He looked up at her. "'Bout Ivy? I guess I think none of us would be stupid enough to mess around with her so I don't really know why we're having this conversation. Some old gossips in town probably saw when me and her had that business breakfast a week back...which you told me to go to, Pop, if you'll recall." He looked to Gideon who nodded grudgingly. "I reckon that's likely where all this is coming from."

"But the rumors aren't about you and Ivy," Gideon said. "They're about Ivy and 'one of my sons.' If folks thought it was you, why wouldn't they just say so?"

Jake shrugged.

Gideon sighed. "All right, just each of you boys look me in the eye and tell me you ain't with her and I'll leave it be. But don't lie to me. Ain't never had a problem with my sons lying to me."

He looked first at Boone, whose expression had sobered. "I swear, Pop. I ain't been with Ivy."

Dallas said, "I ain't been with Ivy."

Cody said, "I swear. I never been with Ivy."

Jake said, "I've never been with Ivy."

Gideon gave them each a once-over. And then he nodded and went back to finishing his dinner. Clara relaxed. Her boys wouldn't lie. So the rumors must be just that.

The Turner's ranch hands ate their dinner in the bunk house. The Turner dinner table was family only. It was rectangular, but small. Ivy's father, Jared, sat at the head of the table, closest to the wall. Her mother had always sat at the opposite end, closest to the kitchen. And Ivy had sat on the side. She couldn't identify at what point she'd assumed her mother's spot at the table, but she noticed it that evening.

"When did I move to Mom's chair?" she muttered.

"What's that?" Jared asked over a mouthful of steamed broccoli.

"Nothing. Do you like the chicken?"

"Kind of bland."

"That's what your heart wants, Daddy. Bland food. Don't insult the cook."

Jared smiled as he took another bite. "Myra Tidwell paid me a visit this morning."

"For God's sake, does she never stop?"

"How are you holding up?"

Ivy didn't want to talk about it. She had an MBA and single-handedly ran the business side of the ranch, a job that had formerly belonged to her mother. And since taking over the work, Ivy had managed to grow their business in terms of productivity and profitability. She'd proven herself adept at increasing efficiency as well as sales and marketing. Until yesterday, she walked with her head held high. "I'm rather pissed, if you must know."

Jared chuckled. "Well, you ought to conduct your affairs with more discretion."

Heat flooded her cheeks. She opened her mouth to defend herself, but thankfully she remembered that her father didn't know—couldn't have known—of her little folly. He was only teasing her, of course. She forced a laugh and said, "I was overcome with desire."

Jared shook his head. "The idea of my girl going after a cowboy...everyone in this town knows you don't swing that way. Why would they lend credence to this stuff?"

"People love juicy gossip, that's all. It'll pass."

"I just hate to see your name dragged through the mud. I know how much your reputation means to you."

Ivy shrugged. "It'll pass." There really wasn't any more to say on the subject.

But then Jared looked up, making eye contact for the first time since they'd sat down. "I want you to know, if it turned out you did like one of those boys—"

"Dad, please. Come on. I've got a city-girl soul. I'm not interested in cowboys, you just said so yourself."

"Now we both know that's bullshit. You *want* to have a city-girl soul, but you're a hundred percent country stock, through and through."

Am not, am not, am not. Ivy worked up her coldest glare.

Jared sighed. "I know you say you don't want a cowboy, I just want you to know...it wouldn't bother me.

Your mother and I were both so proud of the woman you've become. We were at ease. I trust you to make your own decisions."

Ivy clenched her teeth against the brief pang of sadness in her throat before nodding. "Thank you, Daddy."

He smiled and went back to eating. Ivy exhaled slowly, relaxing now that the conversation had passed. Open-minded or not, Ivy hoped her father never found out what she'd done, and with whom she'd done it.

It Took A Rumor

Genetics had obviously been good to the Deathridge boys. So much so that three of them took it for granted. Jake barely glanced up when women made passes at him. Cody had a collection of polite rejection lines he cycled through. Dallas didn't go out unless he wanted to get laid, at which point he went to a bar, picked out a woman like a puppy in a pet shop, and took her home.

Boone didn't understand any of them. Maybe it was because he was the youngest. He'd watched the others go before him and wanted what they'd had. And maybe it was because he was the only late bloomer among them. Sixteen came, then seventeen. Eighteen. Nineteen. Yes, he, Boone Deathridge, brother to Dallas Deathridge of the infamous School Nurse Affair scandal, didn't lose his virginity until he was twenty.

It hadn't been for lack of trying. He'd mimicked every one of his brothers' moves in his attempt to score. At the age of twenty, quite by accident, he finally learned that valuable life lesson that everyone must realize in order to reach self-actualization: be yourself.

At a loud, smoke-filled party, Boone had looked around the room at the women he usually made passes at, the kinds of women his brothers went for, the kinds of women who rejected Boone roundly and regularly; something inside of him had despaired. A voice had said to him, "You'll never have that." He'd given up.

He'd been about to leave when he noticed a young girl, likely fresh out of high school, hovering in the corner, smiling at her friend, but glancing around shyly. The girl looked sweet and innocent. Normally Boone's eyes would have passed right over her, but in that moment, he'd paused to look a little closer. Nothing wrong with the girl. Underneath her demure sundress and cardigan, she had a pretty nice body. A spark ignited inside of Boone, something he would later come to recognize as the spark of inspiration. Likely Michaelangelo had felt it when he'd first picked up a paint brush, or Beethoven when he'd first touched a piano. Boone saw this girl and realized he'd been going after the wrong prey. He'd been using the wrong tools. Sure, Jake and Cody could act like they didn't care and have women falling at their feet; and Dallas could act like he was doing a girl a favor talking to her; but Boone didn't have that kind of prowess. He had a sweet face and a non-threatening air about him. That night, instead of seeing those attributes as weakness, he'd chosen to turn them to his advantage.

He'd approached the nice looking girl and struck up friendly conversation. He hadn't leered, but instead had bashfully offered her compliments, giving a little something, and then pulling back so as not to come off predatory or desperate. He'd dropped little bread crumbs of seduction, just hints at a time, camouflaged under a veneer of mostly fake innocence, until the girl had followed him out the door and into the back of his car.

Now, five years later, Boone still remembered that night as the best of his life. The most amazing thing about the whole situation had been that the girl had moved away a week later, making it easy for him to shake her off.

It Took A Rumor

Other women over the years had proved more challenging, and his one regret, now that he looked back on it, was that he hadn't planned better for how to get his conquests to move on. The trouble with preying on nice girls was that they were all very commitment-oriented, and nowadays, Boone had a rather bad reputation as a wolf in sheep's clothing.

Which was probably why so many people thought he'd been sleeping with Ivy. He had a meeting with Ivy that night, only an hour after the dinner where he and his brothers had solemnly sworn that they were up to no bad. Boone reflected on those promises. Jake and Cody would be telling the truth. If they swore they weren't fucking Ivy, then that was that. But Dallas was lying. Maybe not about Ivy, but he was lying about something. Just like Boone was.

He drove down the highway that sprawled between Deathridge and Turner property, reflecting on the fact that an informal poll on the Fair Grove Times Facebook page (run by Myra Tidwell) had Dallas beating out Boone as the suspected lover by about twenty votes. It was an insult. Ivy was not the kind of ass that Boone couldn't get. He could easily have her if he wanted her. She just happened to be the one woman, besides his dear mother, whom he respected.

He made a left down a dirt road—barely a road—that led down the fence line between the two properties. He drove past fields on either side and down to the tree line where he put the truck in park and waited. A minute later, he heard the distant buzz of an ATV engine. A moment later, Ivy topped the ridge, coming into view with her long, blond hair flying out behind her, and dark sunglasses on despite the dimming of the evening light.

Boone got out of the truck, leaned against it, and waited until she parked and turned off the motor. She swung her leg over and approached, hand-extended.

Boone was used to her formal behavior. She'd always had the manners of a southern gentleman.

"Boone," she said by way of greeting, and offering him a firm handshake over the fence rail.

"Ivy. Thanks for coming."

"Sure."

He looked her up and down. Jeans and a t-shirt for a change, but still nothing that would excite his fancy. Maybe if she dressed like a country girl once in a while he might have put some truth to those rumors. But then again, no. Even as pleased with himself as he was, Boone still knew that Ivy deserved better than him. "How are you holding up?" he asked.

She hooked her thumbs in her jeans and glanced out at the sun. "That why you called? See how I'm holding up?"

"I do kind of feel like this is my fault."

She cocked her head. He couldn't see her eyes through the glasses. "How do you figure?"

He shrugged. "Molly did use your truck to meet me at the hotel last night. I mean, maybe that's where this rumor is coming from."

Her lips pressed together. "You're a pig."

"Hey, she's a big girl."

Ivy shook her head and looked away. "I don't know. If that's where the rumor is coming from, then I'm screwed. I can't rat her out."

"I just want you to know I'm real sorry, and to thank you for, you know, keeping me and Molly's secret."

She turned her face back to him. He assumed she was looking at him, but again, it was hard to tell. "Just do me a favor and if people ask you if you're fucking me, be honest and tell them no. No more joking around."

"Sure. Of course, Ivy. And maybe I can make a statement on Myra's Facebook page or something."

Ivy waved her hand. "Just...answer 'no' if anyone asks. Otherwise, leave it alone. Maybe it'll blow over, soon, and people will quit treating me like the whore of Babylon."

Boone hated to hear this. She'd never done anything to deserve that sort of disrespect. Even if she had slept with one of his brothers, she didn't deserve this. He frowned, this new thought occurring to him.

Had she?

He hadn't even entertained the idea since this was Ivy Turner, professional to a T. Suddenly, he couldn't help cracking a grin. "You know, I assumed this was on me and Molly, but…have you? Did you?"

Ivy's cheeks turned red and she lifted her chin. "Have I, did I, what, Boone?"

"You know what."

"I can't believe you have the nerve to stand there and ask me if I've slept with one of your brothers. You've known me all your life, and you ask me something like this? Have you no respect?"

The wicked notion died like a frostbit flower, and Boone lowered his head. "Aw, Ivy, I was just teasing. Don't take offense, okay?"

She eased back, her shoulders relaxing. "Sure. I'm just sick of the insult, you know? I had a boyfriend for over two years and no one treated me like a slut for sleeping with him."

"Maybe everyone assumed you'd be waiting for marriage."

Her eyebrows went up. "Do you think? Do you think that's what people assume about me?"

He shrugged. "Yeah, I figure. Because you're so upstanding, you know."

"So if an upstanding woman has a one-night-stand, she's automatically a whore?"

He laughed and looked away. "Ain't my rules, Ivy. Blame society."

She grumbled something and turned back to her bike. "Are we done here?" she asked.

"Yeah, except…"

She climbed astride the ATV. "Except what?"

"Except…tomorrow night. Molly wants to meet again, and—"

"And can she use my truck?" Ivy laughed. "Can I cover for her again? You seriously came here for that, even after you just said that you thought this might be responsible for the rumors ruining my reputation."

"I think I'm in love," he lied.

She snorted. "You're so full of shit." She started up the bike.

"Ivy? Will you cover for us?"

She pulled the sunglasses up to the top of her head and hit him with her beautiful, blue eyes. "She's my best friend."

Unfortunately, that was all the answer he would get. Ivy backed her bike up and drove away. He watched after her, hoping she would come through for him. With any luck, this affair could last quite a while. He didn't think he would tire of Molly very soon.

Pastor Allen had originally been a missionary. He was in Papua New Guinea for a while, and then Tanzania. Twice a year, a bus arrived full of American college students from Christian universities that helped sponsor his mission work. Two years ago, a beautiful young woman with honey-colored hair and sweet, wide eyes had stepped off the bus and stolen his heart. They'd married immediately and when her classmates returned home, she'd stayed with him.

He'd been foolish. The girl was young and her passion for missions untested, so that after a year, when her passion died like a malnourished sprout, she began complaining. Pastor Allen loved his wife, though, and would therefore withhold nothing from her. As much as he wanted to spread the word of God to those who had little or no access to it on their own, the Bible had strong words about how a husband was to treat a wife.

Fortunately, the pastor at the community church in his wife's hometown of Fair Grove was retiring, leaving an opening. Richard Allen had sent his audition video as well as a letter from his wife. He'd received an invitation to try out, two weeks later. Two weeks after that, he had a job.

They'd been in Fair Grove for three months, now. At first, his beautiful young bride had barely seemed to improve. Nothing he did made her happy. But she'd taken a turn, recently, for the better. Now he sat in his study, listening to her bustle about the house, humming and singing to herself. He smiled and counted himself a lucky man.

His wife popped her head in the door of his study and greeted him with a bright, dimply smile. "I hope you don't mind, but I'm going to spend the evening with Ivy, after dinner. She's having a really hard time."

"Of course, Molly. You're a good friend. Tell her if she needs anyone to talk to, I'll be happy to listen and offer counsel."

She bobbed her head and went back to her housework.

"Don't do this," Ivy implored. She sat on the edge of her four-poster bed that she'd meticulously made up that morning, same as every morning of her life, minus the few years she'd spent living in college dorms. Even then, she'd always been a tidy person.

Molly was letting down her hair and fixing her makeup in front of the vanity mirror over Ivy's cherrywood dresser. She'd come over a little before sundown. "It's Boone Deathridge. For four, miserable high school years he didn't even know I existed. I have to do this."

She'd already done it, was the thing. Molly had had her night with Boone, and Ivy, as much as she hated the whole situation, had been willing to cover for her friend that once. It hadn't occurred to her that the affair would continue.

Ivy smoothed the soft, worn comforter beneath her hands, more to comfort herself than to straighten any wrinkles. The pink, floral pattern had faded long ago, now a shabby image of its former self, almost sepia. But Ivy wouldn't replace it. She had fond memories of decorating this room with her mother. From the eyelet lace window dressings that were once pure white, to the floral wallpaper that they'd fought over—at the age of twelve, Ivy had thought it Victorian and classic while her mother found it stuffy and old-fashioned—her mother's memory infused the room.

Molly's thick, soft-brown hair fell into a natural wave. If Ivy were a vain woman, she'd have been jealous.

Molly was tall with a figure that could only be described as dignified. She seriously looked like the cover model for a 1950's copy of Good Housekeeping.

There had to be something she could say to convince Molly not to cheat on her husband again. She was Molly's best friend by default, the other friends driven off by Molly's selfish, narcissistic behaviors. And frankly, as secure as Ivy was as a daughter, a business manager, and a citizen, she did feel a little weak in the friendship department, and Molly's attention made her feel good.

Truth be told, Ivy didn't have any other girlfriends. Growing up, she'd spent most of her free time on the ranch with the men. She went to college, worked hard, and by the time she got back home, most of the girls she'd gone to high school with had married and begun families. It wasn't that that precluded them from being Ivy's friend, it was just that they seemed to look at her with distrust once she'd arrived home in her business clothes with her business degree. She'd set herself apart by choosing career over family, as if one couldn't have both, and was therefore outside their sphere of interest.

Molly was the one exception, probably because her bad attitude and behavior had driven everyone else away. And probably partly because she was a preacher's wife, which always held with it a sort of social exile. Regardless, Ivy was grateful for Molly's friendship. It made her feel a little less pathetic.

"Richard is a good man," Ivy said lamely.

"Richard is a good man," Molly agreed. "And I love him. But I need this. I knew the moment Boone turned those heat-filled eyes of his my direction that there was no quenching this urge except to be with him. It'll run its course and Richard will be none the wiser. We'll all live happily ever after."

Shit, what was she supposed to say to that? It was so delusional and yet so straight-forward. "Well at least don't meet at the same hotel."

"What other hotel is there? This is Fair Grove."

"Go one or two towns over. Eldridge. Oak Bluff. Anywhere but here."

"It's not a big deal. I'll have your truck and the night manager doesn't know us. We're being careful, trust me."

Did the woman not even think about the consequences of her actions? Even barring the infidelity sending her straight to hell, what about how it was affecting Ivy? If indeed their first rendezvous had been the start of the rumors, then Molly might consider Ivy's feelings. Hell, Boone had at least had the decency to own up to his part in it, though it didn't seem to be stopping from continuing in sin.

Ivy sank back on her bed. It was an abuse of her friendship, wasn't it? Molly stood there preening, not a care in the world. "You know, my truck parked next to Boone's truck outside that hotel…that's probably where Myra got this idea that I was sleeping with one of them."

"Oh, psh." Molly fluffed her hair in the mirror. "Myra's an equal opportunity gossiper. She tells stories about everyone."

"Don't blow this off. It's a big deal to me."

With a long-suffering sigh, Molly came and sat on the edge of the bed. She took Ivy's hands. "I'm sorry an old hag no one listens to is defaming your good name. But why don't you just acknowledge it? So what? Say you slept with Dallas, he sleeps with everyone. That's the secret to gossip. Once you put the truth out there, it stops being interesting."

"That wouldn't be the truth. It would be a lie. Because I haven't slept with Dallas."

"So make the lie a truth and sleep with him. What's the harm? He's hot. He'll do it. Then you can go forward in church on Sunday, repent of your sin, and be welcomed back into the community. No big deal."

"You're a very different person than me."

"Don't be a bitch. You know it's more fun being me than you."

"I can forgo the kind of fun that hurts people."

Molly threw her hands up and returned to the mirror, taking up her eyeliner. "You should have married the preacher. You'd both have a lot of fun up there, the sole occupiers of the moral high ground."

It was on the tip of her tongue to tell her to fuck off, but Molly gathered her things, blew her a kiss in the mirror, and left.

Of course it was appalling what Molly was doing. It left Ivy mildly nauseous and continually desiring a shower, not that a shower could wash away this kind of dirt. But the worst part was that Molly was right. She really did have more fun. Not that Ivy approved of her kind of fun, but she did kind of, maybe, just a little bit wish she could cut loose for a little while. Just stop being the person she was and carry on a reckless affair.

How unfair was it that she couldn't even enjoy the memory of her one, reckless moment without having her personal life plastered all over Myra's blog? Yet Molly got to continue an affair of far more scandalous proportions without getting caught or gossiped about.

She closed her eyes. It was for the best. She wouldn't want him anyway, at least not long term anyway. She might like to feel his strong, calloused hands skimming up her breasts one more time. Maybe more than once.

But she wasn't Molly. She had a conscience. Values. And frankly, she was too busy with work to bother with an affair right now anyway. And that was the absolute truth.

It Took A Rumor

The great thing about Jake was that he didn't let his ego get in the way of shoveling shit.

Dallas found him in the horse stalls the morning after they'd all promised their father that they hadn't been screwing Ivy Turner. Dallas had taken extra care to study Jake's features during that moment because, if the rumor had been true, he was pretty sure Jake was the one she'd pick. And Jake not being one for lying, he surely would have shown a twitch or a bead of sweat or something. Nope. Cool as a cucumber, that Jake. So for the most part, Dallas believed him. For the most part, Dallas didn't really care. He was there this morning seeking out his older brother for the purpose of betraying him.

Which would have been so much easier if Jake weren't such a stand-up guy.

The temperature was down from the day before. They were in for a cool spell, oddly low temperatures for August. Dallas always felt the weather changes in a way that the other men in his family didn't seem to. Maybe he was more sensitive. Maybe he wasn't cut out for the outdoors. He had a bit of a fever-chill when he approached his brother.

"You couldn't get Boone to do that?" Dallas asked.

Jake turned, startled. "Couldn't find the little shit. It's his turn."

"So leave it until he shows up."

Jake snorted and went back to work. The idea of putting off a chore was anathema to Jake. Dallas couldn't understand it. Horse shit was a never-ending encumbrance...why hurry to clean it up? "Wanted to talk about you and Ivy."

Jake turned a little faster this time, his brow furrowed. "Huh?"

Still not a total guilt-reaction. If Jake had lied about fucking Ivy, he'd definitely be showing more reaction. "The meeting from last week?"

"Yeah? What about it?" Jake replied, still cool and calm.

"What did she say?"

Jake shrugged. "She made an offer. Tried to convince me to convince Pop that they'd maintain the integrity of our ranch and—"

"Yeah, but how much are they offering?"

Jake sighed and shoveled some soiled straw into a wheelbarrow. "Half a million for the land. Another quarter for the business."

Dallas had to fight to keep from reaching for his chest. His heart thundered. Split five ways, that gave him a hundred fifty grand. Of course, it wouldn't be five ways. The land belonged to Gideon and after him, to Jake. So Dallas wouldn't see any of that. But still, the quarter million would be split five ways, which meant fifty thousand. More than enough to get him the hell out of Oklahoma and started somewhere bigger. Better. He could get a college degree. A job in a suit in a high rise building. A girlfriend who sipped champagne instead of beer, wore heels instead of boots, smelled like expensive perfume rather than ordinary, everyday shampoo.

"I don't guess the old man would hear the offer?" Dallas asked.

This time when Jake turned, there was anger in his eyes. "Would you? It's bullshit. You can't put a price on family, Dallas. Old Man Turner ought to know that by now."

Dallas shrugged. "I guess when it comes down to it, it's not a lot of money considering we'd all have to find new jobs."

"That was part of the offer. We'd stay on as hired hands. On our own fucking land, can you believe the nerve?"

"You're telling me they're offering all that money and jobs? Would we get to keep living in the house?"

"Yeah. They said they'd deed off the land with the houses on it. Mighty generous of them." Jake spat and shoveled. "You might grab a shovel if you're just gonna stand around gabbing, man."

Dallas was not grabbing a shovel. He took a step back. "I don't understand why the old man wouldn't at least listen to an offer like that. Doesn't sound like it would change our lives that much."

Jake stopped, again, and gawped at Dallas.

"What?" Dallas asked, hoping to sound and look innocent.

"You don't seriously think we should consider it, do you? This is our livelihood. Granddad built this with his own two hands. He sweated and bled for this land. You think you can put a price on that?"

Dallas knew for damn sure he could put a price on it. But he wasn't about to say so to Jake who looked just about to deck him. "Of course not," Dallas said, backing away a little more. "It's just they ain't gonna give up. Old Man Turner is stubborn as a mule. And that little bitch of his is a real bulldog."

Before he could even register what was happening, Jake dropped his shovel, lunged at Dallas, and swung his fist. Dallas' head whipped to the side and he stumbled backward, nearly falling. His ears rang and his jaw ached, but once he recovered his balance, he was grinning ear-to-ear. Jake stood there, shoulders squared off, chest heaving with deep, fast breaths. "Wow," Dallas said. "Kinda sensitive about little Ivy, ain't ya?"

"I'm just trying to knock some sense into you. This ranch is our life. You'd best remember that."

"Oh, I'll remember that. And I'll remember not to call Ivy a bitch anymore."

"Call her whatever you want." He turned to retrieve his shovel. "Just don't do it around me. She might be trying to destroy everything we love in this world, but she's still a lady."

"Yes, sir, gentleman Jake, sir," Dallas said with a mock salute. As he walked away, his laughter faded in the wake of the conundrum before him. How to get Gideon to sell the property. And how to keep his hands clean doing it.

"Turner Cattle Company," Ivy said into the office phone. She shifted in her seat, stretching her black pencil skirt a little further down her thighs. The morning was a little cooler than expected, and she wished she'd worn slacks.

"Ivy, dear."

Ivy no longer needed the slacks as the sound of Myra's voice made her blood boil. "Yes, Ms. Tidwell, what can I do for you?" she said through her tightly clenched teeth.

"I just wanted to inform you that I'll be publishing the latest reports of your exploits. I don't suppose you care to tell me which of the brothers you spent last night with?"

"None of them, Myra."

Myra laughed, a throaty, sophisticated, utterly arrogant sound. "Oh, dearest. If you want to keep your affairs secret, you really ought not to conduct them in the only motel in town."

Damn Molly!

Damn Boone!

"It's nobody's business."

"Of course it is. We're a community, aren't we? We concern ourselves with each other's lives. It's called love."

Such bullshit! Ivy felt her nostrils flaring like a bull about to charge. "I disagree. I wish you would just leave me alone."

"I'm sorry you feel that way. I'll give you one more chance to weigh-in, and then I'm publishing."

Ivy didn't even consider spilling Molly's secrets. Molly was married. There was a huge difference between a single girl fornicating and the preacher's wife having an affair. So she said, "I've got nothing to say."

Almost as soon as she hung up the phone, the office door opened. Ivy lifted her head in hopes of seeing Edna returning with coffee and pastries. It was hard not to stress-eat when your reputation was being dragged through the mud all because of your misplaced loyalty to an increasingly selfish friend.

But it wasn't Edna. Waltzing in the door like he owned the place, with absolutely no concern as to what people might say, was Dallas Deathridge. He flashed a charming smile and turned his ball cap backwards before reaching out for a handshake.

Ivy composed herself, stood, and took his hand. She leaned to the side to see out the window. "I see you rode Storm Shadow." Storm Shadow was a buttermilk buckskin whose coloring was uniquely stark. The white of his body was pure against the ebony black of his mane and tail. He'd won some trophies in horse shows in his time. As a result, most folks around town knew him by name. More importantly, they knew he belonged to Dallas.

"Aw, don't worry, Ivy. I'm sure no one will see him here."

There wasn't typically a whole lot of traffic down the highway outside her office, but at that moment a car passed by. Followed by two trucks. She arched a brow at Dallas. He shrugged as if it were of no concern to him. "What do you want?" Ivy asked.

Dallas's cocky half-grin would have made a weaker woman's knees buckle. But Ivy's knees had done enough buckling lately.

Dallas said, "I want to know whose bright idea it was to seduce Jake. Yours? Or your old man's?"

Her knees buckled. She covered it by taking a step back, folding her arms over her chest, and arching both brows. "I don't know if you've been keeping up with Myra the Mouth's blog…but I've taken quite a lot of unjustified shit because of you boys. Why do you feel the need to add on to it?"

Dallas ducked his head, his grin vanishing. He hooked his thumbs in his pockets and shuffled his feet. "Yeah, you're right, Ivy. I'm sorry."

"Good. Now, is that why you came in?"

"No, ma'am."

The 'ma'am' relaxed her. She dropped her arms to her sides and dried her palms against her skirt.

"I came in because…because…" he took a deep breath, met her eyes, and said, "I wanna sell."

A laugh escaped her lips. "Sell what? You don't have anything I want, Dallas."

"Yeah. Yeah, I know that, Ivy. But...Jake told me about your offer. The money. The jobs. It just seems more than fair, that's all."

"More than fair." She tasted the words. Frowned. Nodded. "Yes. I agree. Unfortunately, you're the wrong brother. And the right one is as stubborn as his father. So, what is it you think you can do for me?"

"I think I can find a weakness. I mean, the ranch is doing fine...it's definitely worth what you're offering, so, don't get me wrong..."

Ivy smiled. She could feel the smile on her lips. The predatory rictus of it. The primal satisfaction of the smell of blood. The whetting of the appetite. It was all she could do not to lick her lips.

"...But," Dallas continued, "there's not a lot of room for error. I mean, one bad year and we'd be in pretty deep shit. What I mean is, with the six of us, we don't have any extra. Money's tight. So..."

Ivy cocked her head and waited. Dallas wasn't the sharpest Deathridge by a mile. But he might be useful.

"The thing is, I think I can convince him."

"Do you, now?" Ivy sank back into her chair and crossed her legs, not bothering to tug her skirt down when it rode up her thighs. Dallas' gaze dropped for a moment before bouncing back up to her eyes.

"Yeah. And, if I do, then I want more money."

"Oh, really?" She didn't bother masking her amusement. "Exactly how much do you think your assistance is worth?"

"An additional fifty grand."

"No kidding? You think you've got something worth that?"

"The fact is, Ivy, I want the fuck out of this town. And I'm about to take a risk for you that might just get me cut off from the family funds. So...I'm going to need money. Just something to get me started."

Ivy bit her bottom lip in thought. Dallas wanted out? Where exactly did he think he was going to go? The man had "farm boy" written all over him. He was over thirty. It had probably never occurred to anyone in his family that he wasn't content working the ranch. "How long have you been wanting to leave the ranch?"

Dallas sighed and dropped his head back. "For as long as I can remember."

Another car drove by outside, the hum of its tires barely penetrating the noise of the window air-conditioning unit. Ivy tapped her fingernails on the arms of her chair. "I'd be willing to shake on fifty-grand. But only if you can prove you're actually helping me. I don't want lightning to strike all your cattle dead and you come to me taking credit for it. Understand?"

Dallas nodded. "Yes, ma'am."

"And just to be clear, you're talking about convincing your old man to sell, right? You're not planning sabotage or anything? Because we want the ranch in tact."

"Of course. I mean, yeah. No sabotage. I'm just going to talk to him."

Ivy studied him for a moment longer before standing and extending her hand. "Deal."

Dallas hesitated. "Are…are you authorized to make this deal? I mean, how do I know you're not just blowing smoke?"

"You're insulting my integrity now?"

"No. Of course not, Ivy, it's just…"

She dropped her hand. "You came to me. I can take or leave this deal without much care or concern. You want to get paid for helping us get what we want, then I'm in. Otherwise, get the hell off our property before someone sees your horse outside and jumps to the wrong conclusion."

Dallas gulped and extended his hand. Ivy shook it. "Deal," he said.

She smiled, thanked him, and watched as he left the building, mounted his horse, and rode away. She wouldn't get her hopes up too high. But if Dallas could end this cold war between her father and his, it would be worth a finder's fee of fifty thousand.

It occurred to her that she'd become the unofficial guardian of the Deathridge brothers' secrets. Well, all except for Cody, who probably didn't have any.

It Took A Rumor

Cody had a secret.

He walked, cutting through the fields to the fence that separated his family's property from the Turner's. He always took walks in the evenings after dinner. But recently, his destination had changed. Instead of aimlessly wandering, enjoying the crickets and the cool evening breezes, he was headed to an old barn the Turners hadn't bothered to tear down. His heart raced, his blood buzzing so loudly he couldn't hear those night sounds he usually enjoyed so much.

The sun still hovered over the horizon as Cody approached the barn. No sign of anyone there, but then, there wouldn't be. The person he was going to meet would be discreet.

Cody walked inside and stopped in the light of the doorway. Streaks of dust-filled sunshine criss-crossed through open slats in the roof and broken boards in the wall. Light and shadows painted the room and the young man standing in the middle of it.

"I didn't think you'd come," said the man, his voice barely a whisper.

"Said I would, didn't I?" Cody replied.

The man wiped his palms along the thighs of his worn jeans. Jordan Shaw was the newest ranch-hand for Jared Turner. The kid was only nineteen, but hard work had shaped his body into that of a full-grown man. He was lean and almost as tall as Cody, with fair hair and hazel eyes. Cody's mouth watered at the sight of him.

They'd met at the bar. Cody and his brothers had no problem hanging out with the Turner's ranch hands so long as Gideon didn't find out. Cody had been shooting pool with a worker named Reno when Jordan had walked in. The connection had been instant. They'd had beer together for weeks before Cody got up the nerve to invite him for a ride. They'd gone out in his truck and made out for hours.

It had been two months since they'd first met. This was their third hookup in the past week.

He approached Jordan, who stood still, likely overwhelmed with some combination of fear, anticipation, and lust. Their first time together, Jordan claimed was his first time ever, and Cody believed him simply because of how the kid had clung to him afterwards, trembling and weeping. That should have been fair warning. Cody didn't need to get involved with someone sensitive. Someone with feelings. He could barely afford the risk of his usual out-of-town hookups. Jordan was a little too real. A little too close to home.

Therein lay the problem. The kid had been so good…felt so good…Cody couldn't resist a second visit. And now a third. If Jordan lived a hundred miles away it would be so much easier to deny himself.

He reached for the boy, cupping the back of his head and kissing his jaw.

Jordan clung to Cody's shirt. "I've never met anyone like you," he whispered.

Cody didn't answer. Couldn't answer. Instead, he pushed Jordan's shirt up and off. He removed his own, then held still as Jordan's hands slid up and down his abdomen and chest. Cody watched the young, callused hands touching him. He wondered, for a moment, what it might be like to link fingers with Jordan, just as he had with so many girlfriends in the past. How different to have his hand intertwined with that of another man. A young, beautiful, sweet-hearted man.

"Is everything okay?" Jordan asked, the concern in his voice and his eyes so sincere it made Cody's heart ache.

He kissed Jordan hard and furiously on the mouth. They fumbled at each other's jeans, unbuttoning and unzipping and groping and moaning. Cody filled his hands with Jordan's length and tugged, making the younger man cry out. Cody bit his lip, his jaw, his chest. He sucked hard, leaving a mark there purposefully, because every chance might be their last, and he wanted the boy to remember him.

Jordan cried out. "You're different," he gasped. "Different than last time."

Last time had been slow. Exploratory. Sensuous. Yes, this was definitely different.

Cody spun Jordan around and pressed his palms against the wall. "Stay," he said.

Jordan's breathing was rough and ragged. Cody found his jeans and searched them for the condom he'd brought. He ripped open the packet, rolled on the condom, and stroked himself a few times as he studied Jordan. He found his lube in the other pocket, squeezed some into his hand, and began massaging Jordan, who pushed back on his fingers, quite a bit more boldly than last week.

When Cody could stand it no longer, he slid his way in, using every ounce of restraint he had left to gently stretch his young lover.

"Oh, God!" Jordan moaned.

At last, Cody lost to himself to his own passion, pounding and thrusting, fighting back the need to come. When Jordan's sobs became heartfelt, Cody took pity and wrapped his arms around him. Jordan laid his head back on Cody's shoulder. Cody took Jordan's erection and stroked in time to his own thrusts.

With a cry, Jordan painted the wall in front of them with his semen. A moment later, blinding pleasure took Cody out of himself. He clung to the high, wishing like nothing else he could stay there instead of crashing down into the muck of post-coital bliss tainted by self-loathing, loneliness, and the knowledge that he'd likely never attain a lasting happiness.

For a moment, there was only breathing. His and Jordan's. Cody held his lover for a long moment. He kissed him beneath his ear and ran his hands up and down his sweat-slick chest and abs.

"Cody, I think…I think I'm in love with you," Jordan whispered.

Cody's hands froze for just an instant. Love? What could love possibly mean to two men in their situation? Was he supposed to go to his father and say, "Sorry, Gideon, I'm gay, but since it's love, maybe you can forgive me?" It would have been laughable if it hadn't been so devastating.

He finished the kiss he'd begun before whispering into Jordan's ear, "If you ever wanna fuck again, you'll not say that to me. Not ever. Got it?"

Jordan tensed. His breath hitched. "Got it," he said in a shaky voice.

Cody pulled out and backed away. He pulled up his pants and searched for a way to dispose of the condom. In the end, he had no choice but to tie it off and pocket it.

"Do you maybe wanna go out for a drink or something?" Jordan asked.

Cody turned and gaped at Jordan who was holding his jeans in front of his crotch, twisting them nervously. "We drink together at the bar."

"Yeah, but, I mean, just the two of us. Like a date."

"A date? You're joking, right?"

"Well, we can't just keep meeting for booty calls, right?" Jordan's nervous laugh was a thin mask for the vulnerability in his eyes.

How could the guy be this naive? "You want to go on a date...like a couple?"

Jordan gulped. "Yeah. I like you. I thought…maybe…"

Cody couldn't look at him anymore. He turned away. "Look, kid, this is all there is, okay? You wanna meet and fuck, I'm your man. But that's all I've got for you. Okay?"

Jordan's voice was tense. "Sure. I get it."

"Do you?" Cody asked. He turned and closed the distance between himself and Jordan. "Because I can't have this getting around to anyone I know. And if it does, I'll hurt you, Jordan, do you understand me?"

Jordan nodded, anger and pain in his expression. Cody just added it to the list of reasons to hate himself. The sick thing was, he *would* hurt Jordan. He'd do anything to keep his family from finding out his secret. Nothing was worth the pain of the rejection he would surely face from his father. And Jake. That would be the worst, really. Disappointing Jake.

Cody let go and backed up a step, keeping his eyes on Jordan. "I mean it. If one person makes a suggestive comment or joke to me, I'm coming straight after you."

Jordan's jaw tightened. "You've made your point," he said through his teeth.

Cody nodded and was about to zip up his pants when someone shrieked. It was too high-pitched to be Jordan, but Cody looked at him anyway. Jordan standing there completely naked and Cody with his pants undone, both turned wide, stunned eyes to the source of the sound.

It Took A Rumor

Ivy's life was spent managing people and numbers. That alone was stressful enough for an introvert, but add to it the public humiliation Myra Tidwell was inflicting upon her and it was enough to paralyze her emotionally.

She gathered her book, a bottle of wine, and a flashlight, and saddled up her horse, Mitzy. She rode Mitzy to one of her favorite reading sanctuaries. Most often she went to the big flat rock down by the creek, laid out a blanket, and relaxed to the sound of water trickling over rocks. But a certain Deathridge brother had ruined that spot for her. Not necessarily in a bad way. It was just that now she couldn't go there without thinking of him. She'd sit there staring at the same page in her book for an hour until she realized what she'd been doing. She'd simultaneously wish he would show up and pray he wouldn't.

And thinking of him was a waste of time. She couldn't have him. Didn't want him if she could. She needed to get her head in the here and now.

So she chose the old red barn she used to use as a hideout when she was a little girl. Funny, she recalled Boone being among the kids who used to meet her there to play and make trouble. That was a long time ago.

By the time she arrived at the barn, the sun had sunk behind the horizon. She took her book, wine, and flashlight and went into the darkening barn. Her first reaction at the man-sized motion to her left was to scream in fright. But as her eyes adjusted, she recognized the two men. Jordan and…Cody?

She dropped everything, slapped her hands over her eyes, and said, "Oh, God, I'm so sorry! I didn't see anything. Just…just pretend I wasn't here." She turned and fled, leaving behind yet another reading sanctuary she'd likely never be able to use again. Since she still had her eyes squeezed shut, she fumbled at Mitzy's reins and misplaced her foot three times before finding the stirrup.

No sooner had she scrambled into the saddle then a strong pair of hands pulled her down. She kicked and thrashed, albeit half-heartedly. "I don't care," she said. "I don't wanna know. I won't say anything."

"Shh, settle down. Let's just talk," Cody said.

She opened her eyes. He had on his shirt, hanging open. "It's none of my business," she said softly.

He nodded and then squinted out at the horizon, his blue eyes sparkling in the light. He looked like a goddamn cologne model. Where did these brothers get off being so sexy?

He took Mitzy's reins in one hand. His free hand he placed low on Ivy's back, walking her back toward her house. "Listen, it's your business now, like it or not."

"It's not. It's really, really not." She had to pry her eyes from him. Her brain was making adjustments to her reality. This new reality in which Cody Deathridge was gay. A gay cowboy. Banging her new ranch hand. In her second-favorite reading spot.

"The thing is, you're a good Christian girl, Ivy, and maybe you think it's your duty to tell someone like Pastor Allen or something…try and save my soul."

"Oh, no. Not at all. I could care less about your soul. Do with it what you please. Just don't make me the guardian of another secret."

He grabbed her arm, spinning her to a halt. They were only a few hundred feet from the barn. No sign of Jordan. Perhaps he'd snuck out and gone off toward the bunkhouse. "*Another* secret?" Cody asked, leaning on 'another.'

Ivy knew when to keep quiet. She closed her mouth and made a vain promise to God never to open it again.

Cody studied her, the crease between his brows deepening. "Ivy, I need this kept quiet. My dad, he'd…"

The choke, the fear and vulnerability, went straight to her heart. "Listen," she said, taking control of the moment, "This is nobody's business but yours and Jordan's. I don't care except to wish you both the best, that's all."

He glanced around for a moment before meeting her eyes again. "You don't think I'm going to hell?"

Of all the things for him to worry about. Ivy grinned and leaned in, lowering her voice conspiratorially. "I quit believing in hell back when I found out Santa Claus wasn't real."

Cody nodded and swallowed. He stepped back. "Yeah. Okay. Then…thanks. And…I'm sorry for…trespassing or whatever."

"It's okay. Use the barn anytime you want. After seeing that, I don't think I'll be going back there. Ever." She mounted Mitzy, vaguely aware that she was leaving behind her book and wine in the barn. More than vaguely aware that she held yet another Deathridge secret. The business woman in her thought she ought to be spending her brain power figuring out ways to parlay these secrets into a deal on the Deathridge ranch. But Ivy could no more give in to that instinct than she could sprout wings and fly. Besides, her father wouldn't approve. He was a good man. An honest man.

No, she would simply have to keep these secrets to herself.

She rode home and ran a hot bubble bath since her reading session had ended in disaster. She sprinkled lavender oil in the water and lit a scented candle. Then she turned off the lights, dropped her clothes, and sank into the steaming hot water. Nothing was more relaxing than watching candlelight flicker through the shimmering bubbles surrounding her.

She closed her eyes and wondered. Wondered what he'd feel like behind her in the tub, his strong, wet limbs embracing her. Wondered what he'd look like bathing alone, his stetson shading his face, only his cocky smirk showing. Wondered what he would do with her if he had the whole night. Would he lift her from the bath and dry her before carrying her to bed? Would he take her right there in the water, no care whatsoever to how much of it splashed onto the floor? Would he just hold her as she did what she was doing right now, easing the ache between her legs with her hand?

The steam swirled around her, her body temperature rising to match the water as she fantasized about him and massaged herself. When she was finished, she sank back into the water, dunking completely under.

After her bath, she dried, put on panties and a t-shirt, and climbed into bed. Her phone pinged with a text message from her father.

"Myra updated her blog. So sorry you're being put through this," the message said.

Ivy loaded the blog on her phone.

And the winner is...

If any of you didn't see this coming it was your own fault. The frontrunner in the polls, Dallas Deathridge, was spotted inside the Turner Cattle Company office where Ivy was working. Alone.

Could this be the end of the mystery? Or is Dallas looking to make a different kind of business deal? We shall just have to wait and watch as Ivy's little drama unfolds.

Ivy should have been upset. But the pleasing after effects of her bath had taken hold. Her body felt heavy and relaxed. After all, did it really matter? The damage was done. If people thought it was Dallas, maybe they'd finally get bored, and Myra could move on to fresher stories.

She turned off her phone and fell back on her bed. Her mind shut down, shortly followed by her body, after which she dreamt about the only Deathridge brother she'd actually been with.

It Took A Rumor

Jake had deceived his dad exactly twice in his life.

The first time was when he was eight. He took his dad's shotgun outside in the woods, desperately wanting to fire it and knowing no one would let him. He set up a target back behind a hill and downwind of the house, hoping the sound wouldn't travel far.

He lifted the shotgun like his dad had shown him with his pellet gun. This was heavier, though. He tucked the butt into the hollow of his shoulder, held a steady aim, and fired. The very next moment he was flat on his back, ears ringing and shoulder aching. No one came to get him, though, and after he lay there for some time, he rose, gathered the gun, and headed back home. He managed to reload the shotgun and replace it without anyone seeing.

But at dinner, somehow, his father knew; Jake could see it in his eyes. He forced every bite of his beef stew down his throat, each bite pushing the last one further down. The food soured in his stomach and as everyone left the table, Jake knew he was supposed to stay. He sat and waited for Gideon to speak. "Well?" Gideon finally said.

Jake burst into tears and confessed everything.

That was the one and only time Jake had deceived his father, until the other night at dinner—until Gideon had turned to each of his sons to ask if they'd slept with Ivy Turner.

That was three days ago and the lie weighed heavily on Jake. The only reason he didn't spill the truth, though, was that he was pretty sure his actions with Ivy ten days ago hadn't been the cause of the rumors. He'd listened to, and read, the gossip. Several people had mentioned a hotel and late nights. Jake and Ivy had been in a field in the middle of the day, so why were the rumors about a hotel?

No, it had to be something else.

After his shower, he settled into his recliner in front of his big screen television. He'd bought it himself, that way if his brothers ever got wives and moved out, there'd be no dispute as to who got the TV. In fact, most of the things in the home he'd bought himself. For that very reason. It didn't occur to him that maybe his brothers were mooching off him. But he did want to establish ownership in the event any of those losers actually found a woman and moved on.

He found ESPN just as Gideon stormed in the front door. Jake's heart honest-to-God stopped beating. But when Gideon's rage-filled eyes landed on him, Jake knew the rage wasn't for him.

"Where's your brother?" Gideon snarled.

Jake stood and looked around. Which brother? "Umm…"

Boone came from down the hall, just then, freshly showered, shirtless and in his pajama pants. Jake glanced at Gideon and saw that the anger wasn't for Boone, either. "Hey, Pop," Boone said.

"Where's Dallas?"

Jake answered. "In his room. What's going…"

Gideon stormed past him, down the hall, and came back frog-marching Dallas into the living room. "Jesus, Dad, what's going on?" Dallas asked.

Gideon shoved him away. "What were you doing at the Turner's earlier today?"

Jake's attention narrowed to Dallas. What *had* his brother been doing at the Turner's earlier that day?

"Dad, what are you talking about?" Dallas asked.

"Someone saw you there, and now it's all over town that the mystery's all but solved as to which one of my sons Turner is using his daughter to lure away."

"I…I didn't…it wasn't…"

"Spit it out, boy!"

Dallas drew himself up and cast an imploring glance at Jake. Unfortunately for him, Jake had zero sympathy, just then, and a whole lot of suspicion. When no one spoke up, Jake said, "Maybe he's trying to make a deal. A sly deal behind our backs. Is that it, Dallas? You want out and you're gonna throw us to the wolves to do it?"

Gideon stepped menacingly toward Dallas.

"No!" Dallas said. "Honest, Pop, I'd never do something like that. It's just, I thought maybe I could help get her and her old man off our backs, that's all."

It was a stupid excuse. The Turner's weren't 'on their backs' to speak of. They'd merely renewed their yearly offer to buy out the Deathridge ranch. So Dallas was covering something up, but Jake couldn't figure what it would be.

Cody arrived, just then, back from one of his evening walks. A little later than usual. He froze as soon as he hit the wall of tension in the room. "What's going on?"

"Dallas, here, is just about to explain why he paid a visit to the Turners today," Gideon said.

Cody remained silent and edged toward the hallway, likely leaving room for Dallas in case he needed a fast getaway out the back door.

"It's just like I said, Pop. I was just trying to get her to back off."

"Why is it you think she'd listen to you? You ain't ever been friends with her that I can recall."

"Well, you see, it's just…" Dallas looked around the room, meeting the eyes of all his brothers. Jake glared at him and waited, certain whatever came out of his mouth next would be a lie. Dallas rolled his shoulders back, looked his dad dead in the eyes, and said, "Ivy and I have been sleeping together."

For a moment there was silence. At least for everyone else there was silence. For Jake there was the roar of blood rushing to his ears. "That's a damn lie," he said in a harsh whisper.

Dallas slumped, putting on an act of penitence. "We didn't mean it to happen. It didn't have anything to do with business. It's just, we got to shooting pool at the bar one night and...things just sort of happened. Our mistake was meeting at that damn hotel."

Boone snorted.

Jake glared at his youngest brother, then at Dallas.

"How come you're just now fessing up?" Gideon asked.

Dallas shrugged and hung his head. "It's just, I really like her. I didn't want what we have cheapened by all this gossip. I just thought maybe we could keep our relationship a secret, that's all."

Jake's emotions were strangling him. There was no way Dallas was telling the truth, but having to stand there and listen to Ivy's honor get besmirched by his asshole brother was almost more than he could take. What was worse, Gideon seemed to be buying into it.

"Son, you can't trust a woman," Gideon said, putting his hand on Dallas' shoulder. "You may think she's falling in love with you, but the timing's just a little too coincidental. I'm betting she's using your feelings for her to worm her way into this family. You can't let that happen."

Dallas shook his head. "I'm sure she's not like that."

"We all like to think that. But trust me, she's not after anything but our ranch. Promise me you'll keep your distance from now on?"

After a long, heartfelt moment of silence, during which Dallas pressed his fingertips against his closed eyes and sniffed a couple of times, he at last nodded. "I promise, Pop. Anything for the family."

Gideon slapped him on the back before turning to Jake. "I want you to meet with her again. I talked to the bank. They'll give us a loan to buy that Hampton property from them."

For a moment, Jake's anger at Dallas vanished in the wake of his surprise. "You want me to offer to buy a thousand acres from the Turners?"

"Well, yeah. Only makes sense. It's inconvenient to them, since they can't get their cattle there without going over the highway. They can't grow their ranch this direction since we ain't selling. This way we solve their problem, and we grow our operation. It's win-win."

Jake shuffled his feet. "You sure you aren't just pouring salt in the wound? Goading them?"

"What did you just say to me?"

Jake stood up straight, fighting the inherent urge to duck his head and take his licks. He was going to inherit this ranch one day, he had a right to some say in how it was run. "Take offense if you want, but I never heard you talk about buying that property before. Or grow our operation. Seems you could've done it back when it was for sale."

Gideon squared his shoulders to Jake. Boone, Cody, and Dallas all took steps backward. "Now I don't take to my own boy questioning how I run my business."

Jake fought back the urge to roll his eyes.

"So," Gideon continued, "You're gonna meet with Ivy tomorrow, like you did last week, in a coffee shop, out in the open so no one can accuse you of sneaking around." He shot a reproving look at Dallas. "And make that offer."

"And what if they take it? You're prepared to go into debt? Hell, Pop, that land's worth more than our property and business put together. You wanna borrow against what you already own outright?"

"I don't see how it's any of your concern."

"It's my damn livelihood, Pop. And guess who's gonna be paying off the majority of that debt? Me, that's who."

Then Gideon did the same thing he did every time he was backed into the corner. He pointed at the door and said, "You don't like how I run things, there's the door."

Jake had never called his bluff, and he wasn't about to start now. Still, it pissed him off. Seemed like an abuse of power. Rather than listen to his grown son who might possibly have some useful ideas, Gideon continued to bully his way through life.

Still, what could he do? Nothing, that's what. "Fine," he said. "I'll meet with her tomorrow." He turned to Dallas. "You want me to convey your undying love, Romeo?"

Dallas glared at him in response. Jake wanted to punch him. But he'd done that earlier in the day and it hadn't made him feel any better.

After Gideon left, Jake started to close the distance between himself and Dallas, only to have Cody block him. "Let's not ruin our nice new carpet," Cody said.

"You're lying," Jake said to Dallas.

Dallas dropped the act and was grinning now. "It ain't no lie. Me and Ivy's in true love."

"Cut the shit, Dallas," Cody said.

"I know for a fact you ain't been meeting her in no hotel," Boone chimed in.

All faces turned toward Boone. "How you figure?" Cody asked.

Boone suddenly went pale. He hitched a shoulder. "I just know, that's all. Ivy ain't like that. She's a lady."

Jake, who had seen first-hand how deliciously unladylike Ivy could be, nodded his agreement. "That's right. She's a lady. So don't go making this worse for her."

"I'll just tell her the secret's out," Dallas said. "She'll be relieved."

Dallas and Boone retired to their rooms. Jake collapsed in his recliner and Cody fell onto the couch. "Where were you off to, this evening?" Jake asked, even as he switched on the TV.

"Just walking. Nowhere in particular."

"You were out a little later than usual is all."

Cody shrugged.

"You think Dallas is telling the truth?" Jake asked.

"Nope. No way."

Jake felt a little better. Of all his brothers, Cody was the one he respected most. Mainly because he was quiet and did his work. "Why you reckon he'd lie about that?"

"Probably because he's hiding a worse secret."

Jake mulled on that for a while. But he couldn't keep his mind from wandering to Ivy. What was she doing? Did she ever think about him? Was it usual for her to hookup the way she had with him?

Ten Days Ago

The diner sat right on Main Street across from the historic City Hall building. A few years back the town had gotten a historic grant from the state, and what had once been a run down brick building with a sagging green awning, now looked like a French café with little iron tables and chairs on the sidewalk out front and a hand-carved wooden sign that read, "River Front Diner, est. 1953."

Inside, the floors were tiled and the tables covered in vintage Formica. There was a table for two directly in front of the large window that overlooked the street. This was where Ivy sat, across from Jake Deathridge. She'd dressed in her usual business attire, a pencil skirt and button-down blouse. Her dark blond hair was pulled back in a loose bun at the base of her neck. She could have worn her contacts, but she felt the glasses made her look more professional. Jake, the eldest Deathridge, was clearly not as concerned about his appearance. He looked fresh off the farm in muddy boots, torn jeans, and a t-shirt. He'd taken off his stetson and hung it on the corner of his chair. He'd ordered a tall stack of pancakes, three fried eggs, two slices of bacon, a side of sausage...and was on his third cup of coffee. He ate heartily to the point that Ivy wondered if he realized she was still in the room.

She nibbled at the vegetarian omelet she'd ordered and sipped her coffee. "So," she said, continuing the speech she'd been giving him for the past ten minutes, "I really think if we could help our fathers communicate, both our families would benefit."

It Took A Rumor

Jake didn't even glance up at her. She'd explained to him the benefits of selling his land; how they would be hired on to help work it and they wouldn't have to give up the house; how Gideon and Clara could retire. She'd even told him the exact offer...a substantial sum that reflected the full value of their property. He hadn't reacted at all.

When the waitress came by to offer more coffee, however, he smiled brightly, held out his cup, and thanked her. As soon as she was gone, it was back to the business of eating.

Ivy sucked in a breath, very close to abandoning professional decorum. "Mr. Deathridge, I—"

"*Are you done?*" *he asked, sitting back in his chair at last, hitting her with dark, suddenly intense eyes.*

She found herself closing her mouth and stiffening her spine. "I suppose so."

"Good, then I can tell you what I could've told you before we even sat down. We ain't selling."

She wanted to bang her head on the table in frustration. "We're just here to discuss the possibility."

"Listen, honey, there is nothing...nothing...you have to offer that will tempt us to sell. This ain't about money to us, it's about family. So I'm sorry you've wasted your time—"

"Oh, you are?" *she asked, her temper hanging on for dear life.* "Why exactly did you sit there and let me go through the whole spiel if you weren't even going to participate in the discussion."

His lip quirked up at the corner. "Seemed like you were really into it."

Her temper slipped even further, now hanging off the ledge by only four fingertips...three...two...

She grabbed her purse and started thumbing through for her credit card. As the waitress walked past, Ivy signaled her for the check. She couldn't even look at the cocky cowboy across the table from her, though she felt his eyes on her, laughing at her.

"Hey."

Ivy looked up, then, just daring him to push her the rest of the way over the edge.

His smile had faded and he was looking at her curiously.

"What?" she asked, a little more snap to her voice than she'd wanted.

"Do you remember when you were little and our moms took us all to the State Fair?"

Ivy sighed. He'd successfully neutralized her temper—it was regaining its grip and crawling back up over the ledge and onto solid ground. But she didn't want to chit chat with him. "Not really."

"You'd have been pretty small," Jake said. "Maybe four or five. You held my hand. I took you on the little kid rides and bought you cotton candy. You don't remember that?"

It Took A Rumor

"I really don't," she said. The waitress brought the ticket and Ivy handed over her card.

"I'll get mine," Jake said, digging his wallet from his pocket.

"It's fine. It's a business expense." She nodded to the waitress to take her card and go.

Jake frowned at her, sliding his wallet back in his pocket. "You called me Mister Jake, that day." He grinned. "Ain't that funny?"

She glared at him, debating the merits of spitting in his face and walking away. But then, out of nowhere, she did remember. It was a golden memory, washed over from the brightness of the sun that day. She remembered him, though, seemingly gigantic, towering over her. She couldn't remember his face. But his hand holding hers, making her feel safe and cared for, even though he'd wanted nothing more than to go hang out with his friends. "You got stuck babysitting while Mom and Clara sat in the shade."

He grinned. "That's right."

"There was a girl you wanted to hang out with, but you couldn't."

"Yep. You really killed my social life that day."

"You weren't mean about it."

"Wasn't your fault."

She found herself smiling at the memory. At him.

But something about the way he was looking at her caused her stomach to unsettle and her cheeks to heat. "You sure have changed a lot," he said.

She stiffened. "I'm an adult, now, of course I've changed."

His grin widened. "Adulthood looks good on you."

She slammed her hands on the table and stood, just in time to take the receipt from the waitress. "I'm leaving. If you ever decide to be reasonable and have a conversation about how our two families can cooperate, give me a call."

She walked out as quickly as her three inch heels would allow, confused as hell at the turn that conversation had taken.

It Took A Rumor

Jake drove his pickup through the field toward the creek on the back of the property. The unevenness of the ground jostled him, rattling his already pounding head.

He'd met with Ivy Turner that morning. She'd taken over for her dearly departed mother running the business. Now it was her job to deliver the annual offer to purchase the Deathridge ranch. And since Gideon didn't want to meet with her, he'd sent Jake.

Jake hadn't enjoyed the meeting and having his and his family's inadequacies as ranchers thrown in his face. He had, however, enjoyed the way Ivy's heeled foot occasionally brushed his shin under the table whenever she was crossing her legs. And the way the tendrils of her hair curled along her elegant neck. And the way, sometimes, when she leaned forward, her blouse would dip just a little too low.

Yes, sir, the little girl next door had gone and grown up sometime when he hadn't been looking.

The overall effect of the meeting had been a confused mix of emotions that married together to create a pounding headache. Jake figured the best cure for a headache was work...at least, that's what his Pop had always claimed.

They'd had a sick heifer, a few days earlier. The vet had diagnosed her with hemlock poisoning. It was odd because typically the cattle didn't eat the stuff unless there was a severe drought, which there wasn't. Still, that cow had wandered from the herd for a few hours during a move to a different field...never would have happened if Jake hadn't left Boone and Dallas to do the job. When they found her, she'd been near the creek.

So that was where Jake was headed. The creek bed was flat where the cow had been, so Jake was able to drive right up to the bank. He was about to get out when he looked up through his dirt-smattered windshield and froze. Beyond a broken fence separating Deathridge and Turner property, lounging on a large, flat rock with her feet dangling in the water, was the little girl next door. In a yellow sundress. With her hair down. Miles from the uptight businesswoman she'd been earlier that day.

She had an open book in her hand, but was staring at him in shock. Jake grinned, got out of his truck, and splashed through the shallow part of the creek toward the broken fence. "Whose responsibility is this fence?" he asked, as though he even cared.

"Sell us your property and it'll be ours." She met him at the fence, her book abandoned on the rock, and rested a hand on her hip. She was standing ankle deep in creek water, goosebumps spreading up her legs. The dress was thin enough that he could see other evidence of the chill, too. Jake forced himself to look up at her eyes.

"No chance," he said.

"Then I guess it's all yours. Because I'm sure as hell not fixing it."

He nodded toward her side of the creek. "See that brush over there?"

It Took A Rumor

She turned to look.

"There's hemlock growing in there. It's all along that side of the bank on both sides of the fence. We nearly lost a cow because of it."

"Huh. Weird. Well, thanks for the head's up. That why you came down?"

"Yup. What about you? Kind of early in the day to be taking off work."

"I had a rough morning. Some stubborn ass won't make the best business deal of his life. It's frustrating watching good people make bad decisions."

He fought back a smile as he stared at her smart mouth. He leaned to the side to see past her. "Good book?"

She edged over to block his view. "Yes, as a matter of fact it is."

"Is that a romance novel? You don't seem like the type."

"I read serious literature."

"Just not today?"

"It's not a romance, it's..."

"I see a gray cover with a tie. Now I don't know much about books and reading and all that, Miss Ivy, but that there is a romance novel."

She stomped and huffed. "You know what, there's nothing wrong with an intelligent woman reading romance novels. It's very...liberating."

"Whatever you say, ma'am," he said, with a tip of his stetson.

"At least I'm literate."

He studied her and decided to let her have the win. Her defiant chin was just too much. He wouldn't want to break her spirit even if he could.

"Well," he said, taking a step back. *"I guess I ought to work on this another time. Wouldn't wanna keep you from...liberating...yourself."*

He winked, enjoyed her sweet blush for a moment, and turned away.

"Wait." She ran back to her rock and returned with her cell phone. She stepped over the broken part of the fence, the creek water now calf-deep on her. She thumb-tapped on her phone and then turned it to face him. *"What do you think of these numbers?"*

He studied them, giving nothing of his surprise away. "That's the land and the business?"

"Yes. And quite honestly, it's very generous. I didn't even want to offer it, but Dad said if I got a chance to talk to you again, he wanted to give it a try."

Jake's jaw muscles ticked. He nodded. "Very generous. I'm not sure what part of 'You can't put a price on family' is unclear to you, Ivy. But we ain't interested."

"You can speak for your father on this? On these numbers?"

"On any number."

It Took A Rumor

"You won't even try?"

"I don't even want to."

She threw her hands up and let them drop to her sides. "You know, it's one thing to have principles. It's something else to be just plain stupid."

"My granddad built this business—"

"With his own two hands. Blah, blah, blah. Wake the hell up, Jake. It's all fine and good to have grand ideas, but eventually reality comes knocking. This is reality." she held her phone up.

"You can take your reality and shove it where the sun don't shine!"

"Oh, my God, how do you live like this? How do you make your decisions based on these laughable, outdated ideas of family loyalty?"

"Maybe because I have a soul! You've got nothing in there but a cash register." He pushed two fingers against her chest, over her heart.

"I'd rather have no heart than no brain." She pressed two fingers against his forehead.

"Your momma'd be mighty disappointed in you right now."

"Don't you dare bring my momma into this!"

"You think she'd be happy about you trying to tear a family apart?"

"I'm not trying to tear you apart! This wouldn't be tearing you apart!" She held up her phone again.

This time, Jake grabbed the phone and chucked it up the creek. It landed with a short splash on her side of the fence. He stared after it, frozen in shock at his own rashness.

Ivy watched it's progress before turning wide, enraged eyes on him. "You son-of-a-bitch!" She shoved him hard in the chest.

Maybe it was because he wanted to shove her back but couldn't, her being a girl and all. Maybe it was misplaced emotions. Confused switches in his brain somewhere crossing the signals. Whatever the reason, he grabbed her by the hair and pulled her in for a kiss. A hard, angry kiss. A kiss meant to punish, though he wasn't sure which of them he was punishing.

He let her go and pulled his lips away.

She gaped at him, lips parted, breasts heaving. An instant later she was in his arms, her mouth hungrily taking his, her legs wrapped around his waist, his hat falling into the creek. He turned, moving toward his truck, intending to open the door. Somewhere in his brain there was a voice of reason, but when you find yourself pleasantly between a woman's legs, instinct tends to take over. Instead of getting her into the truck, he slipped on a wet rock and wound up slamming her against the door instead. She cried out.

"You okay?" he gasped.

She nodded and mumbled something unintelligible before burying her fingers in his hair and taking his mouth again. He shoved the skirt of her dress up over her hips and pulled one side of the bodice down, baring a breast. He groaned in agony. He covered her breast with a greedy hand. For a moment, it shocked him back to reality. Here he was groping little Ivy Turner's breast out in the open for God and anyone to see, except there wasn't anyone here. Her breath came in hot bursts. He looked up. Their eyes met and for a moment he thought she would ask him to stop. But then she smiled. It was a split-second of camaraderie in the midst of a turbulent storm. In a blink, it was over, and her blue eyes darkened with lust as she smashed her mouth against his.

There was thin lace beneath her skirt. Fragile lace. He broke from her lips and growled, "How much do you care about these panties?"

"They're my favorite ones—" She cried out as he ripped them off, and laughed as he fumbled with his belt, button, and zipper. After that, she wasted no time pushing herself onto him, meeting his thrusts passionately.

There was nothing he could do. No way he could hold back. If he could speak, he'd beg her to slow down and let him have the reins. But she kept pulling at him, sucking at his ear and neck, kissing him, riding him. Moaning. Breathing. "Jake!" she gasped as her muscles rippled around him and he lost the little bit of control he had, coming hard inside of her.

For a moment she clung to him, her arms and legs around him, her head on his shoulder. Small and vulnerable in his arms. The torrent of their breaths and heartbeats and moans subsided. Now there was only the trickle of the creek, the breeze rustling the leaves, and a nest of young sparrows singing nearby. Basically, silence.

Jake held her. Her small, vulnerable body was plastered to him and he felt like a protector. Like a hero. He breathed in the scent of her, felt her hot breath on his neck. Never in his life had he felt like more of a real man than in that moment.

He kissed her on the cheek and neck, cherishing her for a moment. Caring for her. He pressed his hand to her back feeling the fragile swell and contraction of her ribcage as she breathed and wondered how this moment felt like so much more than it should have. More than an indiscretion. More than an impulsive, foolish act. More...but what?

Ivy moaned and dropped her legs, sliding off of him. She slipped past him. He pressed his palms against his truck, closed his eyes, and took a breath to steady himself. When he turned, it was to see her kneeling in the creek water, her skirt gathered in one hand while her other hand was busy washing between her legs.

They hadn't used a condom.

"Oh, hell, Ivy, I'm so sorry."

He couldn't see her face. Her hair curtained it. "It's okay," she said in a weak voice. "Not my smartest moment. But I'm on the pill. And you're healthy, right?" Her words were confident, but her voice shook like a leaf in the breeze.

He knelt in the water next to her, not caring about getting his jeans wet, touched her chin, and turned her face towards him. "Perfectly healthy," he promised.

She nodded and went back to washing.

"I'm so sorry," he repeated.

"Oh, stop. I totally jumped you. Let's just...let's just leave this here. Okay?" She stood and dropped her skirt. It clung to her wet thighs.

He stood and faced her. "Absolutely," he agreed. Then he cleared his throat, suddenly nervous. This wasn't courtship, he knew that good and well. But Ivy wasn't some random woman he'd met at a bar and would never see again. She was his neighbor. The little girl he'd once bought cotton candy for at the fair. And beyond all that, a good woman. He stood a little taller, cleared his throat once more, and asked, "Could I walk you home?" It was supposed to be, 'Will you have dinner with me,' but he just couldn't quite pull that off.

Ivy smiled. "You're a real gentleman. But no thanks. In fact, I'd rather just forget this happened."

He frowned over at his truck as though he could see the ghost of what had happened there. She wanted to forget it happened? Well, that sucked. "Um, yeah," he stammered, not sure how to answer.

"No need to acknowledge it anymore? No need to talk about it?"

He nodded, still frowning, still wishing he could have a moment to formulate what he wanted to say. He wasn't above trying to convince her to see where it would go. "Sure, Ivy. Whatever you want." The words were distant and insincere.

She bent down and picked his hat out of the water where it had hung up on a rock. With a grin, she plopped it on his head. He closed his eyes as water dripped down the sides of his face and neck, and opened them again in time to see her skipping through the creek and over the fence.

He watched her gather her book and boots, take her horse by the reins, and walk over the hill and out of his sight. There was self-recrimination. How could he have dishonored and endangered her like that? There was also satisfaction. Because holding her in his arms had easily been the most meaningful moment of his life. But more than anything, there was regret. Because that might have been the only window of opportunity Fate would put in his way, and the thought of never holding that girl again made him suddenly weak and achy.

With a sigh, he forced himself back into a mindset of work. Romance or no romance, sex or no sex, the chores had to be done.

It Took A Rumor

Present Day

Ivy knew that their second breakfast meeting at the diner would be all business, but she couldn't seem to get that message across to the part of her brain that picked out her clothes, because she ended up in the same sundress she'd worn at the creek that afternoon, in the same boots she hadn't been wearing. Not the same panties, though. Those had been shredded.

She smiled at the memory.

Then she berated herself for smiling at the memory. She couldn't quite bring herself to change clothes, though. Perhaps he would recognize the dress and be thrown off kilter. Perhaps he wouldn't even notice it.

She drove to the diner where he was already waiting, in a corner booth this time. He didn't stand, which was unusually ungentlemanly of him. He did lean forward as though he was about to stand and changed his mind at the last minute.

Ivy slid across from him, flipped her coffee mug over, and pulled out her phone. When in a business meeting with a bullheaded cowboy, a good way to get the upper hand was to hold a high-tech gadget and pretend you were completely interested in what was on the screen. "Old man have a change of heart?" she asked without looking at him.

"Not exactly," Jake answered.

When he didn't volunteer any more information than that—a power play, Ivy was certain—she let out an exaggerated sigh and placed her phone on the table. "So why am I here?"

Jake opened his mouth, but paused when the waitress came by to fill their coffee mugs. "Can I get you two anything else this morning?" she asked, reaching for her order pad, eyes only for Jake.

"Just coffee, thanks," Ivy said firmly.

The waitress cast her a pressed-lip smile and turned away. Jake didn't appear to have noticed the waitress at all. Instead, he was giving Ivy a rather intense once-over, his eyes narrowed and roaming her face. "Something's different," he said.

"Just say what you got to say, Jake." She didn't pick up her coffee cup. Her hand might tremble, and she wasn't about to show weakness here.

Jake gave himself a shake, his focus returning to business. "Yeah. So, the old man has a counteroffer."

Ivy leaned back. The old man has a counteroffer? That was a far different approach than he'd taken ten days ago when it was all "we" and "us." Ivy allowed herself a little smile. There was blood in the water, she could smell it. With her now steady hand, she lifted her coffee mug to her lips. "Let's hear it," she said, and threw in a quick glance at her watch, just for effect.

Jake's eyes narrowed, again, as he leaned forward. "Your hair's down," he said.

Her coffee sloshed. "The counteroffer?"

"He wants to buy the Hampton property."

Ivy smirked. "*He* wants to buy the Hampton property?"

"I mean, we."

"Of course you do."

Jake slumped back in his seat like a pouty child who'd just been gotten the better of. Ivy could have laughed at him, then, but she had more important stakes to drive home. "First of all, Jake, the Hampton property has been the Turner property for ten years, now, and it ain't for sale. Secondly, what's Gideon think he's gonna do? You all own your property free and clear. Why would he borrow against that just to send a 'screw-you' to my old man? And how can you, as the heir apparent, even pretend to support a decision like that? You know your grandchildren would be paying that off."

Jake was all-out scowling, now. His big arms folded over his big chest. Not many men could look anything but menacing or childish when they were pouting…Jake was dead sexy. His dark eyes bored into hers. "It's the dress," he said.

"I beg your pardon?" She sat her coffee mug down. It rattled once on its saucer. She withdrew her hand and folded it in her lap.

"The dress. I know that dress. Intimately."

"Listen, if you don't want to talk business, then—"

"If you wanted to talk business you'd be in one of those prissy black skirts with your hair in a bun and your nails all manicured."

"This is ridiculous." She turned and started to scoot out of the booth before he could see the heat in her cheeks. But he propped his boot on the seat next to her, trapping her. "Move your big, dumb foot, Jake."

"Know what I think?"

"Nope. And I don't care." Time to get the hell out of there and have a ritual burning of that bad luck dress.

"I think you're angling for another off-the-books meeting down by the creek. That what you want, Ivy?"

"We agreed never to mention that."

"You got a lot of nerve wearing that dress in here," he said with a smirk. "You wanted me to mention it, admit it."

"Let. Me. Go."

"I'd be happy to meet you again, you know. Been thinking about asking you out."

Ivy searched her mind for the low-blow and found it. "It's not that I'm not interested, it's just that I don't think I can spare the two and a half minutes."

He dropped his foot and his smirk, his eyes widening and the color draining from his face. "That was a mean thing to say, Ivy."

She snorted as she stood and grabbed her cell phone. "Don't get your ego in a twist, baby. At your age, there are worse problems to have." With a wink, she turned and sashayed the hell out of there before he could think of a comeback.

On the drive back to her office, though, it wasn't her verbal victory that played over in her mind. It was the fact that he'd offered to meet her again…that he'd admitted to having wanted to ask her out. Why would he admit that to her? Had he been trying to play her? Or did he really like her?

For some reason, Ivy spent the rest of her day glancing at her phone. Whether she was hoping for him to call or deciding whether to call him, neither happened.

Jake finished his coffee. He wasn't sure why. He didn't want it. In fact, it kind of burned his stomach. Maybe it was simply that after being figuratively kicked in the balls, he wasn't sure he'd be able to walk. Even after he finished that cup, he signaled the waitress for a refill.

"Where'd your girl go?" the waitress asked as she poured.

"She's not my girl." He frowned down at the black liquid swirling in his cup.

"Well, it's her loss."

Jake pulled his cell phone from his pocket and stared at it, not sure what he'd find there. He had Ivy's number. He could text her. It wasn't really pride, stopping him. Her remark had definitely deeply offended him and awakened in him the itch to prove to her that he could last a hell of a lot longer than two and a half minutes; but more than that, it had cast doubt in his mind. Considering that the brief history of his relationship with Ivy consisted of her walking away without looking back, he couldn't help questioning whether her feelings for him matched his for her. And no man wanted to put his heart on the line when there was the potential of it getting ruthlessly stomped on.

Still. There was the dress.

Why would she have worn it? She had to have known he'd recognize it. He'd had his hands all up in that dress. Then again, she hadn't originally worn it for him. She'd worn it for comfort on a warm day when she'd been headed out to relax and read. Maybe the same was true to today. Maybe she'd worn it because she was taking the day off after their meeting. Maybe she hadn't intended to send his head straight to fantasyland and make him hard as a steel rod right there in a public place.

"Well, well, well. Mr. Jake Deathridge."

Jake looked up from his coffee to see Myra Tidwell sliding into the booth across from him, her cell phone and stylus out and ready. Never one to blend into the background, Myra had on black and white striped leggings and an aqua blouse with a matching aqua turban. Her array of plastic bracelets clacked together as she thumb-tapped her phone.

"You sure are tech-savvy for a little old lady, Mrs. Tidwell," Jake said.

"I'll take that as a compliment. Do you have any comments on your brother's relationship with Ivy?"

Jake looked into her zealous blue eyes and just shook his head. "Ain't you got any grandkids or quilting partners or something to spend your time on?"

"I do, as a matter of fact. But social reporting is my passion. Now…about Ivy and Dallas."

"I just met with Ivy, just a couple minutes before you showed up. Didn't anyone report that to you?"

Myra's ears perked up. They actually, literally moved.

"How come," Jake continued, "you don't assume because she was talking with me, just now, that I'm the one sleeping with her?"

"Are you?"

"You know what else? I saw Ivy and Molly Allen having tea together through the window of the shop up the street just a couple days ago. Maybe Ivy and Molly are sleeping together."

Myra's eyes narrowed.

"Hell, maybe Ivy ain't even actually human. Maybe she's an alien bodysnatcher come to seduce unsuspecting cowboys into impregnating her so she can populate the earth with human-alien-cowboy hybrids and end the human race as we know it."

Myra leaned back and pursed her lips. "You have a terrible attitude, young man. I wonder how your mother would feel about you behaving so rudely."

"I'm sure I'll find out tonight after she watches your newest video."

Myra clucked her tongue and slipped her phone into her purse. "Be a stubborn mule if you want. I'll get to the bottom of this mystery."

Jake had been the subject of Myra's gossip blog off and on for as long as he could remember. All of his brothers had. As well as most of the people in town. It really didn't bother anyone. Myra's words didn't typically make much of a splash. But he couldn't help being offended on Ivy's behalf. "You know, she doesn't deserve this." He frowned, surprised that he'd said that out loud.

Myra looked up, interested once again. "Doesn't deserve what, dear?"

"Having her name slandered. She's a good person. A hard worker. A devoted daughter. And I promise you she didn't do anything unethical with any of my brothers. So...can't you ease back? Find some fresh meat?"

"It sounds to me like you care for Ivy."

"I don't know what you mean by that, but I do respect her. And her father. They're good people, both of them."

"Is Jared Turner trying to buy your ranch?"

"That's old news, Myra. Jared Turner has been trying to buy our ranch for over ten years, now."

"Why won't your father consider selling?"

Jake pressed his lips together. Myra had just stepped foot onto family business. She was the biggest mouth in the state of Oklahoma. But then, maybe if he gave her something else to chew on, she'd leave poor Ivy alone. He knew the answer to her question. Gideon didn't want to sell because he loved their small-time ranch and wanted to pass something down to his sons, simple as that. But Myra didn't have to know that.

So instead of the truth, Jake asked a question. He frowned as though deep in thought and said, "You know, I'm not sure. Turner's offer is good. I just wonder if maybe there's something else going on…some kind of old rivalry or something. You know?" He leaned back, frowned a little longer, then let out a laugh. "But that's silly. I'm sure I'm overthinking it. Anyway, it don't matter. We ain't selling. And you can just get off poor Ivy's back, because as much as she and her father want our property, they'd neither one of them use a mercenary marriage to get it done."

Myra had clearly stopped listening to him after the part about an "old rivalry." As he'd said the words, her eyes had gone wide and her gaze distant. She was already drumming up the possibilities.

After she left, Jake smiled to himself. It felt good, doing something nice for that cold-hearted man-eater whom he just could not stop daydreaming about. He didn't think much past that. If Myra stirred up things between Jared and Gideon, it couldn't be as bad as what she'd done to Ivy.

And once the heat was off Ivy, maybe she would give him a chance to beat his less-than-stellar record of two and a half minutes.

Part 2: A Busy Sunday

Myra's Blog

It's been a week abundant in delicious gossip. As we go into this Lord's day, I want us all to reflect on ourselves as a community. Some criticize me and my blog as being petty or harmful, but I disagree. Gossip brings us together. It forges friendships. It solidifies values. It's part of the fabric of community.

Through gossip, we learn who needs help and who needs prayers. We feel connected with our fellow citizens. It's ingrained in each of us to want to be a part of each other's lives. To feel important in the greater story of our community.

So with that in mind, stay tuned, because I have some juicy news coming up this week. Hint: what's the most common reason for two old men to spend forty years feuding?

See you all tomorrow!

"And Adam said, This is now bone of my bones, and flesh of my flesh: she shall be called Woman, because she was taken out of Man. Therefore shall a man leave his father and his mother, and shall cleave unto his wife: and they shall be one flesh." Pastor Allen's voice boomed from the pulpit as he read from the book of Genesis.

In Fair Grove there were only two churches of any significant size. On the south side of town, there was The Path. They had a rock band with a stage and lights and fog machines. You could go there in your jeans and t-shirt and drink coffee during service. In spite of that, most of the cowboys and their families still chose to attend Fair Grove Community Church on the north side of town. Ivy never could figure it out. Her only theory was that the cowboys would rather dress up and sit in uncomfortable, hard-backed pews than find themselves sitting next to hipsters and college students.

Of course, Ivy couldn't criticize. She'd tried to attend The Path just on principal. As much as she was and always would be a country girl, she considered herself a progressive country girl. If she was being honest, she might even admit to feeling slightly superior to the other ranching families in the area. After all, she'd left home, gone to the city, gotten a degree, and experienced life around more diverse people than anyone else in Fair Grove had. But even with all that experience, The Path was just too different…too far removed from the traditions she'd grown up with.

"We call this the first marriage," Pastor Allen continued. "The entire foundation of our Christian teachings on sex and marriage is based in these verses. What do we glean from these verses? First, we see that woman was created from man. That she was made equal to man, but for the purpose of supporting him."

Ivy sank into herself a little. It was so conflicting, hearing those words, because she disagreed with them. And yet, wasn't that what she did? She came home to take her mother's place in support of her father.

She looked up at Jared, sitting next to her, his eyes trained on the pastor. Her father was a good man. Even if he did agree that women were created solely to support men, he never made her feel that way. He'd paid for college. Encouraged her to pursue anything she wanted. Never made her feel that she needed to find a husband and produce babies in order to be of any worth.

Ivy's eyes wandered across the aisle and up a few rows. The Deathridges occupied the same pew every Sunday. Gideon sat in the aisle seat, with Clara next to him. Clara—definitely a subservient woman. Ivy knew her to have devoted her whole existence to supporting her husband and boys. Next to her were Boone, Dallas, Cody, and Jake, lined up youngest to oldest. All with their hair washed and combed, no hat rings today.

Jake. What kind of man was Jake? Did he want a wife who would cook and clean and bear children and rub his feet at the end of the day? If so, then surely he knew Ivy wasn't the woman for him. Hell, he'd probably figured that out as soon as she'd jumped him. An old-fashioned guy like Jake probably wouldn't even consider marrying the kind of woman who expressed her sexual independence by having fast, hard anger sex in an open field in the middle of the day. *Been thinking about asking you out,* he'd said. Asking her out for a date? Or asking her out for a booty call?

"Second, we learn that marriage is meant to be between one man and one woman. Not one man and many women. Not one woman and many men. From this we derive our beliefs on fidelity and fornication."

On the front pew, like a good little preacher's wife, sat Molly Allen. Her straw hat cocked demurely to the side, hiding her face from Ivy. It didn't matter. Ivy knew what was on her face. Nothing. No guilt. No self-recrimination. Molly was missing something in her soul. Whatever that thing was that made a person willing to sacrifice her own desires for the good of another person, the same thing that had Ivy keeping secrets for other people even when those secrets hurt her—Molly didn't have it.

Neither did Boone, apparently. Ivy could see just enough of his face to make out a smirk, his eyes aimed directly at the back of Molly's head.

"Third, we learn that marriage is meant to be between one *man* and one *woman.* Not a man and a man. Or a woman and a woman. Every verse in the Bible after this on the treatment of homosexuality by Christians comes from this foundation."

It Took A Rumor

If Ivy wasn't mistaken, Cody shifted a little. And why shouldn't he? He was a mouse in a house full of cats.

Behind Ivy and Jared was a pew full of cowboys—ranch hands who worked for the Turners, all with their hats in their trucks and Bibles in their callused, sun-browned hands. She didn't look back, but she cringed at the thought of poor Jordan hearing these words. Of course, he'd probably heard them before. The sermon was fairly standard. Nothing new. Still, Ivy wondered at how, well into the twenty-first century, it could still be going on.

Perhaps it was simply tradition. A traditional belief that hadn't yet sloughed off with the rest of the dead traditions. But still, did Pastor Allen not realize how many people he'd excluded in just this one, basic, traditional sermon? Did he not understand how many people now sat in his congregation feeling like they didn't belong? Like they couldn't be saved?

"It is not too late to be saved!" Pastor Allen concluded. "If you're in the congregation today, and you've found yourself struggling with sexual sin, I implore you, come forward. Let the blood of Christ cleanse you. And if you're struggling with ongoing sin, such as homosexuality or infidelity, again I implore you, come forward. You do have a choice. You can be saved."

Everyone stood as the piano started playing "Washed in the Blood."

After that there was a prayer and the congregation began dispersing. Ivy followed her father into the aisle.

The building had a high ceiling and plenty of air circulation, but there was something stifling about this particular day. Probably a combination of the sermon and the judgmental cold shoulders of everyone who'd bought into Myra's gossip that week. On a normal Sunday, it would take Ivy up to a half hour to make it from her pew to the back door, just because of all the stops for conversation along the way. Today, it didn't appear it would take her very long at all. Her father received some attention from friends, but she herself was roundly dismissed. Almost like she didn't exist.

The Deathridges filed past, Gideon casting a glare at Jared who didn't appear to notice. Ivy felt something slip into her hand. A piece of paper. Jake's fingertips trailed over her knuckles as he walked by. He cast her a subtle smirk and a wink, and then he was gone.

Ivy's heart thundered. She slipped the paper into her purse and glanced around, worried someone might have noticed. But no one was looking. She was a complete pariah at this point.

Anxious to look at the paper, she slipped past her father, out the back doors, and into the parking lot, headed for her father's car.

"Ivy?"

She turned to find Dallas jogging toward her. He took her by the shoulders, shocking the hell out of her at the physical contact. "Why are you touching me?" she asked.

"Just play along," he muttered.

It Took A Rumor

"What...?"

He kissed her. Ivy's eyes flew open, the heat of rage surging through her system. She was about to jam her knee into his balls when he pulled back. "Ivy, honey," he said, loud enough for passersby to hear, "I can't see you anymore. I'm sorry to do it like this, but I just can't carry the burden any longer. We had some good times, baby, but it's over." He trailed his knuckles down her cheek.

Ivy choked back a wave of nausea as she glared at Dallas, who, though he was putting on a pretty good show of sadness, had a mischievous light in his eyes that made Ivy want to punch him. Hard.

With a wink only for her, he turned, head and shoulders bowed, and walked away. As soon as he left her field of vision, Ivy found herself staring straight across the parking lot at Jake.

He stood by the open door of the truck he'd driven to church with his brothers, and his shoulders rose and fell with his breath like a bull about to charge. Ivy's mouth dropped open, instinctively preparing to defend herself, though he was too far away to hear her, and she wasn't sure it would do any good anyway.

The parking lot was filled with people frozen in various postures of leaving. Nearby a man had one foot in his car. Another couple had their hands on their doorhandles. And of course there was Myra, phone up and recording, a smile of pure, voyeuristic ecstasy.

Ivy felt herself on the verge of snapping. She sucked in a breath, took a step toward Myra, and...

"Hold it together." Molly stood in front of her, took her by the arm, and led her to her car. "I'll drive you home. Come on."

"I am not going to stand here and be ruined by that jackass!"

"Shhh." Molly was all but shoving her into her car. Ivy found herself seated and sheltered. She looked up to see Molly holding quiet conference with Jared. Ivy's father nodded, then waved to Ivy before heading to his truck.

Being in the car took a lot of tension out of her. Whatever the hell had just happened was over now. She looked around and saw the Deathridges had gone. Molly got behind the wheel and started driving.

Rather belatedly, Ivy dragged her sleeve over her mouth. "Eww! Just ew! How dare he? I'm going to start my own damn blog and—"

"Listen, this is good for everybody, okay? He made it look like he broke up with you, so now everyone believes he was the one who got the rumors going. So Myra will stop and the gossip will phase out. And it also keeps me and Boone safe, as long as we don't go back to that hotel."

Ivy turned to look at her friend. "I hope you don't plan to go anywhere else with him at all."

Molly sighed heavily. "Richard has been getting suspicious. I mean, I don't think he suspects I'm cheating on him, but last night he said he wanted to talk. Said I was growing distant and he was afraid I might be making some bad choices. This, by the way, is based on my wearing too much makeup when I went out the other day." She rolled her eyes.

Ivy wanted to care, she really did, but at the moment she could only muster up concern for one thing. "So you're done with Boone?"

The look on Molly's face said everything. Ivy knew before she said it what she was going to say. "I think I'm falling in love."

"Oh, for God's sake!" Ivy threw her hands up and her head back against the seat.

"You're not being very supportive right now!" Molly shouted back.

"Molly, Boone is not in love with you—"

"You don't know him. He's so generous to me—"

"He's a wolf and everyone can see through his sheep's clothing but you. Don't do this to yourself. Don't do this to your husband. You had some fun, now why not move on?"

Molly didn't say anything else. They rode the rest of the way home in silence, Ivy clutching her purse, torn between fury and helplessness, and the itch of curiosity as to what was on that note Jake gave her.

Ivy got trapped into sitting through lunch with her father who was nothing but sympathetic to her plight. But as soon as she could get away, she hurried up to her room, opened her purse, and pulled out the note from Jake. She could only imagine what it said. Some declaration of her beauty. Some poetic confession of love.

The note said, *Meet me at our spot at one.*

Ivy's shoulders sank. Seven words. But then, what did she expect? He was a cowboy. A roughneck. A man of few words. Besides, their last meeting had been more of a contest of wills than a courtship. It was a little unrealistic to expect love poetry at this point. She should probably be grateful it wasn't an invitation to a duel with pistols at dawn.

Ivy gave herself a shake. It didn't matter. It was ten minutes past one, now. Whatever his reasons for wanting to see her, she could use the chance to explain what had happened between her and Dallas that morning. Or what hadn't happened.

She slipped on some boots and ran downstairs and out the back door. Her ATV was faster and closer than her horse, so she ran to the shed, climbed on, and drove it into the field.

Halfway to the big, flat rock it occurred to her that he probably wasn't there. The fact that she was late combined with his very clear anger that morning might have resulted in his deciding to give up on her.

It Took A Rumor

Would that be bad? Surely it would be better to let this thing between them go by the wayside. He was never going to break free of the influence of his father, that much Ivy knew for sure. She'd known men like him. Loyal to a fault. Any attempts at a relationship would only end in heartache.

But he's so cute, a little voice in her head said.

So are skunks, but that doesn't mean they don't stink to high heaven, said the logical voice in her head.

He didn't stink. He smelled really, really good, said the other voice.

"Aaarrgghhh!" Ivy shouted in frustration, her voice drowned out by the loud motor of her four-wheeler.

She drove faster, the wind stinging her eyes so that she had to wipe the tears away. As she approached the tree line along the creek, she slowed.

His truck was there on his side of the fence, but he wasn't in it. On second glance, she saw a pair of booted feet dangling off the open tailgate. She let out a breath, parked her bike, and killed the motor. She walked with as much control as she could, climbed the fence, and stood by his tailgate.

He was flat on his back, staring up at the trees above him. "Didn't think you were coming," he said.

"Well, I'm here. What did you want?"

"I wanted a roll in the hay, but I've since changed my mind."

Ivy's face went hot. "A booty call? Your stupid note was a booty call? Who do you think I am?"

He sat up, hopped off his tailgate, and towered over her. "I think you're a girl who doesn't mind screwing around, that's who I think you are."

She was as much surprised by the sound of her palm across his cheek as he was. She held her hand in her other hand, staring down at it as tears blurred her vision. Her palm stung, so it was some comfort knowing his cheek probably stung, too.

"Ivy, I..."

All she knew was that she didn't want to hear it. She stomped on his foot and turned, leaving him hopping and cursing behind her.

She made it all the way over the fence and to her bike before he caught up to her. He didn't touch her, but reached around and grabbed the key out of the ignition. She turned to face him, distraught that she couldn't keep a couple of the tears from showing.

His cheek was red and his expression was stern. "Tell me what I'm supposed to think. Dallas has been going on and on about how you two have been sleeping together. I don't wanna believe him, but the fact is, I don't know you, Ivy. I don't know what you're capable of. And you sure didn't have any hesitation about jumping me—"

She raised her hand, again instinctively. This time he caught her wrist.

"Ivy, I know I deserve it. I know. But don't hit me again. Come on, let's just talk about this."

"I hate you," she snarled through her teeth.

His jaw ticked. As she relaxed her arm, he loosened his grip on it. "I can see that. But I gotta know. What's going on with Dallas?"

"I don't owe you anything."

"I know that, too. I know, Ivy, I really do. But the fact is, I ain't been able to get you out of my head since that day. I don't know why, but I've got it in my head that you belong with me. Did...did you feel that way after...?"

Damn him and his earnest expression and his blatant honesty. Ivy's heart melted like butter on a hot biscuit. She slumped and sat back against the seat of her bike.

"Just...please tell me what kind of girl I went and fell for," he said softly.

Ivy took a deep, cleansing breath, and exhaled slowly. "You're right. We don't know each other. So this once I'll defend myself to you. But if that doesn't earn me some good faith with you, then I don't want anything to do with you."

He nodded quickly. "I understand."

She stood, rolled her shoulders, and took one more breath. "Okay, I can't tell you what Dallas is hiding, but for some reason he's decided to hide it under the pretense that he and I have been sleeping together. Which is the furthest thing from the truth because…eww." She shivered.

Jake smiled.

"So he fake broke up with me and I had no idea what was going on. I still don't."

"So he's using you for cover? Do you know what it is he's hiding?"

She looked at him, hoping he wouldn't ask her any more on the subject.

His expression grew more stern. He nodded. "Okay. Why can't you tell me?"

"It's a confidence. You wouldn't want me telling your secrets, would you?"

"I don't have any secrets."

She grinned, arching a brow. "You have one, at least."

He bit his bottom lip and looked her up and down. "Yeah, I guess I do."

Ivy felt herself blush down to her toes under the heat of his appraisal.

"Okay," Jake said. "Then, whatever he's hiding has worse consequences than sleeping with you would."

Ivy shrugged. "I guess that's a matter of perspective."

He studied her for a long moment, eyes narrowed. After what felt like forever, he relaxed. "Is there anything else I need to know?"

Ivy was filled with the urge to tell him everything. Of course, she wasn't stupid enough to give in to such an urge. Just because he was approaching her with honesty and the most gorgeous brown eyes on the planet didn't mean it was time for her to bare her soul to him. So she shrugged and said, "Nope. I think that's it."

"Doesn't solve the mystery of why your truck's been seen parked next to one of our trucks at that motel."

Ivy pressed her lips together.

Jake raised his eyebrows.

Ivy slumped back. "I do know the answer to that, but I can't tell you."

"You could if you set your mind to it."

She grinned down at her boots. "Jake, I ain't sleeping with any of your brothers. Or anyone else, for that matter. That's really all you want to know, isn't it?"

"It's part of it." He reached down and tipped her chin up. "Do you like me, Ivy?"

Her face went hot again. She shrugged, looking down at her boots once more.

Jake chuckled. "If you want me to walk away, just say so. But you gotta look me in the eyes so I know you're serious."

She lifted her gaze to his. "I don't want you to walk away."

His Adam's apple bobbed. He nodded once. "Good. I won't."

"Good."

She shrugged.

He shrugged.

They stood there, suddenly unable to hold eye contact.

"So, uh," Jake stammered, kicking at the ground, "how do you want to do this?"

"Reverse cowgirl?" Ivy said, hoping to shock him, even though she blushed to her ears doing it.

His eyes went wide and his jaw dropped. And then he laughed. "Shit," he said to the sky.

Ivy laughed with him. "You don't like doing it that way?" she asked, moving into him.

"I like that way just fine."

She giggled, holding onto his hips, her head dropping almost all the way back as she looked up at him.

He brushed her hair aside. "Obviously that wasn't what I meant."

"Obviously."

His expression sobered, some. "How do you want me to, um...court you?"

"Court me?"

"Yeah. Do you want to take it slow? I mean, we can't go on traditional dates, but we could meet. Have picnics here at the creek. Hold hands."

"Hold on, why can't we go on traditional dates?"

"You kidding? My old man would disown me."

Ivy stepped backwards, dropping her hands from his hips. "You're a grown man. You're almost forty, for Christ's sake."

"I'm thirty-six...what's that got to do—"

"You're standing there, a grown man, telling me you can't date me because it might upset your daddy?"

Jake's cheeks reddened slightly. "I said he would disown me."

Ivy snorted. "You're being overly dramatic."

"That ranch is my life, Ivy. I date you, it's gone. Do you get that?"

"That's ridiculous. He's not going to take that away from you just because you date someone he disapproves of. He's all talk, Jake. He loses you, he loses his livelihood."

But what she saw on his face was that, whether Gideon would or wouldn't disown his son in actuality, Jake genuinely believed he would. And as a result, Jake wasn't going to take a risk that might lose him the one thing he loved more than anything else in the world.

Ivy pondered on this. She turned it over in her mind. Turned it over in her heart, drawing from a deep well of compassion. She took in a deep breath, met Jake's vulnerable gaze, and said, "Fuck you, Jake Deathridge! If you're too afraid to so much as have a beer with me in public then you can go fuck yourself! God, I can't believe I even came down here."

She hopped on her bike and reached for the key, which wasn't in the ignition. She shoved her open hand out to him.

Jake's stone cold gaze didn't waiver as he dangled her key in front of him and took a step backward. Then another. And another.

"Stop screwing around and give me my key," she said.

He frowned, seemingly thoughtfully, and shook his head. "I don't think so. We're gonna talk common sense like adults, you're gonna apologize for being mean to me, and then we'll have a nice, passionate kiss goodbye. Then you can have your key."

"You condescending son-of-a-bitch! I'll…I'll…I'll…"

He laughed. "You'll what?"

"I'll tell your mother!"

All humor left as his jaw dropped. "What the hell is with all the low-blows? You ever try being nice?"

"Give me the key, Jake!"

"No! You're so damn self-righteous, you stand there and tell me why I should risk my livelihood to go on a date with a woman I hardly know?"

"Because I'm a woman you want to get to know. You just said you liked me. You said I belong with you. So?"

"So let's see each other quietly…discreetly for a while. Figure out what we want from each other. Figure out if there's even anything we can work with here. Then we can talk about going public and the consequences of that."

Ivy frowned at him as she got her temper under control. It made sense. He wasn't asking for anything unreasonable. But damn it, there was no romance in it!

She should sacrifice her ideas of romance for him. It was the right thing to do. "I don't…" she stopped, thinking her words through. When she spoke again, she was quiet. "If you and I were to become something long term, I don't think I could look back on this moment and respect myself for agreeing to what you're asking."

His eyebrows went up. "I'm asking to get to know you. How is that unreasonable?"

"I want romance."

"Romance?" he said the word as if pronouncing it aloud for the first time in his life; uncertain, unsteady.

"Yeah. Romance. Gestures. Boldness. Courage."

She may as well have been speaking in Swahili. He stared at her blankly for the longest time. "I don't think I understand."

She fisted her hands, but worked to keep control of her emotions. "It's not rocket science, Jake. If you wanna see me, you can knock on my door, hat in hand, like a gentleman. If not, then we got nothing more to say to each other." She lunged forward and snatched her key from his unresisting hand. Though she moved fast, she hoped he would stop her. Wished he would step forward and give her what she wanted.

But she rode home, angry, tired, and deeply disappointed.

Jake remained in a perpetual state of shock all the way through dinner that night. As he stared sightlessly at the plateful of roast beef with carrots and potatoes his mom had dished out, he kept going back to that word. Romance. Was it reasonable for her to want romance from him? Especially when they didn't even know each other. Jake was no Romeo. Never even wanted to be. And Ivy was a born and bred ranch girl as well as a business woman…she should be above such ridiculous notions.

"I do hope Ivy isn't too brokenhearted," said Clara.

Jake looked up and opened his mouth, but closed it swiftly when he realized his mother wasn't talking to him.

Dallas let out a heavy sigh, his cheek resting on his fist as he dished second helpings onto his plate. "Of course she's brokenhearted, Mom. We were falling in love."

Jake frowned at his blasphemous brother for taking the name of Love in vain. He himself couldn't exactly say he was in love with Ivy just yet, but he knew for sure the seeds had been planted. All that wanted was some nurturing and, apparently, some romance.

Boone snorted at Dallas's remark.

Clara smacked the back of Boone's head. "Don't mock your brother. Love isn't a joking matter. Why, I can't imagine how I would have survived if I hadn't been allowed to see your father."

"Thank you, Mom," Dallas said. "Your understanding means so much to me."

Punching him in the face would only elicit more questions that Jake couldn't answer. He'd watched Ivy, earlier that day, take control of her temper by breathing deeply, so he decided to try it. He made it to the end of his inhale when Gideon spoke again.

"I did you a favor, son. Ivy may be a pretty girl, but she ain't a lady."

Clara gave a sad, resigned sort of nod.

"Ivy's a lady," Jake said, because his brain-to-mouth filter tended to malfunction at the sound of Ivy's name.

Gideon snorted in response. "If she was a lady, she wouldn't have been sleeping with Dallas, now, would she?"

Dallas darkened at the insult, but otherwise remained silent.

Clara reached over and patted him on the shoulder. "Don't say things like that, dear. Our Dallas is every bit the gentleman, aren't you?" She pinched his cheek. He grinned at her.

"Yes, ma'am."

Gideon merely shook his head and speared a forkful of roast beef. "Nah, that girl's smart. Only reason she'd go after Dallas is to weasel her way into our good graces. He's the only one dumb enough to think her sincere."

Jake could no longer inhale or exhale, his teeth were ground together so tightly. Dallas pushed his plate away, leaned back in his chair, and got that distant look in his eyes that all the boys got from time to time. It was a way of shutting down, anesthetizing against Gideon's cruelty. Clara sat up straighter, glancing between Dallas and Gideon as though confused by the situation; as though she hadn't sat in that same spot all their lives and heard Gideon call Dallas "dumb" nearly every day.

"I guarantee you," Gideon went on, jabbing at a piece of potato and a carrot, "that if she thought she could get her hooks in Jake, here, she'd have done it. She probably tried. Am I right, boy? Did she try flirting with you?"

Jake stared blankly at Dallas. "Not that I can recall."

Gideon ignored the response and pointed his fork at Dallas. "I repeat…I did you a favor. She was playing you for a chump. You ought to know better than to think a girl like that would want anything to do with you. She's a social climber, that one. Got her fancy clothes and college degree. You just go ahead and thank me right now, son, and be done with her. Go on."

Dallas said, "Thank you, Pop."

"You're welcome. You're right welcome."

Jake got up and left the table.

"Honey, where are you going?" Clara shouted. "You didn't eat your supper!"

The screen door slammed on her last word. He skipped the two porch steps, his boots landing solid on the gravel driveway. He followed it to the county road toward his house. The gravel crunched beneath his feet. The sun hovered over the tree line, gradually dipping, taking its summer heat with it.

Jake stopped, turned around, and started walking the other direction. He passed his parents' house without incident and followed the county road all the way to where it intersected with a small highway. Three miles didn't slow down his heartbeat or his intentions. The farmhouse came into view, big and beautiful, way more house than the two people living in it needed. Even when Mrs. Turner had been alive, she'd had to hire help to keep it clean. Three stories tall with a two-story wrap-around porch. Mrs. Turner used to talk about turning it into a bed and breakfast, but Jake doubted her introverted husband and daughter would do any such thing.

Jake jogged up the steps to the double doors and rang the bell. Ivy would open the door and he'd grab her and kiss her good and hard. He'd do it fast before her brain had a chance to ruin the moment. He'd kiss her so wildly that she'd beg him to take her to her room. Then he'd make love to her way longer than two and a half minutes. He'd blow her mind. Rock her world. Conquer her so thoroughly that she'd never want to leave his side.

The door swung open and Jake choked on his next breath. "Uh, hey, Mr. Turner."

"Good evening, Jake. What brings you by tonight?" Jared, as amiable as ever, stood comfortably in his doorway, holding the screen door open.

"Umm…" Jake couldn't help glancing past Jared's shoulder to the interior of the house.

"Are you looking for Ivy?"

"What? No, of course not. Why would I be looking for Ivy?" He laughed nervously, cleared his throat, and schooled his expression. "No, sir, I came by to, um, to…to warn you. Right. About the thing on Myra's blog."

"What thing?"

"Myra caught me at the diner the other day and, well, at the time, she was asking about Ivy and Dallas. And I thought she'd done enough to poor Ivy, so…I suggested to her there might be some rivalry between you and my dad."

"I see. You thought that would take her attention off Ivy."

"Yes, sir."

"In that case, no apology necessary. Ivy's a strong, self-confident young woman, but the gossip was really beginning to get her down."

Jake swallowed and nodded.

"I don't suppose you happen to know how the rumors got started in the first place?"

Jake gulped again and shook his head.

Jared chuckled. "Son, if you wanna see her, she's just upstairs."

"See who? Ivy? I don't even know her. I just came by, like I said, to apologize." He started backing down the steps even as his eyes wandered upward. Somewhere up there in one of those rooms was a smallish girl with blond hair and warm skin and soft lips and a loud mouth...

"She isn't doing anything important. I could call her down."

She'd grown up up there, just a few miles from him. He'd spent all his life on that one patch of land and here she was, all the time. He remembered seeing her as a baby. A toddler. A little girl with braids. She'd grown up and gone to school with Boone. One summer, when she was sixteen, he'd seen her swimming in the river with her friends, climbing up on rocks and jumping off. He did remember that—her lean, bronzed body glistening in the sun; her smile big and innocent and unspoiled. He'd seen her in passing at church every Sunday, in the grocery store, at the diner, socializing at fairs and carnivals and parties. All this time. "I wouldn't want to bother her," he said, barely conscious of having said it.

"Jake."

Jake's head cleared and he met Jared's gaze. "Yes, sir."

"Are you in a relationship with my daughter?"

"No, sir." That was an easy question to answer.

"Do you want to be?"

Not an easy question to answer. Jake laughed nervously. "No. Of course not. I don't, like I said, even know her. I just..."

Jared blinked and folded his arms over his chest. "Just what?"

"I just never noticed her before, that's all."

"But you're noticing her now?"

"No. I mean, yeah, but…but you wouldn't want that, I'm sure. Right?"

"Well, for the most part, I want Ivy's happiness. Do you intend to make her happy?"

Jake stood there in the dirt at the foot of the porch steps looking up at Jared leaning against the front door. What was he doing? He wasn't a teenager asking to take the guy's daughter to prom. He was a grown man who wanted a grown woman. He'd never realized before how much he cowered on a daily basis. He'd always called it respect. He respected his father, therefore he did as he was told. But that was wrong all along. He knew this now because he wasn't afraid of the man who stood in front of him. He respected him.

So Jake climbed the steps and faced Jared Turner like a man. "I'd sure like to try, sir."

Jared grinned. "How long's this been going on?"

Jake thought back. "I guess two weeks or so? Happened when you sent her to meet with me at the diner that first time."

Jared nodded.

"Mostly she just yells at me, though. So, I'm not sure if she's interested."

"No time like the present to find out. I'll go call her down. Can I get you something to drink? Iced tea? A beer?"

Jake grinned at the word "beer," and Jared nodded, disappearing inside. There was a porch swing at the end of the porch, facing inward. Jake sat and rocked slowly. A couple minutes later, Ivy came out, carrying two beers. Her hair was loose. She had on shorts and a thin, flowing tank top, no bra…clearly clothes to be worn when settling in for the evening. Jake stood as she approached, sat when she sat, and opened her beer for her. He rested one arm along the back of the swing, framing her with it, making her a part of his space.

"I'm sorry about all of this," he said.

"All of what?"

"All of the drama."

She shrugged and drank deeply from her beer. "Why are you here?"

"I don't know. I was going home. Turned around and came here instead. Missed you." He brushed her hair aside so he could watch her blush.

"We don't even know each other."

"I was remembering, just now, all the times I noticed you in the past. Just brief moments where you made an impression on me. There's a lot of them. You were a little kid for the longest time, though, so I don't think I ever made that transition in my mind to looking at you as a woman."

She looked up at him. "I guess my jumping on you down by the creek fixed that for you."

"Yes, ma'am."

She scooted closer and relaxed into his side. How she could be so casual was beyond him. The mere feel of her warmth had his heart racing. With her body pressed against his, he was dangerously close to cardiac arrest. "I'm calmed down from earlier," she said, "but I haven't changed my mind. Dating is one of those basic steps into adulthood, and if you can't even break away from your father enough to do that, then I'm not going any further down this road with you."

"I know. I get it." A breeze blew in. Her hair tickled his neck. The scent of it filled him deeply.

"So? What's your plan?"

He blew out a breath. He really hadn't thought this through. "You need a plan right now?"

"I need an intention right now."

"Okay, well, I intend to give you what you want. I just don't quite know how, yet."

She brought her feet onto the swing and curled against him, his reward for saying the right thing. No, that was the wrong way to look at it. What he'd done, was earn a bit of trust. Enough trust that she was willing to relax against him for a while.

"I've been doing some remembering, too," she said. "I remember I had a crush on you when I was twelve."

Caught off guard, he momentarily forgot his lust and laughed. "Really?"

She shook her head. "I used to lie in bed at night, hug my pillow, and cry over how much I was in love with you. Stupid teenage girl stuff, but still…it's kind of funny."

"How'd you come to even notice me?"

"I tripped and fell running around in the church parking lot. You picked me up, helped me to the bathroom, stood by while Mrs. Harper applied antiseptic. Then you walked me to my car."

"Twelve. That would have made me, what, twenty-two? I didn't realize I was so gentlemanly back then."

"You had a girlfriend. I was heartbroken."

"Oh, yeah. Melissa, I think."

Suddenly, she sat up and swung around, straddling him. She reached to set her beer on the porch rail, then took his and did the same. Jake just focused on breathing. Her knees hugged his hips. He had no idea where to put his hands. "You don't have a girlfriend now," she said with a sly grin.

"No, ma'am."

She ran her hands up his neck and into his hair. His eyes rolled shut and a low groan escaped his throat. When he felt her breath on his lips, he opened his eyes just long enough to watch hers close, and then melted into her kiss. In so many ways, he lost consciousness of the outside world as all his senses turned inward, attuned to all the nerve endings in his body that were now lit up like Christmas lights. In other ways, he was more fully aware than he'd ever been. He felt the vertebrae of her spine shift with her subtle, seductive movements. Through that touch, in his mind, he visualized her moving, undulating against him. His other hand cupped her jaw and felt its movement and its fragility. How could something be so delicate yet so strong?

When she kissed her way to the base of his jaw, he opened his eyes to see as much of her as he could. Her hand on his chest, fisting in his shirt. Her bare thigh against his jeans. She was all soft curves and mouthwatering flesh.

He touched her reverently, cupping her shoulder and sliding down to her elbow, watching the light from the sunset filter through the fine hairs on her arm, giving her a soft glow. He kissed her shoulder softly.

"Oh, Jake," she whispered. She nipped at his ear, and he hissed in a breath. She did it again, this time licking along the outer edge.

"Ivy," he groaned, and wrapped his arms around her, squeezing her tightly. This was such a dense concentration of want and need that he thought he might burn up in the heat of it. "You're trembling," he whispered.

"I think that's you." She pulled back and smiled at him, her cheeks flushed pink. "Look how turned on you are. It's no wonder you don't last very long."

"Don't make fun of me, Ivy," he said, because she was right. He was so turned on it hurt, and he only wanted her kindness and her body, just now.

Her expression sobered, her lips still parted from the smile. "I wasn't meaning to. I just think it's strange..."

"What?" He stroked her hair. Tucked his hand in the small of her back beneath her shirt, bare flesh warm and damp with sweat. "What's strange about it?"

She laced her fingers behind his neck and hung on. Her smile faded. Her lips were swollen and wet. For a moment, he saw her as a tousled, uncertain girl. He knew she wasn't a virgin. Obviously. But in that moment, she looked like one. "It's strange to see you..."

"See me what, Ivy?"

She shifted on his lap, and he hissed in a breath, still on edge and not sure how long he would last with her sitting on him like this. Her wide eyes sparkled. "To see you such a slave to desire."

He grinned at that. "I try not to be. You've caught me unawares."

"I'm glad. I like it. I like seeing you weak."

This time he laughed and brought her against him in a firm embrace. The moment changed, no longer blistering with heat, but rather warm and soft. She rested her cheek on his shoulder. He rubbed her back up and down. "I like you like this," he said.

"How's that?" Her voice was barely more than a whisper.

"Quiet."

She laughed and squeezed him tighter. "This relationship is going nowhere."

"Mmm. We'll see."

"You're not usually passionate. I'm not usually quiet. Clearly this is just a fling."

He turned and kissed her hair. This wasn't just a fling. "I'm passionate when it counts. And it happens I like you when you're loud, too."

She sighed. "Can we just stay like this forever?"

They couldn't.

Later, as he walked home in the dark, he tried to remember how the time had ended. It seemed as though one minute he was high as a kite, holding her, swaying in the swing with the evening breeze cooling their skin, and the next, he was trudging down a gravel road in the dark. She hadn't invited him inside. He hadn't asked. At some point, they'd separated, and they'd stood, straightened their clothes, and parted.

Now, here he was, halfway home, his head clearing at last, and reality slowly returning to the forefront of his mind. He'd run away, is what he'd done. Run off on an impulse and done something that made him happy. But the plain fact was, dating Ivy was going to cause strife, and for a peacemaker like Jake, that prospect didn't sit well.

He arrived home, grabbed a beer out of the fridge, and sat on the porch, vaguely wondering where his brothers were, this time of night.

It Took A Rumor

If anyone had the right to storm out, it was Dallas. But since Jake did it first, Dallas was obliged to sit through the rest of the meal with his food burning in his belly and a volcano of rage in his soul on the verge of erupting. As soon as Clara called Boone to help with the dishes, Dallas took off.

He cut through the field as though he were headed home, but rerouted when he was out of sight of the house.

Dumb. It was the reason for everything. Gideon wouldn't pay for a college degree because it'd be a waste on someone so dumb. Dallas would never get a respectable woman, since he was too dumb.

Maybe if he'd been born first, being dumb wouldn't matter so much. It sure didn't matter in Jake's case. Jake was dumb as shit and the old man didn't seem to care. Boone wasn't dumb, but he was a damn idiot. Dallas had never done a thing to earn his father's prejudice. It was just a box that he stuck Dallas in back when he was a five-year-old boy who accidentally lit his momma's curtains on fire, and now he was stuck in it.

The sun was setting, but he had his phone on him for a flashlight if it got too dark. He picked up his pace until he caught sight of the tree line by the creek. He jogged until he reached the edge of the shallow creek, and followed it toward the Turner property.

Jake had left trash bags full of those poisonous weeds there. Tons of them. From the low light, Dallas could see that the gallant bastard had even gone to clean out the stuff on the Turner side of the fence. There were at least a dozen large trash bags, but Jake would notice if one was missing. He loved those cows like his own children, so he'd have made sure to count, not wanting any of the poison to make its way back to the cattle.

Dallas leaned back against a tree and pondered. He'd have to take some of the weeds out of each bag. Jake would notice a missing bag, but he'd not notice a little missing from each bag.

He couldn't very well carry it by hand back and forth, so he'd need to drive the pickup out here. Trouble was, if he got caught, how could he explain himself?

This quandary kept him occupied for the better part of five minutes, and just as the sun dipped below the horizon, he had it figured out. Of course. The bags had to be hauled off. That was likely to be Jake's first chore in the morning. He'd simply volunteer to do it for him. Show a little brotherly love.

Dallas smiled to himself. Brilliant. He'd get Ivy her sale and be off this property in a week's time.

Dallas strolled back toward his house. It was full dark when he arrived and found Jake sitting on the back porch, three beers in.

Dallas plopped next to him on the steps and grabbed the fourth beer out of the six pack. "Where'd you run off to?" he asked.

Jake frowned at him. "Here. Been here the whole time."

"Is that so?" Dallas asked, laughing at the lie. He twisted the cap off his beer and chugged half of it.

"Yeah, that's so. You got something to say?"

"Nope. Not at all." No sense pushing his luck. He didn't really care where Jake had run off to.

Jake shook his head and finished off his bottle.

"So…what's on the schedule for tomorrow?" Dallas asked, as casually as possible.

It must not have sold, because Jake gave him a funny look. "What are you talking about?"

Dallas shrugged and stared out into the night. "Just wondering what chores we gotta do first thing?"

Jake kept staring at him. "You were born and raised here same as me. If you don't know what's gotta be done by now, boy, you oughtta put together a resumé and find another job."

Dallas laughed nervously. "Yeah, I guess you're right. I just meant, you got anything needs done that ain't been done yet? I mean, I know you were gonna fix that fence down by the creek."

"I fixed that a week ago."

"Yeah, okay." He waited, but Jake was not forthcoming. "What about all them weeds you were wanting to dispose of?"

"I pretty much did all the work. Just gotta haul it out to the dump."

"I'll do that for you," Dallas said.

This elicited outright laughter from Jake. "What's your angle, man?"

"No angle. Just looking for something to do that gets me out of shoveling shit."

Jake nodded. "Yeah, well, you can do that *and* shovel shit."

Dallas laughed, just to keep things light. "Yeah, whatever," he said. With Jake's suspicions aroused, he thought he'd better act a little more unconcerned. "I'm sure you'll have it shoveled before I'm even awake."

"Prob'ly." Jake popped open another beer.

Dallas exhaled slowly. He wouldn't say anymore on the subject. He finished off his beer and went inside.

It Took A Rumor

I wanna see you.

Cody had sent the text ten minutes ago. He sat in Ivy's abandoned barn, sure that Jordan wouldn't refuse him. It hadn't occurred to him that the kid might not answer.

After five more minutes, he dialed Jordan's number. It went straight to voicemail. "It's me. Call me. Please." He hung up and waited.

The itch had grown unbearable. He regretted everything he'd said to Jordan. All he wanted was a moment with him. Just one moment. One fix.

His phone vibrated.

I'm not interested.

Cody stared at it. *I know that's not true.*

No more answer came. Cody sat leaning against the wall, uncertain what to do. At last, he texted again, *I'm at the barn. Jordan, I know you want this. Meet me, please.*

It was as much desperation as he was willing to show.

After dinner he'd casually mentioned he was going for his walk. He'd established a nightly habit of taking long walks just for this purpose. Sometimes he used the time for peace and quiet. Other times he used it for hookups. But since it was a habit, his family never questioned it.

After listening to his Dad, Cody had a lot of frustration to burn off, and he wanted to burn it off on Jordan.

The sun sank slowly, darkening the barn. Cody closed his eyes and sank into the ache of unrequited need.

"What do you want from me?"

The words were spoken softly, in a deep, young voice. Cody opened his eyes. Jordan stood over him, holding a flashlight. Night had fallen. "I can't stop thinking about you," Cody admitted.

"Fuck you. I said as much to you last week and you…you hurt me, Cody. I'm not like you. I don't do hookups. I thought we had something real."

Cody stood and looked down at Jordan. He brushed his knuckle along the newly grown stubble of his jaw. "You trying to look tough with this?" Cody asked.

Jordan didn't smile.

Cody did. "I like it. Makes you look older. More experienced."

Jordan's blue eyes softened in the glow of the flashlight.

He'd shown up. Cody took that to mean he was still interested. That he still had feelings. So he leaned in to kiss him.

But Jordan backed up. "I won't let you use me."

Cody straightened and rolled his shoulders back. "What are your terms?"

"Terms?"

"Yeah. What do you need from me to be with me?"

Jordan let out a laugh and fell back a step. "Is this how it works? Negotiation? I want to date like normal people, Cody."

"We're not normal people."

"Sure we are. What about Harry and Martin. They're married. Nobody bothers them. They've got lots of friends. They go to parties and bars together. Chad Baker…he's gay. Openly. Goes to bars to hook up. Even goes to that other church on Sundays."

"They don't have Gideon Deathridge for a father. I've stayed under the radar for almost thirty years, I'm not about to rock the boat now. I like you, Jordan. A lot. I wanna keep seeing you. But if you think there's some chance of the two of us having a 'normal' relationship, then I…I just feel sorry for you. You're never going to have that in this town."

Jordan shook his head and started walking toward the door. "Then goodbye. I don't want to do this with you."

Cody grabbed his arm, panic seizing his throat. "Please," he begged before he could stop himself. "I need this. I need you. Please, Jordan."

Jordan's eyes welled. "If you want me, you can ask me on a date like a man. We'll go to dinner, have a few drinks, and fuck like animals in the back of your truck. But I'll be damned if I'm going to be your dirty little secret."

With that, he left, and with him, Cody's breath. Cody sank to the ground, leaned against the wall, and waited for the pain to pass. It didn't, though, not entirely. It swelled like a mushroom cloud and then shrank back to a small ache, but it didn't disappear. He stood and walked back home.

It Took A Rumor

Molly paced the floor, staring at her phone. He hadn't called or texted in days. Days. Was he finished with her?

The light in the sitting room was dim, which fit her mood. She was going crazy, desire and fear warring within her. This was a need. A fundamental need. She'd become hooked on Boone Deathridge and now he was withholding from her. She'd texted him a dozen times. Left six voicemails.

"Honey, is something bothering you?"

She looked up. Richard stood at the edge of the room. He rarely came in. Through some unwritten agreement they'd decided that this room was her private space. Richard had always respected that. "I'm fine," she said.

"You seem distracted. Upset."

"No, it's nothing. I'm fine."

"Honey, I'm worried."

"Well, don't be," she snapped.

Richard stepped into the room. He took her by the arm and led her down to the sofa. "I'm worried about us."

"Why? What's wrong?"

"I think you know what's wrong."

"Don't talk to me like I'm a child!" she snapped. She squeezed her eyes shut and inhaled deeply, struggling to control her temper. "I'm sorry," she said more calmly. "I just need some time alone."

Richard sighed. Instead of leaving, he leaned back in the chair. "One of my jobs as a pastor is to counsel people.

I counsel a lot of couples. Molly, honey, something's not right between us, and I don't know what. If it's something I've done, I wish you would tell me."

Molly tried to push the guilt away. Usually this wasn't a problem with her, but this time, she couldn't manage it. She fought as hard as she could, but still ended up weeping into her hands.

"Molly, talk to me. I promise, there's nothing you could tell me that would make me love you less."

"Oh, Richard!" she cried. She turned into his arms. He held her. Rocked her. Kissed the top of her head.

And then her phone buzzed in her pocket.

It Took A Rumor

Boone waited until everyone was asleep. He hadn't been planning on contacting Molly anymore. He'd been getting kind of bored with her, truth be told. But after three days and no luck at the bars that weekend, he was beginning to get the itch. Besides which, all the tension at the dinner table gave him that antsy feeling of wanting to run away or do something bad.

Granted, screwing the preacher's wife had become rather blasé, it was still the baddest thing he was doing at the moment. He texted her and waited. After about fifteen minutes, she texted back.

Where do you want to meet? She asked.

Motel?

Someone will recognize my car.

Use Ivy's truck.

The phone rang. "Hey, beautiful," Boone answered.

"Richard's getting suspicious."

"You want to cool things off for a while?"

"Honestly, Boone, I thought we already had. I thought you were done with me."

He flicked a piece of lint off his jeans. "No, baby, of course not. How could you even think that?"

"It's just you haven't called—"

"I've been really busy. But I've been thinking of you the whole time."

He heard her sigh. And sniffle. Maybe this was a bad idea. He'd thought she was cool, but if she was getting too attached, he should let her go. When she spoke again, it was in a soft voice. "Okay, I can meet you tomorrow night. I'll see if Ivy can help me, and I'll text you a time and place."

"Perfect. I can't wait."

"Me, either. Boone?"

"Yeah?"

"I just want you to know…you mean so much to me. So much."

"Uh, yeah. You do too, babe. See you tomorrow." He hung up, tossed his phone on the nightstand, and went into the bathroom to take a shower before bed.

Part 3: Tangled Webs

Myra's Blog

As promised, I have some inside information to share. But who would have thought Sunday would yield such drama?

Ivy Turner has now been spotted in public with two of the four Deathridge boys, which narrows things down considerably. Of course, Ivy is a modern girl. Perhaps she's seeing them all. In any case, the most likely candidate is the bestower of a very public kiss...one Dallas Deathridge. Although it does appear to have been a goodbye kiss. Is our Ivy broken hearted? Or will she simply move on to the next brother? Time will tell.

But folks, that's not what I want to talk about today. It's come to my attention that there might be more to the Turner/Deathridge rivalry than a patch of land and a daughter of ill repute. I can't say for certain, but my vast experience when it comes to angry, competitive men, says that there is a woman involved. Did the two men once battle over little Clara Deathridge? Or was it the lovely Penelope, rest her soul?

As always, I'm thrilled to hear from my viewers if anyone has information on this or any other juicy topics.

Ta-ta, for now!

Ivy's relationship with Tim, her boyfriend from Tulsa, had been a practical affair. They'd spent two years having practical conversations and practical sex and practical goodbyes. It wasn't in her nature to behave in a dreamy manner. But the next day, no matter how she tried, she could not come down off the high of being in Jake's arms. So she stubbed her toe, locked her keys in her truck, forgot the main thing she went to the grocery store for, and just overall botched the day. Edna at work didn't say anything, but she cast Ivy occasional, suspicious glances.

It was through sheer force of will that Ivy refrained from calling Jake, or even sneaking over to his ranch to find him and throw herself at him. No, she was determined to be a lady and wait for him to pay proper suit. Still, if she'd known what obstacles were about to present themselves, she might have thrown her principles to the wind and seized the impulse.

Her first hint of trouble happened that evening. At six, she started dinner preparations. It was a quiet time for her, her father still out with the cattle while she put together a heart-healthy dinner for him. Tonight it was a thin slice of marinated chicken breast with a side of arugula salad and whole grain croutons. The great thing about cooking for her father was that the meals were in line with her own dietary preferences. Although she did occasionally sneak out for a pizza now and then.

As she was plating dinner, there was a knock at her front door. Rather, a pounding. She hurried to open it, finding Reno Yates, one of her ranch hands, frantic and out of breath. "Ma'am, I'm sorry to bother you. There was a fight at the bunk house. Jordan's bleeding pretty bad."

"Oh, my God. Can he be moved? Do we need..."

Just then, Reno stepped aside, making way for three men. Two were ranch hands with Jordan's arms over their shoulders, practically dragging him between them as blood poured from his nose down his mouth and chin. Ivy rushed into action. She ran to the laundry room where she had a basket of towels fresh from the dryer. She grabbed an armful and covered the couch. The boys lowered Jordan while Ivy wet one of the towels to start cleaning up Jordan's face.

"Is there anything besides the broken nose?" she asked, cleaning Jordan as gently as she could.

"I don't think so," Jordan rasped.

"If he doesn't have a broken rib or two, they'll at the very least be severely bruised," Reno said.

"Let's get him cleaned up and to the hospital," Ivy said. "One of you guys call the police."

Jordan shook his head. "No police. It's just a fight."

"It's assault. You'll press charges, of course."

"No. Come on, Miss Ivy. Let's just handle it among us. Please."

She looked into his blood-shot, watery eyes. Men. Of course, it would be a whole lot easier if they did handle it themselves, but Jordan deserved justice. She'd better figure out what happened first.

Having got the worst of the blood off Jordan's face, Ivy reclined him against the arm of the sofa with an ice pack and a whole lot of tissues. Then she turned, took in a deep breath, and faced the three ranch hands. "All right. Spill."

The two behind Reno ducked their heads and shuffled their feet. Reno cleared his throat. "Beau and Wylie."

Ivy nodded, not at all surprised. "Okay. So how did it start?"

For this, Reno looked to Jordan, who closed his eyes and said, "They found some gay porn on my phone."

"Why did they have your phone?"

"Beau just grabbed it from me. Wanted to check baseball scores or something."

Ivy sighed. It was all the more reason for them to handle things in-house. Spare poor Jordan the embarrassment of being outed to the whole town. "You're sure you don't want to press charges?"

"What would they do, a couple nights in jail? Pay a fine? Not worth it. Just leave it, Miss Ivy."

She studied him to make sure he was serious. Then she nodded. "Okay. Well, let's get you to the hospital and checked out. Terry, you and Billy wait here for Jared. When he gets back, give him the whole story, okay?"

"No hospital. It's just a broken nose," Jordan said.

"We want to be sure there's no other head injury."

Jordan started to object again.

"It's non-negotiable, Jordan. I'm your employer and I won't risk it. Reno, you'll come with us?"

"Yes, ma'am," Reno said.

The guys helped Jordan to the truck while Ivy gathered her purse and keys.

On the ride there, as Ivy drove, Reno cleared his throat again. "Uh, so, are you really gay?" he asked.

Ivy bit her tongue as Jordan turned and glared at his coworker.

Reno put his hands up. "I'm not judging. I got a cousin who's gay. Of course, she's a lesbian, so it's kind of hot."

Jordan dropped his head back and pressed the ice pack to the bridge of his nose. "You're an asshole."

Reno laughed. "Yeah, but that's what you like, right? Assholes?"

"Jesus, Reno," Ivy said, though she found herself fighting back laughter.

When Jordan started laughing, it gave Ivy and Reno permission to let loose. By the time it was over, Reno was giving Jordan's shoulder a friendly squeeze and promising to watch out for him on the ranch from now on. Ivy didn't tell him it was completely unnecessary. Beau and Wylie would be gone by morning.

At the hospital, Reno and Ivy sat in the waiting room while a doctor examined Jordan. Ivy decided it wasn't her place to contact Cody, so she waited until the doctor was finished and went into Jordan's room.

"Will they do X-rays?" she asked.

"Yeah, that's next." His voice sounded restrained. The swelling in his nose made him sound like he had a bad cold. Ivy could barely look at him. The bruising spread beneath his eyes and over his nose.

"I was wondering if there's anyone you want me to contact?"

"You mean my folks? No way. This'll be all healed up before I see them next. Thank you, though."

"Okay. What about Cody?"

Jordan's head snapped to the side as he frowned at her. "No. Thank you."

Ivy bit her bottom lip. "I can't help thinking he'd like to be here for you."

Jordan laughed bitterly and looked away. "Nah. That's over. But thank you for thinking of it."

Ivy might have argued, but the guy was so damned polite. She simply said, "You're welcome," and returned to the waiting room.

All told, they spent almost five hours in the ER. The X-rays revealed two cracked ribs. Reno reminded Ivy that Beau wore steel-toed boots. The image hit Ivy with clarity, and her emotions suddenly burst through the protective layer of shock that had helped her remain so level-headed. She took Jordan home, giving him a room in the main house for the night. Once he was settled, she went with Reno and her father, who kindly let her be the one to fire Beau and Wylie.

The two men argued with her, which only fueled her anger. By the time she was finished with them, they were packing their things and starting the long walk to the bus station in town. Ivy wasn't sure if they feared her or were simply anxious to get away from the crazy screaming lady, but either way, she felt better.

Unfortunately, it was nearly eleven by the time she got showered and settled into her bedroom. All afternoon, she'd harbored the hope of another connection with Jake. But he'd have gone to bed hours ago so he could be up at the crack of dawn to work and sweat and just generally be the man he was meant to be. Still, with a sigh, Ivy lay back on her bed and lifted her phone screen. She pushed the home button and smiled.

I wanna see you.

The text had come three hours ago. It must have disappointed him not to receive a text back. At least she hoped it did. She hoped he stared at his phone a good fifteen minutes before setting it aside. And then stopped to check it every time he walked by it throughout the evening. And then lay in bed staring at the ceiling just hoping and yearning. Poor man! He could very well be awake and torturing himself.

Ivy started texting him back, but jumped when the phone rang in her hand. She tapped the green button and pressed it to her ear, smiling in spite of her best efforts to remain calm. "Hello," she said. She almost said, "Hello, Jake," since she hadn't seen the name on the screen.

"Ivy, it's Boone."

Her anticipatory fervor vanished. "What do you want?" she snapped, more harshly than was necessary.

"Is Molly at your place?"

"No, Boone. Why are you still seeing her? I thought that had fizzled."

"Shit," he muttered. "She was supposed to meet me an hour ago. She was gonna walk up to the covered bridge from her house, and then I was going to pick her up."

"So she decided not to come. What's the big deal?"

"She's not answering her phone."

"Boone, she's probably changed her mind. There's plenty of other fish in the sea, right?"

"I'd feel better if I knew she was okay. You're right, it's not that big of a deal. But she's never failed to show up or answer her phone. So, I mean, could you check on her?"

Ivy sighed. "I'll call her in the morning. If she doesn't answer, I'll drive by and see."

Silence.

"Boone, seriously, it's almost midnight."

"Something doesn't feel right."

"Fine. Stay there. I'll call you back."

It Took A Rumor

Ivy hung up, found Molly's number, and called. No answer. She thought about calling Richard, but what was she going to say? *Hey, Richard, your wife failed to show up to meet her lover, do you happen to know where she is?*

She lay in bed, hoping her phone would ring. After a while, though, she sat up and swung her legs out of bed. It was ridiculous. Nothing. Molly was likely sleeping soundly in her room. Besides, if she knocked on the door, Ivy would be confronted with the same dilemma as a phone call: what to say to Richard.

Even so, she dressed and quietly slipped out of the house. Her father slept on the opposite side of the house on the second floor. A jackhammer couldn't wake him up between the hours of ten and four.

Ivy drove towards the parsonage. It was weird being out at night. It took more effort, maybe because she was tired, or maybe because the whole world was asleep. But as she drove, she only got sleepier and more doubtful of her actions. It just didn't feel right.

She parked at the church building, got out, and walked the little trail through the woods that led to the house. Naturally, all the lights were off. Molly's car was in the driveway next to Richard's. Ivy hesitated at the edge of the front lawn. The night air cut right through her sweatpants and t-shirt. The grass was wet and so was the air, dampening her skin and chilling her to her bones.

Some of the windows in the house were open. Perhaps she could get a peek inside. She took one step and stopped. Nope. This was going too far. She wouldn't trespass to assuage her curiosity. She would simply wait until morning like a sane person.

Retreating into the woods, she called Boone.

"Find her?" he asked.

"I was going to peek in the windows of her house, but figured that was going too far. Her car's here. The lights are out. I'll just check on her in the morning."

"Ivy, please. Just see if she's in there."

"I can knock on the door, but it's going to look pretty weird."

"Don't. Don't knock. Just go look in the window."

Ivy sighed. "If she's home, she's home. If she's not, what do you want to do?"

"I'll keep looking for her. If something happened to her because she was walking through the woods alone in the dark to meet me, I'll…"

"You'll what? Suddenly sprout a conscience?"

He sighed. "Please. Please just look."

She hung up again, took a breath, and used the flashlight function to work her way around the edge of the yard to the side of the house. She'd been to Molly's plenty of times and knew exactly where the bedroom was. As she got closer to the house, she turned off her phone light, fought to control her breathing, and tip-toed up to the window.

Fortunately, a shaft of moonlight shone straight into the open window and onto the bed. Unfortunately, Molly wasn't there. What was more, neither was Richard. The bed was made and not a sign of anyone in the room.

Ivy backed away, frowning. She pulled out her phone to text Boone. She barely heard the footsteps rushing up behind her before something blunt slammed into her head. The rest was blackness.

Ivy woke up to bright lights and the wrong Deathridge brother gazing down at her with deep concern.

"And you say she fell?" asked a female voice.

"Yeah. We were getting kind of rowdy, dancing. I spun her, she fell, hit her head on the corner of a table," Boone said. "She gonna be okay?"

"Let's check her out. Ivy?"

Ivy turned her eyes to the female voice. "I was just here," she said, because it was true. Hadn't she just been in the hospital with Jordan?

"Let's get you sitting up."

The doctor and Boone pulled on her arms. She laughed as they pulled her upright. The room seemed to rock. "Are we on a ship?"

"Is this normal?" Boone asked.

"Confusion is a symptom of a concussion. Ivy, I need you to focus on my finger and follow it with your eyes."

Ivy squinted and followed the doctor's movements. "I'm getting seasick."

It came on her fast. But somehow, there was a trash can in her arms just as she vomited. A cool cloth touched her lips. Ivy suddenly felt sleepy.

"Stay awake, honey," Jake said. She couldn't see him, but she was sure it was him. Who else would be with her right then?

"I'm sorry I didn't text you back earlier," she said.

"Ivy, open your eyes."

She obeyed with great effort, and then frowned. "Boone? Ugh." She closed her eyes again.

"What the hell does that mean? Open your eyes, Ivy."

She got one open, but as she got the other open, the first one fell back down. She laughed all the way to the CT Scan. Throughout that process, she started to regain some of her clarity. By the time the doctor was giving her diagnosis, Ivy's confusion had gone, leaving her with an excruciating headache and a very bad attitude.

They sent her home with pain medication and orders to return in twenty-four hours for a checkup. At five in the morning, Boone Deathridge was driving her back to her house.

"My truck's at the church."

"I'll take someone and get it for you."

"Just take me. I can drive it home."

Boone just gave her a look and went back to frowning at the road. "Never found Molly."

"I'm sure she and Richard are just away."

"Somebody hit you on the head, Ivy."

She breathed. "Yeah. They did."

There was nothing else to say. Neither of them knew who'd done it. Ivy hadn't heard nor seen anything useful. If she'd been anywhere else, she'd be scared shitless. But she'd been trespassing. Could have been a groundskeeper taking out an intruder, then running away when he saw it was harmless Ivy Turner. Who knew? But one thing was for certain, in Ivy's mind anyway—there was a perfectly logical explanation for it. And for Molly's absence.

Boone pulled into Ivy's driveway as the dark sky was lightening to blue. He rushed around to her side and scooped her into his arms.

"Put me down right this minute," she said, but the yawn kind of ruined the effect. She rested her head on his shoulder and let him carry her up the steps and into her house. She'd initially intended to walk up to her room, but since Boone was inclined to be a gentlemen about the whole thing, she went ahead and let him.

"Your old man must still be asleep," Boone whispered as he lay Ivy in her bed.

"He won't be for long. I need to make him breakfast."

"You need to rest. Text me when you wake up."

"Why?"

"Because I wanna know you're okay. You check in with me, or I'll come over and check on you."

"Okay," she said, curling into her pillow. "Night, Jake."

"Wrong brother, honey." He stroked her hair.

She was asleep before her door clicked shut.

Jake slept fitfully at best, achingly wishing for some contact from Ivy. They'd left on such good terms, he was sure she wasn't purposely ignoring his text.

When four-thirty rolled around, he gave up and got up. He fixed his coffee, drank his coffee, dressed, and dragged himself down to the stables. Ivy wanted to be properly courted, and though it was early in the morning, he still intended to see her. He saddled up Old Gray, who was substituting for Jake's mare. Eloise was due to foal in a couple of months and Jake had quit riding her. He walked her regularly, but didn't want to take any chances on hurting her.

He rode out to a little pond on the western part of the property where he knew there to be a bunch of Forget-Me-Nots blooming. He hopped off his horse, gathered some flowers, then found a thin vine to wrap around the stems, making a beautiful, blue bouquet for Ivy to wake up to.

He might leave it on her windowsill, if he could figure out which was hers. But barring that, he'd leave it in the handle of her front door. No note. She'd know who they were from.

Smiling to himself, he adjusted his Stetson, climbed back in the saddle, and rode through the fields, jumping the fence between his property and hers. Old Gray's hooves pounded the earth, and wind whipped through its mane and Jake's hair. The thrill of riding never ended, not since the first time he'd ridden as a child, except now it was equally as peaceful as it was exciting.

As the top of Ivy's house came into view, Jake slowed. The sun hadn't yet breached the horizon, but the sky was becoming a lighter shade of blue by the second. Still, it was dark enough that Jake could see a light in one of the upstairs windows. He brought his horse to a stop just outside the picket fence around the yard. He couldn't see the front door from where he stood. When the light went out in Ivy's room, he smiled to himself and hopped off his horse. Perhaps she'd be coming outside. If not, he felt comfortable knocking since he knew she was awake.

He jumped the picket fence and made his way to the corner of the house, just about to round to the front. The door swung open. He stopped and stepped back. Because coming out of Ivy's house, as casual as could be, was his youngest brother.

Jake spied on him until he'd driven away. He leaned back against the siding of the house and frowned. What the hell was going on? Jake could think of only one good reason to be in this house at this time of morning, but that didn't make any sense. He wanted to trust Ivy. The fact was, he did trust Ivy. She said she wasn't sleeping with his brothers, so there must be another explanation. But then again, Boone was a charming kid. And hadn't the two of them grown up together? Gone to school together?

Maybe he should knock. Maybe he should leave and gather his thoughts. No, he should definitely knock.

Jake slowly blew out a deep breath and jogged quietly up the front porch steps. He stared at the door for a solid minute. Then he tucked the bouquet of flowers in the screen door handle. He got back on his horse, rode home, and hoped for the best in spite of the fear burning in his stomach.

Clara Deathridge knew something was wrong with her boys. She'd thrown out more leftovers in a week than the past thirty-some years combined. No one was eating. It was an abomination.

Thinking she needed to up her game, Clara scoured Pinterest for new recipes to try. She'd never done it before, and what she found was that the world of country cooking had changed drastically. There were still good ole fried foods, but nowadays people had salads with them. And not just chopped up iceberg lettuce with carrot shavings on top. No, these were much greener, much more complex salads. Perhaps this was the sort of thing that would jar her boys out of their funks.

Clara went grocery shopping, full of energy and enthusiasm. Tonight, she would fix a meal fit for modern cowboy kings. The shopping took longer than usual since there were so many unfamiliar ingredients. Once she had what she needed, though, she picked up her pace and headed straight home to begin cooking.

She boiled pasta for the individual spaghetti bakes she was making in the new ramekins she'd bought. One thing she learned from Pinterest was that you could spice up an ordinary food just by preparing it a little differently.

She hand-rolled pasta to make ravioli which she then breaded in preparation for frying, later. As mealtime approached, she got the spaghettis in the oven, slapped a big rib-eye on her griddle, and began frying ravioli. In between batches, she flipped the steak, gathered the salad ingredients, and began tossing them in a large, wooden bowl: arugula, baby greens, sprouts, cherry tomatoes, red onions, and large shavings of fresh parmesan cheese. She'd always bought the granules in the green, plastic container...wow, what a difference fresh was.

She pulled the peppered steak off the grill and let it rest while she finished the last of the ravioli. She sliced the steak and topped the salad with it. At ten minutes until the boys would be coming home, she began setting the table. The salad was the centerpiece, in a large wooden bowl. She put several different dressings in tiny glass pitchers she'd bought just for the occasion. These she placed around the salad bowl. She divided the ravioli onto two small platters so each end of the table could get to them without having to pass them around. Each plate had ravioli surrounding a small bowl of marinara dipping sauce.

After that, she set out the plates, napkins, forks, and knives. She placed a ramekin of baked spaghetti on each plate. With less than two minutes to go, she filled six glasses with ice, poured sweet tea in each of them, and got the last one placed as Gideon walked through the door, closely followed by the boys.

"Smells good. I'm hungry," Gideon said, though the compliment had little meaning since that was what he said every evening.

Clara smiled as she removed her apron. Cooking had been a rare thrill, today. It had actually been a creative experience. Fresh and lively. She gestured her wan-looking boys to take their seats. They all remained standing behind their chairs until she sat. Such sweet, gentlemanly boys. After they were seated at last, Gideon said, "So...what do we got here, momma?"

"Well, there's individual baked spaghettis. Fried ravioli with dipping sauce. And a steak and parmesan salad." She put on a proud smile, though she was twisting her apron string round and round her fingers as she waited for a reaction. All she got from her boys was the hesitant lifting of their silverware as they took careful first bites of their spaghetti. Perhaps because it was served in different dishes they didn't know if it would taste the same.

Gideon merely frowned at his. He looked at the salad. "We supposed to dip that out with our hands?"

"Oh, the tongs." Clara hopped out of her seat and hurried to the kitchen. It was frustrating, but it seemed there was always at least one thing she forgot to bring to the table. She dug them out of the utensil drawer and hurried back to the table. "Here you go, dear."

Gideon took the tongs, stared at the salad in confusion for a moment, then put a few leaves on his plate, followed by most of the steak.

"Dear, think of the boys," Clara said.

"Yeah, Pop, jeez," Dallas said, snatching the tongs and getting as much steak as he could before Cody smacked his hand and took over. By the time poor Jake got to the salad, there was no meat left on top at all.

"I can cook another steak," Clara said.

Jake shook his head. "Not necessary, Mom. Unless you want some."

Clara stared in dismay at the failed salad.

"Where's the parmesan cheese?" Gideon asked. "Didn't you say there'd be parmesan cheese?"

"That's it, there on the salad. It's real. Not the jar stuff."

Gideon grunted, tasted a shaving of cheese, and made a disgusted face. He picked the rest of the cheese off the salad.

Dallas and Boone seemed to be in a grabbing match for the plate of ravioli nearest them. Gideon pulled the other plate to his setting, clearly claiming the entire thing as his own. Jake and Cody didn't get any.

"They're supposed to be for sharing," Clara said, though her words were drowned out by the noise of the tussle.

"You know better than to set the table like this, Clara," Gideon said. "Gotta dish out the food in the kitchen, or the boys always end up fighting."

Clara sank into her chair.

"You snooze, you lose," Boone muttered.

To which Jake gave a completely disproportionate response when he shouted, "You're a selfish asshole, Boone!"

"Whoa! What the hell, man?"

Gideon reached over and smacked Jake upside the head. "You watch your language at the table young man."

"Maybe if you hadn't raised the little shit to think he can have whatever he wants whenever he wants it there'd be enough…food for the rest of us!"

"Jake, honey," Clara said, trying to calm him down. This behavior from him was unheard of.

But it was too late for Gideon, who rounded on Jake. "If you don't lower your voice and apologize this minute, you and me are gonna go out back and have a conversation."

Jake let out a sharp laugh. "Right, like I'm still twelve. I ain't gonna be intimidated by you anymore, Pop. And you," he said, standing and pointing at Boone. "You're about to learn real quick to quit trying to take what's not yours." With that, Jake turned and stormed out of the house. Again.

Clara gasped in her breaths, tears rolling silently down her cheeks. She turned to Boone, surprised to find him pale and staring at the space in front of him. It wasn't like Boone to act rattled. Then again, he didn't often get yelled at by his oldest brother. Clara reached over and gave his arm a squeeze. "It's okay, dearest. I'll talk to Jake and make sure he apologizes."

Boone pushed away from the table and left out the back door.

Clara looked to her other two boys. Cody was sitting calmly, eyes downcast, holding a fork in one hand, his napkin in the other. Dallas had a hand over his stomach, wincing. "I'm sorry, Mom," Dallas said, "maybe all the

It Took A Rumor

yelling is stressing out my stomach." He pushed his plate away.

She looked helplessly back at Cody. When he met her eyes, he smiled encouragingly and started eating. "It's good, Mom. Shame those two had to pick tonight to fight."

Clara smiled sadly. "You all seem so distracted lately."

Gideon sat across the table from her, eating his steak voraciously, and popping ravioli in between bites of steak.

"It's just a phase," Cody said. "We'll get it together."

"I hope so. I don't believe Jake's eaten a thing in days."

"Did you hear about the Turners losing a couple of their ranch hands yesterday?" Gideon asked.

It took Clara a moment to realize he was talking to her. She choked down her sadness, put on a brave smile, and said, "No, dear. What happened?"

Gideon grunted. "Apparently their newest hand is one of them fags. Two of the boys found out and beat the tar out of him. You ask me, Turner fired the wrong ones. Fella wants to be gay, I reckon that's his business, but he damn sure better keep it to himself. You ask me, he had it coming. But oh, no, not Turner. Fancy's himself a man of the world. Fires two perfectly good hands in order to keep some twig boy probably can't even lift a bale of hay."

"I suppose they'll be looking to hire," Clara said, for the sake of conversation.

"I reckon. I figure they were understaffed as it was-"

"Is the kid all right? The new guy?" Cody asked.

Clara saw that Cody had now abandoned his supper as well. Perhaps there was a stomach bug going around. He certainly looked pale and ill.

"The fag, you mean?" Gideon asked. "Hell if I know. Even if he survives this earth, he'll be burning in hell fires for all eternity. Don't figure it matters much when he starts."

"Jesus Christ, Dad!" Cody shouted.

Clara jumped in her seat, because if anyone was going to remain silent at the dinner table it was her gentle Cody boy. "Honey, are you—"

Gideon interrupted her. "You'll not take the Lord's name in v—"

"Fuck that!" Cody leapt to his feet. "I don't care how much you disapprove of someone, they don't deserve to get the shit beat out of them simply for existing. Jesus, I can't fucking believe this family." And with that, he followed Jake's path out the door.

"Mom, can I go lie down," Dallas said.

Clara's mouth was already open, but she didn't have time to respond to him.

Gideon interrupted. "If you're getting sick, you can go rest at your own house. Don't need me or your momma getting sick, too. It's harder on us older folks."

Dallas nodded and stood gingerly, cradling his stomach.

"Gideon, please," Clara said, finally finding her voice. "If he's sick, I'll take care of him."

"No, mom, he's right. Thanks, though. I'll be fine."

She watched as he hobbled out the front door. Fortunately, he had a vehicle to drive, since the others had left on foot.

Gideon continued the business of finishing his meal. "Don't know what's gotten into them lately," he muttered. "Ought to take my belt to every one of them."

Clara left him, muttering to himself at the table. It didn't appear he would miss her. She went to her bedroom, laid her face in her pillow, and cried.

Jake walked down to the creek, across the fence from the flat rock where Ivy had been reading that day. The sun was setting, but he didn't care. He checked his phone for a reply to the text he'd sent ten minutes ago when he'd started walking this way.

No reply.

Twice he'd texted her. Twice she'd ignored him. And twice she'd been in compromising positions with his brothers.

Jake hopped the fence and sank down onto the flat rock. He lay back on Turner ground and stared at the sky through the leaves above him. He couldn't think why of all the places one could sit and read a book, Ivy would choose something as uncomfortable as a rock. But perhaps she enjoyed the trickling of the creek. Or the birds singing nearby. Or the way the breeze whispered through the leaves. He was beginning to understand that Ivy was a romantic at heart.

"Jake?"

He sat up and spun around. "Ivy." He stood and dusted off his jeans. He reached for his hat before he realized he wasn't wearing it.

"I would have texted back," she said, "but I figured I'd just walk on down here."

"You look so beautiful." She had on leggings and an oversized t-shirt with a coffee stain down the front. Her hair hung loose and wild. She laughed at his comment.

"You must be really hard up."

He shook his head as he looked her up and down. Beautiful. It was exactly the word he wanted.

"Did you leave me those Forget-Me-Nots this morning?"

This brought his head straight back to reality. "Uh, yeah. I did. Right after I saw my brother walking out of your house."

Her smile vanished. "Oh."

Jake's heart sank. "Yeah. So…are you gonna make me ask?"

She walked past him, braced herself on a nearby tree, and lowered herself to sit on the ground. He interpreted the careful movements as a reaction over the emotional shock of being caught redhanded. Though he still wasn't sure what he'd caught her at. He sat across from her and waited.

"I hit my head last night," she said, frowning. "And Boone took me to the ER."

He'd have jumped into immediate concern if her story made any sense at all. Still, as he studied her face, he could see a paleness, there, and a darkness under her eyes. "You hit your head," he said. He took her chin gently in his fingertips and tilted her head up.

"It's just a mild concussion. Still, I've been resting all day."

"You shouldn't have walked all this way."

"I was feeling cooped up. Didn't think the jostling from riding would be good for my head."

Jake frowned at her. His righteous ire dampened by warmer feelings. "A concussion. And Boone...he took you to the hospital."

"Yes."

"And then he spent the night at your house?"

"What you saw was him dropping me off back home. Jake, I'm so sorry, that's all I can tell you. And it's more than anyone else knows, and I have to ask you to keep it between us."

"Keep what between us? You're not going to tell me how you hit your head or why it was Boone who was there to rescue you?"

"I can't. Please, you have to trust me."

He let go of her chin, moved a little closer to her, and rested his hand on her knee. "I don't like to think of my brother rescuing you."

"You'd rather I was left alone to fend for myself."

If he was going to pursue Ivy, he was going to have to get used to some things...namely, her mouth. She had a tendency to rush to the offensive that wasn't entirely fair to him. But then, he supposed she must be getting tired of being accused of sleeping with his brothers. "Obviously what I meant was, I wanna be the one to rescue you."

She sighed and put her hand over his. "If it's any consolation, I'm not often in need of rescuing."

"You and he grew up together. Went to school together."

"Yeah? So?"

He looked up at her and saw the stubbornness in her eyes. She was practically daring him to ask her if she'd ever slept with his brother. "You gotta try and see this from my point of view, Ivy. I like you. Hell, I'm crazy over you. But...I don't like going in blind. And if you've...if you've ever..."

She huffed and pulled her hand away, pushing to her feet a little too fast. Jake stood to steady her when she swayed, but she pulled away from him. "I'm fine. Now, what is your obsession with whether or not I've slept with any of your brothers?"

"It's not an obsession, it's just, no man wants to...to..."

"Would you like me any less if I had?"

He frowned at her. Studied her. "All I hear is you dodging the question."

He recognized pride when he saw it, and Ivy had it in spades. It was in the way she lifted her chin, the pinkness that flooded her cheeks, and the narrowing of her eyes. Through gritted teeth she said, "I don't owe you anything."

She'd said those words to him before. They were just as true now as they were then, but he still couldn't stop himself. "I think if you want me to endanger my whole livelihood you owe me something."

She threw her hands up and shouted. "You're infuriating! I already told you I wasn't sleeping with your brothers, and I told you that was as much as I could give you. You said it was enough, but it's not. No, I'm just something to be conquered, aren't I? Just a piece of undiscovered territory you want to plant your flag on first, right? The thrill's gone if someone else has already been there!"

"That's not…"

"That's exactly what this is. Whether or not I've slept with your brothers, Jake, I wasn't a virgin that day that you had me. You know that, right? I've probably…no, definitely had sex with people you know."

"Who?" The question out of his mouth came naturally, but if he'd thought for just a moment, he'd have known better than to ask.

Ivy dropped her head back and laughed. "You don't get to know that. If it matters that much to you, then I don't want to be with you. No, you know what? I'm done with you, Jake." She turned and started walking away.

The words hit him like a Mack truck, slapping him silent. She was done with him? Like, forever? He couldn't breathe as he watched her walk away. She was ten paces on before he finally got his feet to move.

He caught up to her, matching her stride. "Ivy, this is just a fight. You can't drop me every time we have a fight."

She spun on her heel to face him. "This is not a fight. This is a deal breaker. The fact is, Jake, you have too many conditions upon which you're willing to invest in me. I told you before, I want a man who goes after what he wants. If you wanted me, you should have been bold about it. Fearless. Instead, all you're worried about is making sure I'm worthy of your efforts. And *that* based on who I've slept with. You're making me feel ashamed of myself when I've got nothing to be ashamed of. So that, for me, is a deal breaker."

She turned, but he said, "Ivy, wait. Please. Please just hear me out and try to understand where I'm coming from."

She folded her arms over her chest and arched a brow, classic bitch posture, and he had to fight to keep from smiling. She'd look at their children like that, one day. She'd give them that look and they'd spill their guts. She'd give Jake that look and he'd take out the trash or make the bed or whatever else she wanted. He had the sense of knowing her better just for having seen this posture; the sense of having an inside understanding of her.

He thought of her smooth skin on his hands, of her sweet whispers and kisses, of the way she made him see the future as clear as the light of day. "It's just hard for a man to know he's had to share his woman with other men. And with brothers would be a hundred times worse."

"That makes me feel like used toilet paper."

Jake swallowed, breathing slowly, careful with this fragile moment. "I don't want you to feel that way. I think the world of you."

"If that were true, it wouldn't matter who I've slept with."

"It doesn't. It's just...I don't want to be made a fool of."

"Because you'd be a fool to date someone who wasn't a virgin?"

Jake tensed, his own frustration building. She might be the woman he wanted to build a life with, but he still had his pride. And pride wasn't a bad thing. No, it was a necessary thing for a man. Especially a Deathridge man. He lifted his chin, set his jaw, and said, "If you slept with one or more of my brothers, then I want to know. That's all there is to it. That's a deal breaker for me."

"Oh, you're putting your foot down, now?"

"Looks that way."

"Okay, then we're at an impasse. Because I want to know you'd be with me regardless. I won't tell you because you haven't proven to me that I can count on your good faith. I won't tell you because now, if I said I had slept with one of your brothers, I'd always feel like you were holding that over my head."

He stared at her. At that beautiful face and body. At the first woman who'd ever made him feel something more than simple lust. He stared and knew there'd never be another like her. And yet, what could he do? Beg. He could beg. And suddenly, as the reality sank in and he realized he might never have a chance to touch her again, he went toward her. He took her by the arms and kissed her. "Please," he said against her lips.

She sank against him, her arms unfolding from her chest and reaching around his neck.

He kissed her cheek and ear and neck and murmured. "Please just tell me. Tell me so we can be together."

"If you want me, you know what to do," she said, her voice breathy.

"I do want you. More than anything. Don't throw this away because of pride."

"Right back atcha, Jake."

His lips landed on hers. He cupped her face and held her to him, kissing slowly, languidly. This couldn't end. It shouldn't end. Before Ivy, his life had been one hard-working day after the next, and he'd been happy. But how could he ever be happy with that again? It all seemed so dull and pointless without the hope of seeing her again.

She stepped back and he was forced to let her go. She turned and started walking without so much as a goodbye. Jake's grief momentarily faded in the wake of his anger. "So this is it? You can't answer one simple question?"

She kept walking.

"This is stupid, Ivy. You're being stupid!"

No change in her pace.

"I don't know what you think you're accomplishing, but I ain't coming after you. We could have been great, but you're not the only woman in this town I could be with."

He felt like crying. Ivy was a heartless bitch. There was no way she felt for him what he felt for her, not if she was walking away over this. No, she was getting a kick out of this. Getting a thrill out of hurting him this way.

That was what he told himself as he hopped the fence, and stomped off toward home. He knew it was just anger talking, but he also knew it was far better to be angry than that other feeling burning in his chest. Unfortunately, Jake wasn't one who could hold on to anger. He wasn't one to languish or weep or moan. So by the time he reached home, he'd settled into a sort of melancholy that made him just want to crawl into bed and sleep for the next few years.

It Took A Rumor

There wasn't enough pain medication in the world.

Ivy should have known better than to go to him. She'd gone and gotten her hopes and expectations up. As she'd walked, she'd envisioned being wrapped in his arms and made to feel safe and loved for just a few moments. Instead, she'd gotten the same interrogation he'd given her about Dallas.

Granted, it did look pretty bad, her holding all these secrets for his brothers. But still, why couldn't he extend her a little bit of unconditional trust?

Maybe that was unreasonable. Maybe he deserved to know. And maybe she'd consider confiding in him if he wasn't so hung up on her past bedfellows. Of course she'd never slept with his brothers. But just the mere fact that he was unwilling to proceed with a relationship until he found out was evidence enough that he was the macho, jealous type. Ivy was not interested in that type. Very interested in Jake. Just not his attitude.

She made it home, her head pounding, in time to say goodnight to her father, who was headed to bed. She'd lied to him about her head. Said a horse threw her and she hit her head on a rock, drove herself to the ER, and now needed rest. At least the last part was true.

She grabbed some ice cream out of the freezer, sat down in front of the television, and was about to eat straight out of the carton when there was a knock at her door.

With a weight-of-the-world sigh, she sat her ice cream on the coffee table and peeked out the peephole of her locked front door.

Cody Deathridge stood there, looking around like a thief about to be caught.

Normally, Ivy liked Cody best of all the brothers. He had the mildest manner and was the easiest to talk to. But lately she'd become rather overexposed to the Deathridge charms and only wanted a night or a week or a lifetime away from them and their drama.

She hurled open the door. "What?" she snapped.

Cody fell back a step, his eyes widening. "Uh, I heard about Jordan."

"I asked him if he wanted me to contact you and he said no. You need to go home."

Cody frowned. "You okay, Ivy? You look pale?"

"I have a headache."

"I'm sorry. Real sorry to bother you. I just couldn't sleep knowing he was hurt. I needed to hear for myself that he was okay."

"He's okay. Two cracked ribs and a broken nose."

"Oh. Damn."

"Yes. Is there anything else?"

Cody cleared his throat and looked down at his shoes. "I was hoping to see him. Maybe you could set something up?"

"I've asked him and he says you and he are done. I'm not getting in the middle of that."

"Sure. I understand. But maybe, if I could get him to agree to meet me, we could do it here? Like, when your old man is out?"

Ivy shrugged. It was a perfectly reasonable request. As much as she wanted to kick him in the shin and tell him never to darken her doorstep again, she was rational enough to know she was mad at the wrong brother. "Sure. That would be okay with me."

"Good. Thank you, Ivy. Is he safe tonight? Down at the bunkhouse?"

"I fired the two who did it, but he's sleeping upstairs in one of the guest rooms until he's back on his feet."

Cody's gaze traveled past her towards the stairs. "Is he asleep?"

Ivy sighed. "I don't know, Cody. I said goodnight to him a couple hours ago. He's been hitting the pain pills pretty heavily."

"Could I just, maybe, peek in? Check on him?"

"You don't think that's a little creepy? I mean, if the situation were reversed?"

He shrugged. "I guess. I just miss him."

"I didn't realize you had that much going on? I thought you were just hooking up."

When he met her eyes, Ivy saw the same look that was in Jake's eyes when he looked at her. The same emotion that was in her own heart. And she caved. "Fine." She pushed the door wider. "Let me see if he's awake, first."

As it turned out, Jordan was awake after all. He'd slept a while and then awakened to take another pain pill. As it hadn't kicked in just yet, he'd turned on the television to distract himself from the pain.

Cody waited as Ivy came back down the stairs.

"You can go up," she said. "Second door to the left. He's awake and willing to see you."

Cody nodded and looked Ivy over one last time. She'd lost weight. She looked exhausted. He was sorry for his part in burdening her. It must be mentally exhausting to carry someone else's secrets.

He went upstairs. Jordan's door was cracked open, the blue light from the television flickering and casting shadows. Cody rapped gently with his knuckle before going in. Jordan lay still, staring at the television. It was hard to see the levels of bruising, but the swelling around his nose was obvious. "Hey," Cody said, sitting hesitantly on the edge of the bed.

"What do you want?"

"I heard what happened and just had to see you. I'm so sorry."

"You didn't do it."

Cody stared down at where his hand rested on the bed inches from Jordan's. "When you care about someone, it feels like your fault if they get hurt. I don't know what I could have done. Maybe been there to fight for you. I'm angry I can't defend you. Avenge you."

Jordan gingerly turned his head on the pillow, meeting Cody's gaze. "You know, I can throw a punch. I didn't just fall down and take it."

Cody felt the beginnings of a smile working its way to the surface. "You don't strike me as a fighter."

"I'm not. But I've been in a few. I defended myself as long as I could. It was two-against-one, though. There's only so much you can do."

Cody nodded, returning his gaze to their hands. He reached up and enclosed Jordan's with his own. Tension left his body when Jordan didn't pull away. "You should have had someone by your side to make the numbers even."

"We could maybe…be friends?"

Cody's heart pounded and he wanted nothing more but to press it tightly against Jordan's. "You'd be okay with that?" Cody asked.

"Of course. I'd love to be friends with you. But if you want some of this action," he said, grabbing his crotch over his blankets, "you'll have to take me on a real date."

Cody laughed and leaned in to kiss Jordan on the cheek. "You're so fucking cute."

Jordan shifted to the side of the bed and patted the covers next to him. Cody lay down beside him, snaking his arm beneath Jordan's neck, careful not to jostle him too much. Jordan rested his head in the crook of Cody's shoulder, and they both fell asleep watching television.

Part 4: Dire Consequences

Myra's Blog

I try to keep my video blogs tongue-in-cheek and in keeping with a longstanding tradition of small town gossip, but today we have more serious matters to consider. For the official story, there's a link below this video to the Fair Grove Times. If you haven't heard the news, allow me to break it to you: Molly Allen was found dead in a creek bed not far from her house early this morning. According to her husband, Pastor Allen, she went missing two days ago. She'd told him she was going to visit friends, so he had no idea she was in danger.

Early reports say cause of death was strangulation.

I'm shocked. Simply shocked that something like this could happen in our little town. To throttle an upstanding young woman like Molly and leave her face-down in a creek...it's too horrible to talk about. I hope you'll all join me in praying for those closest to Molly, as well as for Molly's soul.

Ivy had been a good patient and taken a day off, but she couldn't bear the thought of sending her father out another day without a proper breakfast. She was up by five and in the kitchen before six, stirring together a vegetarian egg white omelet.

When Jared came in, dressed for work, he hovered at the edge of the kitchen. It was unlike him not to beeline for the coffee pot, so Ivy turned to face him.

"Um," Jared said, clearing his throat. "It seems our friend Jordan had some company over last night?"

Ivy's jaw dropped. She'd gone to bed before seeing Cody out. Surely he hadn't spent the night. "Uh…um…yeah, a friend of his dropped by." Perhaps Jared had only heard the voices, though that would have been unusual since he was such a hard sleeper.

"Honey, Cody Deathridge is upstairs in bed with him right this minute. The door was cracked open. He's fully clothed and on top of the covers, but still, not exactly platonic behavior."

"Dad, he'll just die if he knows you found out. Please, please keep this a secret."

Jared sank into a bar stool, stunned. "Jesus. Gideon'll kill him. I have no doubts about that at all."

"Which is why we have to keep this quiet."

Jared frowned at her. "Of course I won't tell anyone. I'd never out a man like that, especially not a son of Gideon's. But I do intend to let Cody know that I know. I'm sure he could use another supporter."

Ivy turned back to the stove and flipped the burner off. She slid the omelette onto a plate and handed it to Jared. Movement on the floor above them had them both looking up. "I'll go get him," Ivy said.

She made it to Jordan's room in time to stop Cody from climbing out the window. He had the screen out and one foot on the roof when she walked in. "My dad knows," she said without prelude. "He wants to talk to you."

"Shit," Cody said, going pale. He returned the screen to the window, gave Jordan an apologetic look, and followed Ivy back downstairs. She took some comfort in the fact that she wouldn't be the one getting the fatherly lecture. Still, she was a little sick to her stomach on Cody's behalf.

"Are you hungry?" she asked Cody as they entered the kitchen.

If looks could be sarcastic, his definitely was. Ivy shrugged, hopped up on the counter, and watched as Cody stood at the end of the bar.

"Have a seat, son," Jared said.

"I'd just hop right back up, sir."

Jared smiled and pushed his empty plate away. "I'm sorry it's come about like this. I was walking past Jordan's room and the door was cracked. I peeked in just to make sure he was okay."

Cody nodded. "It was stupid of me. I haven't been sleeping much lately. Soon as my head hit the pillow, I was out."

"You're welcome to stay over any time. That goes for Jake as well," Jared said, with a pointed look at Ivy.

Her eyes flew wide and she shook her head frantically, glancing back and forth between Jared and Cody. Jared frowned.

"Jake?" Cody asked, turning to frown at Ivy.

Ivy laughed artificially. "Right? Why would you say that, Dad? That's so weird."

Jared narrowed his eyes at her. He turned back to Cody. "When do you intend to come out to your family?"

Cody's attention snapped away from Ivy. "Never. God, never. I can't even…there's just no way…"

"Son, you're too old to be living under your father's thumb."

Cody laughed. "There's such a thing as too old for that?"

"I see the way he treats you boys. Kept you home all your lives, homeschooling you so he could have your help on the ranch—"

"My dad believes in family, sir. Family's the strongest bond you can have. Nothing wrong with that."

Ivy watched in wonderment as Cody snapped to attention and practically recited the Gideon code.

"Nothing wrong with that," Jared repeated. "But as a parent, you've got to understand that your children are individuals, that they might one day want to go their own way."

"Ranching's my life, sir. I'm happy to live and die on that land."

More recitation. Programmed words. Programmed behavior. Jared and Ivy shared a knowing look. They both understood that whatever Cody's beliefs about himself and his life, they weren't going to get past the fortress that Gideon had built around his mind. Not today, anyway. Seeing Cody like that made Ivy profoundly grateful for her parents. Both her mother and father had always treated her with respect. Treated her as an individual with the right to become whoever she needed to become.

Jared turned back to Cody. "That's good. That's fine. You still ought to be able to be yourself, though. Hiding a thing like you're hiding...that ain't healthy."

"I'm not gay. I just have a problem. I'm working on it, I swear, please don't tell Gideon—"

"Cody, calm down. I'm not going to tell him. I just want you to know, if you need some support, I'll be happy to help. If you decide to tell him yourself."

Cody's shoulders relaxed. "Thank you. That's kind. But there's no reason for me to ever tell him. I've got this under control."

"It's not a drug addiction, son. It's who you are."

"That's not what the Bible says."

Jared laughed in frustration. He shook his head and stood to shake Cody's hand. "You're right. That's not what the Bible says. Just let me know if I can be of any help."

"Thank you, sir."

With that, Jared left out the back door to get to work.

"I'll get out of your hair, Ivy," Cody said. "I'm sorry for falling asleep like that."

"It's not a—"

Her phone dinged on the counter next to her. It was a text from Boone.

Go to Myra's blog. Now.

Ivy frowned. It was unlike Boone to text her at all without it being about Molly, let alone give her a straight order like that. She picked up her phone and navigated to Myra's blog.

"Ivy, what's wrong?" Cody asked. His voice was distant as she listened to Myra's voice. Somehow, Cody was at her side. He reached over and scrubbed the video backwards so he could watch.

After it was over, Ivy said, "This isn't true, right? Myra's a gossip. This is just gossip."

Cody took the phone and clicked the link to the actual news story. He held the phone out so they could both read.

"My God," Cody muttered.

It Took A Rumor

Ivy gripped the countertop and poured all her focus into trying not to vomit. She sucked in a breath, and then the room wobbled. Cody wrapped his arms around her. She rested against his chest, laying her head on his shoulder. "I'm so sorry for your loss," he said.

"She was murdered."

"I'm so sorry."

It had happened the night she'd been hit on the head. Oh, God, how close had she come to getting killed? It seemed selfish to be feeling both fear and relief when her friend was dead.

She pushed Cody away gently and dashed the tears from her eyes. "Um…you need to get home, right?"

Cody glanced at the time on her phone. "Shit," he said, handing it back to her. It was nearly seven, well into the work day for the Deathridges. Ivy walked him out the door. Just before reaching the porch steps, he turned to hug her. "Thank you for everything. And again, I'm really sorry."

Ivy might have answered him if she hadn't found herself staring at Myra Tidwell's iPhone, raised in full video-recording posture with Myra smiling wickedly behind it.

"I've gotta get a guard dog," Ivy muttered.

Cody turned. "Jesus Christ, Myra, don't you ever give it a rest?"

Myra clucked her tongue and put her phone away. "Such language, young man. Ivy, dear, I've been out gathering statements on the Molly Allen situation. I wanted to get one from you, but this is even better. It will give us all something distracting to cheer us up after this senseless tragedy." She pulled a notepad and pen from her quilted handbag. "Now, where were you the night Molly was killed?"

"Myra, you're not the police," Cody said. "And nothing happened here between Ivy and me. If you insist on posting that damned video, would you at least include that statement?"

"Of course, dear. Ivy? Anything to say concerning your relationship with Cody?"

"There is no relationship," Ivy replied numbly.

"Then what was he doing in your house, hugging you goodbye and whispering sweet nothings in your ear?"

"He wasn't…" She trailed off when she realized that, for Cody, gossip about his sleeping with Ivy would go over way better than the truth. "Can you just not post it, please? It's nobody's business."

Myra pressed her lips together and lifted her notepad once again. "What do you have to say about Molly's death."

"Nothing. I have nothing to say. I just got the news a couple of minutes ago and now you're hounding me. Why can't you leave me alone?"

"So touchy. That's very unbecoming in a young lady, you know. Oh, well." She tucked the paper and pen back in her bag and turned to walk to her little, orange bug. "You know how it is, Ivy. If you don't give me something to talk about, I'll simply make something up." She winked, got in her car, and drove away.

She was going to post that video. Jake would see it. Just another nail in her coffin. "I hate my life."

Cody was pacing, his hands in his hair. "So, worst case, people think you and me are together. That'll get me in trouble with Gideon, but he'll believe me when I tell him it's all a lie. What about you? How will this hurt you?"

She looked up at him, suddenly thinking she might could use another day in bed. Jake thought she was the whore of all whores. Her only close girlfriend was dead. A murderer might know who she was. "I'll be fine. Nothing I haven't dealt with before."

Cody studied her for a moment. "You're sure?"

"Yeah. You go on home before you get into trouble."

After a long second, he said, "Okay. Thank you, Ivy."

"No problem."

Dallas only wanted to make the cows sick. Truth be told, he hadn't thought past the point of slowing down business enough to encourage Gideon to sell to Turner. It didn't occur to him that the hemlock might affect some of the pregnant cattle.

There had been three miscarriages so far, and some of the other cows were showing signs of sickness.

The other thing Dallas hadn't accounted for was the horses.

When he'd taken the bags of weeds for Jake, he'd realized that he didn't know how much he needed to make a significant impact on the cattle. Maybe a few handfuls wouldn't be enough. So he'd dropped the bags off in a part of the woods where no one would be visiting, and told Jake that the deed was done. Later, he'd spread some of the dried weeds in the grass where the cattle were grazing. But as he watched, he saw that most of the cows were avoiding it.

So he took the mulcher out to the weeds, mulched them up, and sprinkled two bags' worth in the feeders. That did the trick.

Except somehow, Jake's pregnant mare, Eloise, must have eaten some of it. Now, Jake was on his knees with Eloise's head in his lap, crying while the vet worked to help deliver the premature foal. Night was falling. Boone turned on the lights in the stables, filling the room with a buzzing, white light.

"It's okay, girl," Jake said, over and over. Silent tears spilled down his otherwise stoic face. He looked over at the vet. "She's been acting sick all day."

"Mmm," the vet, a man Gideon's age, but with a kind, bespectacled face. His kind face suddenly turned severe. "Shit. It's breech."

He began pushing the foal back in in order to try and turn it. The mare bucked and whinnied. Jake stroked her and hushed her. "Everything's gonna be all right," he said soothingly.

Dallas stood back in the shadows, sick to his stomach. The lights were too harsh and accusatory for Dallas. Cody was running around fetching anything the vet wanted and making sure Jake stayed hydrated. Gideon was cleaning up, trying to be useful. Boone was pacing.

"She's gonna be okay. You're gonna be okay, girl," Jake said.

Dallas felt like throwing up.

"Have you been riding her?" the vet asked through strained teeth.

"No, sir. I quit when she was about four months along." Jake looked up at his brothers. "Any of you ridden her lately?"

They all shook their heads. They could have been angry at him for asking such a stupid question. Of course they hadn't ridden her. She was Jake's. But the man was in distress, so no one, not even Gideon, was going to further upset him by arguing unnecessarily.

The vet's assistant was late in arriving. He hurried to the vet's side to help. With a grunt of satisfaction, the vet pulled his hands out of the mare and breathed hard. "Got her. Being premature, she's small. That's one blessing, I guess."

"Will she survive? The foal, I mean?" Jake asked.

"We'll see."

Eloise panted and occasionally whinnied. The foal came slowly at first and then slid the rest of the way out. The doctor immediately started checking her vitals. Dallas held his breath. Looking around, he noticed everyone else holding their breath too. Jake's eyes were locked on the foal while his hands continued stroking Eloise. The only sounds were Eloise's stilted huffs and the evening wind rattling the panels on the roof.

"Well, what do you know?" the vet said with a smile. "She's breathing. Right on schedule."

Everyone watched the first risings and fallings of the foal's chest. Dallas closed his eyes and said a silent prayer of thanks.

The vet moved away from the foal and stood, stretching and rolling his shoulders. "The next hour will tell. Hopefully momma will pass the placenta just fine and baby will stand up. But she looks pretty good, Jake. Definitely some lack of development, but not nearly as bad as we'd feared. I'd say she'd have come on her own in a week or so."

For Dallas, it was like the storm clouds of judgment parting and offering him reprieve. But then he looked at Jake, who was intently staring at Eloise, stroking her mane and muttering to her. "Doc, she's gone limp," Jake said.

The vet immediately knelt next to the mare and started checking her vitals. Her whole body seemed to be trembling. Dallas leaned back against the wall.

The vet moved up to check Eloise's face. "She's showing late signs of poisoning. We weren't looking for it because of the foaling. Shit. Ricky, go to the truck, bring in the stomach tube and some of that charcoal. Jake, you move on aside."

"Is she gonna make it?" Jake asked. His face was devoid of color.

"We're gonna do our best, but I'm guessing there's not much left in her stomach. At this point, probably not much to do but hope she survives as it runs its course."

Jake moved out from under Eloise's head, gently resting it on the floor. He stood back, but not very far.

The vet fed the tube down Eloise's throat and sent down some of the powdered charcoal to hopefully absorb any toxins still in her digestive system.

"She's breathing on her own," the vet muttered.

"That's good," Jake said. It was half question.

"Yes. Her heart rate's high, but not dangerously so, at least not for now. We're just going to watch her for a while. Ricky, take some blood, get to the lab, see if you can find out what happened here."

Ricky, the assistant, hurried back to the truck, returning with needles and a tourniquet. While he was busy doing that, the vet stood and turned to address everyone. "That foal is going to need milk, and Eloise is in no position to nurse."

"I've got a bottle in here somewhere," Gideon muttered. He disappeared into a nook where they stored a bunch of miscellaneous supplies.

"The Turner's have had a couple foalings," the vet said.

"I'll text Ivy," Boone said, whipping out his phone. A few seconds later he smiled. "She says they bagged some colostrum for the freezer. She's bringing it over right now."

Gideon appeared, then. "I'll be damned if I accept help from that son-of-a-bitch. What about the Gleasons? I'm sure they got a nursing mare."

"Ivy's on her way," Jake said sternly.

"Then I'll send her ass back where she came from. I don't want no Turner on my prop—"

"It's not your call!" Jake shouted. "The Gleasons live twenty minutes away. Ivy's on her way now. This is my mare, my foal, my call!"

Gideon turned red all the way to his ears. But if there was one thing he hated more than being talked-back-to by one of his sons, it was letting outsiders witness family business. The look Gideon gave Jake promised a near-future conversation that would definitely not go well for poor Jake. In that moment, though Jake didn't appear to give a shit.

Ivy actually took a few minutes longer than everyone expected. During that time, the foal began moving, trying to stand. Its umbilical cord broke and the vet applied iodine to the stump, but otherwise left it alone. Dallas was silently rooting for the little gal to get up on her feet. If they lost Eloise, he'd never forgive himself, but if the foal survived, at least there would be some light amidst all the darkness.

Dallas turned toward the sound of a pickup truck. He peeked out the stable door. Dusk was settling and Ivy's headlights appeared over the hill, her truck bouncing with the dips and ruts in the field. When she pulled up next to the door, Dallas saw that she'd brought her father.

Ivy hopped out of the driver's seat, bottle in hand, and hurried past Dallas into the stables. "Already got it warmed up," she said, handing it to the vet.

"Thank you, Ivy, that's a big help," the vet said. "Looks like she's just about to stand. We'll wait until she does to feed her."

Jared Turner walked in the door, not far behind his daughter. How old man Turner could withstand the hatred evident in Gideon's countenance was beyond Dallas's understanding. Clearly his father wanted nothing more than to beat Jared to a bloody pulp.

But Jared merely shot him a friendly smile and nod before approaching Jake. To Dallas's surprise, Jake met Jared halfway, hand extended. "Thank you, sir," he said.

"That's what neighbors are for," Jared responded, shaking Jake's hand and giving him a pat on the back.

Jake turned to Ivy, hand extended. But for some reason, she folded her arms over her chest, refusing the gesture. Dallas couldn't see her face, but her shoulders were tense and her head tilted up, blond ponytail hanging severely down her neck. Jake frowned, dropping his hand. "Thank you, too, ma'am," he said.

Ivy shook her head, what sounded like a snort of disgust accompanying the gesture. Jake glanced back at Gideon before taking another step backwards, away from the Turners.

"Guys, she's gonna make it," Cody said.

Everyone turned to watch the foal take its first, shaky stand. Jake fell to his knees in front of it, grinning like a proud papa. "Good girl. You're such a strong girl." The vet put the bottle in Jake's hands. He held it about utter level, squeezing a little of the colostrum out of the nipple. The foal licked hesitantly at first, then latched right on and suckled.

"She's making it easy on us," the vet said with a sigh of relief. "That's wonderful, because you're gonna have a long night with Eloise."

Jake stood, holding the bottle in his left hand, shaking the vet's hand with his right. "I appreciate this so much, doc."

"It's what I do. Unless I get called away, I'll stay and monitor Eloise tonight."

"Thank you."

The vet sat next to Eloise, stroking her neck and occasionally checking her pulse. Now that all the tension had died down, Dallas felt a sick guilt coating his soul like a layer of scum on a shower wall. Boone was the first to go.

"I'm exhausted," he said. "I'm gonna get some sleep, then get up early and take a shift with Eloise."

"Thanks," Jake said to Boone. It wasn't grudging at all. In fact, he hugged his little brother. He hugged Cody, too, who promised to take a middle-of-the-night shift. Dallas gulped down the lump of nausea and approached his big brother who had dried tear streaks down his cheeks. Jake hadn't cried since they were children, not so Dallas could see anyway.

"I'm real sorry about all this," Dallas said, his throat husky.

Jake's brow furrowed. "Hey, it's not your fault." He brought Dallas into a hug, not having a clue he was embracing Judas. "Besides, she's gonna be fine. She's strong, she'll pull through."

Dallas left the stables. Halfway home, he fell to his knees and started vomiting. And kept vomiting. Darkness was falling all around, so it wasn't until just before he blacked out that he realized he was losing consciousness.

It Took A Rumor

There had been nothing but gossip being spoken in town that day. Jake had made a trip to the feed store and the market that afternoon. News about Molly Allen was everywhere. People expressed their concern for poor Pastor Allen before diving into the speculation on suspects. The police didn't have anyone in mind, but that didn't mean the average citizen about town didn't have plenty of ideas.

The other piece of gossip released on Myra's blog that day had concerned Ivy and Cody. When Jake had heard that, he'd burst out laughing. It was too ridiculous to believe. Suddenly, he felt like an idiot for ever thinking she was sleeping with all of them. He knew her well enough to know she wouldn't do that. He also knew that if she did, she wouldn't have gotten caught three times in a row. No, something else was going on. Could be better than her sleeping with his brothers, could be worse. Whatever it was, she didn't wanna tell him, and that was that.

So he'd gone home with his supplies, still mooning over Ivy and wondering what might happen with her. That evening, when he'd found Eloise in labor, his whole world turned upside down. He'd been surprised that the first person he wanted at his side was Ivy. The whole time he'd been sitting there comforting Eloise, he'd been wishing for comfort from Ivy. Wishing for her to stroke his hair and tell him everything was going to be okay, same as he was doing with his mare.

Instead, he'd gotten a cold shoulder.

It wasn't surprising. He knew what she wanted as soon as he'd extended his hand to her. She wanted him to embrace her. Acknowledge her. Need her. Want her. She wanted all of that out in the open. She didn't want to be denied like Peter did to Jesus. She wanted to be openly accepted.

As he stood in the middle of the stables watching her back as she walked away, he knew she was right to reject him. He was being a coward. Gideon had questioned him over milk for the foal and Jake had stood strong against him. But when it came to Ivy, he cowered, avoiding confrontation at all cost. It was no wonder she was angry with him.

"If there's anything more we can do…" Jared was saying to Gideon.

"You can get the hell off my property," Gideon snarled.

Jake turned sharply, even as Ivy froze her exit.

Clara covered her face in her hands—likely because she couldn't physically insert her head into the sand.

"Gideon, I don't know what I did to upset you, but we're just trying to help," Jared said.

"You know what I think?" Gideon replied, moving close to face-off with Jared. "That there mare was poisoned somehow, and I think you was the one to do it. You want our land and you'll do anything to get it."

Jared laughed. "Are you serious? Why would I do that? How could poisoning Jake's mare help me get your property?"

"I'm sure this ain't the whole plan. I'm sure you got other things in mind. But I'll burn this land and salt the ground before I let you get your slimy hands on it."

Ivy stormed forward, standing just a step behind her father. "We've done nothing but help—"

"I'll thank you to keep your little girl in line, Turner," Gideon said, not looking at Ivy. "Seems she enjoys causing trouble. I don't much appreciate her sniffing around my boys."

"That's enough!" Jake said, his fear vanishing just as it had when Gideon had tried to deny the foal milk from the Turners.

"Boy, you'd better watch how you talk to me," Gideon snarled.

"You got a problem with me, we'll talk about it," Jake said, "but I'm not going to stand here while you insult people who have done nothing but offer their friendship—"

Jake didn't see the slap coming. Gideon hadn't hit him in years. Best he could recall, the last time had been when he'd come home drunk, having missed dinner and made his mother cry. He'd been twenty-three and Gideon had dragged him into the yard and kicked his ass. Jake remembered because he'd curled up and taken it, knowing he could easily stand up and fight back. He'd thought on it for days trying to figure out why he hadn't fought back. When he realized it was simply because he had too much respect for his father, he'd fallen right in line, desperate not to cause anymore trouble.

Jakes cheek stung, involuntary tears springing to his eyes. He frowned in shock at Gideon. Then he looked down to see Ivy's hand on his chest, her other clinging to his arm, her eyes locked on Gideon and filled with hatred. At his side like he wanted. Supporting him like he didn't deserve. In the time Jake spent acclimating to what had just happened, Jared had inserted himself between Jake and Gideon. "There's no cause to be doing that, Gideon," Jared said.

Jake pulled Ivy back a step, stunned to be defended by not one, but two Turners. He suddenly envied Ivy her father.

"You'll mind your own fucking business unless you wanna take this out back and finish it," Gideon said.

"Finish what?" Jared asked, raising his voice for the first time. "I don't even know what *this* is. I haven't the first clue as to why you hate me and my family so much."

"Oh, come off it, Turner. You're such a condescending prick, sitting on your high horse, taking anything you want."

"What have I taken from you? What? I make an offer on your property once in a while, you tell me to go fuck myself, I move on with my life. What have I taken?"

Gideon dropped his head back and laughed. "You know damn well what you took. You knew she was dating me and you took her anyway."

Jared smiled in confusion, then frowned. "Penny? This is about Penny?"

"You're such an asshole, acting like you don't know this is about Penny. She was with *me*."

Jared turned, shoved his hands through his hair, then turned again to face Gideon. "This is about something that happened nearly forty years ago? You're mad at me because your high school girlfriend dumped you for me?"

"She didn't dump me, you stole her."

"If I recall, Gideon, it wasn't twenty-four-hours later you started dating the lovely woman who is now your wife. You can't possibly still be harboring a grudge about this. You and Penny hadn't even slept together!"

Jake felt Ivy cringe. He pulled her back a few more steps and put his arm around her, hugging her to his side. There was movement out of the corner of his eye. He looked over in time to see his weeping mother running out of the stables. Gideon hadn't even noticed.

"What you did told me right then and there what kind of man you are, Turner. You're the kind of son-of-a-bitch who'll stop at nothing to get what he wants. You don't give a shit about integrity or honor. So fuck you. And fuck that little tramp you call a daughter."

Jake saw red, but he didn't have the opportunity to avenge his lover's honor because Jared immediately launched himself at Gideon. The two old men fell to the floor and rolled, Gideon landing on top and connecting his fist with Jared's jaw. Jake let Ivy go and pulled his father off of hers. Once he got Gideon to his feet, he let go and stepped back. This time, when Gideon turned, Jake saw the hit coming. He caught his father's punch, stepped to the side, and used Gideon's own momentum to send him falling into an empty horse stall.

"That's enough!" Jake shouted, hoping to God his voice held enough authority to make everyone cease their fighting. He kept his eyes on Gideon for a long moment, watching as the rage in the old man's eyes gradually died down to defeat. Imagine that. Gideon Deathridge, defeated. Jake felt a wave of something that felt like guilt, but there would be time to process that later. He turned to Ivy, who was helping Jared to his feet. "Sir, I'm so sorry," he said, hurrying to help.

"You didn't do anything, son."

"I appreciate your help," Jake said. "Both of you." He looked at Ivy, begging her with his eyes to let his apology be enough for now. Her expression was far more mellow, now, tempered by the shock of the moment.

"I'm sorry," she said.

He shook his head. "You didn't—"

"You needed support and I acted like a petty child. If there's anything I can do for you or…" she looked over at the mare, still being tended to by the vet who'd certainly witnessed a hell of a show. The foal was resting, now, curled up next to her mother. "You'll need more milk," Ivy said.

"Eloise is going to get back on her feet," Jake said stubbornly.

"She won't be able to nurse."

Jake wanted to dig in his heels and insist that his mare was going to be fine. But Ivy was right. Whatever was happening to her wouldn't be healed overnight.

"We've got a nursing mare," Jared said. "Foal's a few weeks old. We could take this one—"

Gideon was at Jake's side, then. "You think you're going to take our property?"

Jared closed his eyes and breathed, but Jake saw what he was getting at. He turned to the vet who met his eyes. The vet said, "You probably don't have much choice."

"I've never done anything like that," Jake said. "Will she just latch on to the other mother?"

"She probably will," the vet said, standing and dusting off his knees. "The difficulty is in getting the other mare to accept her. Let's bottle feed her tonight and tomorrow either me or Ricky will take her over to the Turner ranch and work with her and the other mare. Do you have anymore milk?" he asked Jared and Ivy.

"We brought a cooler full," Jared said.

"Thank you both so much," Jake said. They were giving so much with no real reason to do so. And getting nothing in return but Gideon's scorn.

As soon as they dropped off the cooler and left, Gideon grabbed Jake by the collar of his shirt and pulled back his fist. This time, Jake planned to just take the punishment. But it never came.

There was screaming, coming closer, followed by a hysterical Clara running into the stable, tears streaming down her cheeks. "It's Dallas!" she screamed. "He won't wake up. His body's convulsing." She fell to her knees and sobbed.

Gideon and Jake helped her up, shoved her into their pickup, and drove the direction she pointed while Jake dialed 911 on his cell phone.

Ivy woke up with hay in her hair, mostly because she was sleeping in a pile of hay. In a stable. Owned by the Deathridges. The morning light crept in. Ivy scrambled to her knees and dug her cell phone out of her pocket.

Sometime last night, as she'd been about to go to bed, Jake had called. With the whole family at the hospital anxiously awaiting news on Dallas's status, there had been no one to sit with Eloise and the new foal. Ivy had been more than happy to help.

"Any news?" the vet walked through the stable and past her towards Eloise. He'd gone stall-to-stall checking on the other horses, making sure whatever had made Eloise sick hadn't made the others sick as well.

Ivy frowned at her screen. There was a text message from Jake.

He's in ICU. They're running toxicology tests. Said there's not much they can do but make sure his body has everything it needs to heal itself. How's Eloise?

The text had come an hour ago. She turned to the vet. "Dallas is in ICU. How's Eloise?"

The vet frowned. "Did they determine what's wrong with him?"

"Not yet. Jake says they're doing a toxicology report or whatever. Is she doing better?"

The vet frowned for a moment, not really seeing what was in front of him. He gave his head a shake and knelt by Eloise. "Her heart rate is closer to normal. Her breathing is steady. And she's been in and out of consciousness. I'm keeping her tranquilized for the time. Ricky came back with the test results while you were sleeping."

"What did they show?"

The doctor shook his head, seemingly perplexed. "I guess you know, a couple weeks back they lost a heifer due to hemlock poisoning?"

"Yeah. Jake was clearing all that out."

"Well, he must have missed some. Though I don't have the first clue why she would eat it, let alone eat so much of it she nearly kills herself. It's not a good tasting plant. Animals tend to avoid it except in extreme drought situations."

Ivy sat down hard on her pile of hay. "Oh, my God," she said, not meaning to say it out loud. It couldn't be. He wouldn't.

"How long have you been wanting to leave the ranch?"

Dallas sighed and dropped his head back. "For as long as I can remember."

He'd said he wouldn't resort to sabotage. She'd specifically told him she wanted everything in tact. "We have to check the cattle," she said.

"Beg your pardon?"

"We need to check the cattle. Can you leave her for a while?"

"Well, yes, I suppose, but…"

"And the foal? Is she good?"

It Took A Rumor

"Sure. She's just stretching her legs in the coral. Fed her just a moment ago."

"Okay, let's go."

She drove, her truck bouncing and rocking through the fields. Last night as they'd been driving in to bring the mare's milk to Jake, she'd seen the cattle in a nearby pasture. As they crested a hill, she sighed in relief. There they all were, standing around, eating grass within the fenced pasture. But her relief was short-lived.

"Oh, hell," the vet said.

Dotting the landscape, amongst the standing cows, were dozens of downed cattle. Some were laying, feet tucked under them, still conscious. Others were on their sides, and anyone looking on would think they were dead. Maybe they *were* dead.

Ivy kept on the brake and pressed her hands to her mouth. "Oh, my God," she whispered, tears streaming down her cheeks. What had he done? This was…this was merciless. Brutal. Shakespearean in its scope.

"Put it in park," the vet said. "I'm gonna need your help." He jumped out of the truck and grabbed the backpack he'd brought.

He and Ivy spent the next half hour collecting blood samples from some of the downed cows. They checked all of the ones who were on their sides, almost two dozen in total. So far, only two had died. The Deathridges were going to be devastated.

On the ride back to the stables, the vet called Ricky to come get the blood and run tests. After he got off the phone, he said, "How do you want to tell Gideon?"

"I'm not telling Gideon. I'll talk to Jake. But let's get this handled, first. They've got enough on their minds right now."

"We need to get those cattle corralled so I can check them all out. Jesus, what a mess."

"I'll gather some of my ranch hands and we'll herd them in. Then we'll clean out all the feeders—"

"When you do that, make sure you wear masks and gloves. Make sure your ranch hands immediately get out of their clothes and shoes and wash them after."

Ivy didn't have to ask what he was thinking. There was hemlock in the hay. They both knew it, but Ivy had no intention of sharing what else she knew: that Dallas was the one who'd done it.

She spent the rest of the morning doing work she hadn't done since she was a teenage girl. She rode alongside her ranch hands, herding cattle toward the corral. She'd given the vet a couple of helpers to run the cows, one-by-one, through a shoot, administer a charcoal supplement, and corral them in another pen. The rest of her hands joined her in the pasture, cleaning out the feeders, bagging up what was left of the hay, and piling it in the back of a pickup to take to the dump.

It Took A Rumor

When the work was over, Ivy went home, shed her clothes into the washing machine, and showered while she let hot tears slide down her face.

The one person she needed to talk to more than anything was on life support. She really didn't have the first clue how to address the family. And her head was pounding.

She dressed in jeans and a tank top, took some Tylenol, and got back in her truck. Again. Jared was at the Deathridge ranch with the vet, managing that situation. So Ivy was on her own as she drove to the hospital.

The Deathridges sat in the sterile waiting room. In their muddy boots, flannel shirts, and variety of ball caps and cowboy hats, they were a stark contrast to the generic wall art and bright white light. Clara wasn't there. Perhaps she was with Dallas.

All their eyes landed on her as she walked into the room, but it was only Jake's that she felt. His heartfelt, oblivious brown eyes, looking to her hopefully. She pulled a chair up and sat, facing them. "How is he?"

"Stable," Cody said.

Ivy didn't figure that meant anything. It was just a word they could say when asked the question. "Okay. Well, I have some bad news."

Muttered curses. Gideon glared at her like she was the devil. Jake's eyes glistened. "She didn't make it?" he choked out.

"Oh," Ivy cried, grabbing his hand. "Oh, no, honey, Eloise is okay. She's doing better, even. And the foal is walking around like a pro."

Jake dropped his head and blew out a breath. He squeezed Ivy's hand and didn't let go.

"But the blood tests came back. It was hemlock poisoning."

Jake looked up at her, frowning in confusion.

"I thought you cleaned that out, boy?" Gideon growled.

"I did," Jake snapped.

Ivy interrupted. "When the doctor told me that, we decided we should check on the cattle. There are over two dozen down on the ground. Two dead so far."

"What?" Gideon leaped to his feet. "How is that possible?"

Ivy shook her head, not wanting to lie. So she continued. "We've got them corralled. The doctor is running them through the shoot and pumping tubes of activated charcoal into them."

"What? Who authorized that?" Gideon shouted.

Ivy stood, her efforts to remain calm and polite vanishing quickly. "I did, damn you! That's what the vet said needed done, so we did it."

"You got any idea what that's gonna cost me, young lady?"

"Could save you a hell of a lot of money of money in dead cattle, old man."

"All you did was add to the vet bill. You and your father better get your checkbook out."

"Fuck you, Gideon! If those cattle have been poisoned—"

"If! If they've been poisoned. You could be giving medicine to perfectly healthy animals."

"Oh, did you want me to have the vet run blood tests on each one? How the fuck much do you think that would have cost?"

"You impertinent little bitch!"

"Stop it," Jake said, calmly standing at Ivy's side, his hand on her back. It was remarkable what the small gesture did to soothe her nerves. "She did the right thing. It's what I would have done. Thank you, Ivy."

She smiled up at him. Gideon who? There was nothing in that moment but her man gazing fondly down at her.

"Whole thing wouldn't have happened if you'd done your job right," Gideon said.

Ivy's anger rushed back at her as she turned on the bitter old man. She opened her mouth to shout at him in spite of Jake's hand on her shoulder, but the doctor chose that moment to stroll in. He approached the family, business-like, staring down at a clipboard. "No change in his condition so far," he said. "Which isn't good or bad.

But we got the blood tests back. Found large amounts of a chemical that comes from a toxic plant called hemlock…it's what killed Socrates. I've never had a patient present with a diagnosis like this. Do you all have any idea how he managed to come into contact with it."

Everyone was silent, until Jake said, "It was me. I cleared it out, bagged it up. He volunteered to take it to the dump. It was in bags."

"There might have been residue on the outside of the bags," the doctor said. "Perhaps when he picked them up, it entered through his skin. Or maybe he inhaled some."

"Did you tell him to wear gloves and a mask?" Gideon asked.

Jake's face paled. "No. I didn't think…I just assumed he would…"

"Oh, you just assumed? You know good and well Dallas has the IQ of a goddamn rock. You couldn't be troubled to look after him? You shouldn't have given him that job in the first place, let alone without giving him instructions. You might have just killed your brother, Jake."

Jake fell to his chair, burying his face in his hands. Ivy couldn't decide which instincts to heed. Part of her wanted to punch Gideon in the face. Another part wanted to fall to her knees and comfort her man. The turmoil was confusing, but Boone solved it for her by taking her elbow and walking her out of the hospital. They stopped by her truck. He looked older than she'd ever seen him as he ran his hand over his bloodshot eyes. "This is fucked up," he said.

Ivy had no idea what to say.

"I think this is my fault," Boone said.

Her mouth dropped open. "How do you figure?"

"I've been getting threatening texts. I don't know who they're from. Whoever it is keeps saying they know I...I killed Molly."

"You killed Molly?" Ivy shouted.

Boone clapped a hand over her mouth. "No! Are you crazy? I didn't kill Molly. I can't even bring myself to castrate the bull calves for Christ's sake. But this person keeps saying they know I did. They know about the affair."

"What do they want from you?"

"That's just the thing. Nothing. No demands. I asked what the person wanted and all I got in response was, 'Your suffering on this earth.' Which is just a weird thing to say to someone."

Ivy shook her head in awe. It was just too much, all of it. "So, your theory is that they did this to you to cause your suffering?"

"What else could it be? I mean, the old man is always going to blame Jake for everything, that's just how he operates. But you and I know this ain't Jake's fault."

Ivy wanted to offer Boone some comfort, but how to do that without revealing Dallas's secrets? "Just, keep a cool head," she ended up saying. "I really don't think this has anything to do with the texts. It doesn't make any sense."

"Yeah, but, I mean, what if Dallas is only the first? What if this person goes after Jake and Cody? I mean, they're all a bunch of assholes, but I do love them. If someone wanted to create suffering for me, that would be the way to do it. Oh, God...what if they go after Mom?"

"You need to go to the police with this, Boone."

"And say what? The minute I confess to having an affair with Molly, I become their number one suspect in this murder investigation."

"You didn't do it, did you?"

"I can't believe you'd even ask me that."

"Okay, so if you're innocent, they'll find you innocent and move on to another suspect."

Boone laughed and paced away while he shoved his hand in his hair. "God, are you naive. Don't you watch TV? Innocent people get proven guilty all the time."

"Maybe this mysterious texter is the killer, did you think of that? Maybe you're preventing his capture by hiding the affair?"

Boone shook his head. "Listen, if I confess, I'll be lucky to get put in prison for the rest of my life. What scares the shit out of me is Gideon finding out. He'll kill me, Ivy. I'm not even exaggerating."

Ivy dropped her head back, closed her eyes, and prayed for inner peace. "You are all so afraid of your father. Have you ever thought about standing up to him? Together?"

"No. Fucking. Way. Then it would just be a quadruple homicide. Besides, Jake would never stand against Gideon."

"He did last night, didn't he?"

"That was for his horse. He'd die for his horse."

"I promise you and your brothers mean more to him than a horse."

Boone arched a skeptical brow. It was useless anyway, and none of her business. If those boys didn't want to grow up and stand up for themselves, no amount of preaching from her was going to convince them. "Fine. Do what you want. But Boone, you need to go to the cops with those texts. You could be withholding evidence. You could be putting other lives in danger. There's a right and a wrong, here, and the right thing to do is go to the police."

She drove away while he stood there, pensive and sad.

Part 5: The Fall of Gideon Deathridge

Myra's Blog

It's been quite the week, here in Fair Grove. Not only have we lost poor Molly Allen, rest her soul (and by the way, there are no further developments on that story; if you have any information, contact the number below this video), but tragedy has struck the Deathridge farm like a biblical plague. Poor Gideon can't seem to keep his sons out of Ivy Turner's bed...the one exception being Dallas who is still in intensive care, no change on that front either. They've also got a dead cattle count of eight, so far, and many others sick. I'm sure the family would appreciate our thoughts and prayers.

On a lighter note, I have recently been given insight into the Turner-Deathridge feud. I did a little digging and found out that back in their senior year of high school, Penny Turner née Leist spent a few weeks dating Gideon Deathridge. But apparently she had eyes for Jared Turner and the break-up was not amicable. As it turns out, Mr. Deathridge has harbored quite the grudge over that matter.

Poor Clara. To find out your husband has spent the last forty years feuding with a man over another woman...what a blow to the ego. My thoughts are with you, Clara.

Jake spent the rest of his week alternating visiting Dallas at the hospital, Eloise in the stables, and the foal on the Turner property. That latter chore was his favorite since it put him directly into close proximity to Ivy. Nothing had happened beyond some prolonged eye contact and a brief brush of fingertips…there were usually other ranch hands around, after all. But he enjoyed working with her on training the mare to nurse the foal. By the end of the week, it was as though the two were mother and child by nature. Even better, Jake found out what it was like to partner with Ivy. Turned out they worked well together.

On Friday, Eloise got up.

Jake nearly wept as he hugged her neck. He called the vet, first. Ivy second. Both joined him within the hour, the vet checking Eloise's vitals and walking her around to see if she had any nerve damage from the poison. While he was doing that, Jake stood next to Ivy and held her hand.

"It's nice to see something positive," Jake said.

"Dallas will be next. He'll be on his feet before you know it."

Jake put his arm around her shoulders and smiled when she hugged his waist. "You're the best girl I know, Ivy."

She giggled—a rare sound from her. "I like you, too."

He turned, pushing her away just enough to face her. "After we get Eloise settled in, do you wanna go for a walk down by the creek?"

She smiled. "You're really making it hard for me to stick to my principles."

"I'm not talking about sex or anything. I just wanna be alone with you."

She snorted, and justifiably. He could claim all he wanted that he wasn't talking about sex, but there was no denying the hope.

Well, Ivy may have principles, but Jake couldn't afford them. Not when so much was at stake. So he took her hands, lowered his eyes, and said, "It's just been such a hard week, you know? I guess I'm feeling, I don't know, vulnerable."

"Stop it," she said with a laugh.

He sighed heavily, stepping a little closer to her. "Lonely, too, you know? Real lonely. No one to talk to. Share all my emotions with."

"Shut. Up. You are such a manipulative bastard!"

He grinned at her, then, and she grinned back.

"Okay," she said, rolling her eyes and shaking her head. "You win. I can't resist any longer. But I still want what I want, Jake. I still need what I need."

"I know what you want and need, and I'm gonna give it to you, I swear. I just need a little time."

Her smile faded as she nodded.

Eloise tired quickly and the vet led her back inside to rest. Jake took Ivy by the hand, and they walked through the field to a little trail that led into the woods and down by the creek. They followed the creek to the fence that separated his property from hers. For the most part, they were silent. They climbed the fence and sat on the big, flat rock, facing each other.

They kissed tentatively at first. Soft swoops and awkward misses until they fell into sync, landing perfectly against each other, and stuck. Jake threaded both hands in her hair, held her gently but firmly, and sank into the kiss. Just lips for the longest time, opening gradually more and more. Then tongues and penetration and nothing but a hot, wet world of sensation.

It was heaven.

Jake breathed her in. Held her. It was worship. Not like the routine, ritualistic worship of Sunday service. No, this was different. He'd finally found something worthy of his awe and wonder. This was true worship, offering his body to this woman who lifted him out of himself, stripped away his illusions and made him see the world in a different light. She flooded his world, washing away the things that didn't matter and illuminating that which he'd never seen before. He saw things in his imagination…wanted things he'd never wanted before.

Her. Forever.

They stayed on that pleasant plateau, just kissing and loving, for God only knew how long. But then something shifted. As Jake indulged more and longer, he found himself changing from wonder-struck worshiper, to need-fueled possessor. His hands fisted in her hair. Hers fisted in his shirt. He pressed harder against her, crushing her lips with his own, not able to get enough. An itch he couldn't scratch.

She pulled back, gasped in a breath, and groaned when he pulled her back in. His hands were on her back, now, squeezing and rubbing. He felt the line of her bra and longed to unclasp it. Found the curve of her waist and squeezed.

She pulled back again, panting. "Oh, God," she squeaked.

He kissed her open mouth, then moved to her jaw. She tilted her head and he dragged his tongue behind her ear and down her neck, frantically kissing and sucking. It wasn't enough. There was no such thing as enough.

Her hands were all over him and he ached to touch her breasts and slide his fingers into her jeans. "More," he groaned against her. "Please."

She let out a little laugh and more panting. He pulled back and met her eyes. They were both shaking. Both breathing hard. Both gazing at each other like they were seeing God for the first time.

He waited, hoping for some sign from her. Some invitation. But though she gazed at him, there was still a hesitation. A wall. Of course he hadn't earned her trust. He hadn't given her what she wanted.

So he kissed her some more. He pushed towards her and she let him lay her down on the ground and position himself over her. She let him push her shirt up and pull her bra down and take her nipples, one at a time, between his teeth.

Her breathing was shallow and fast. Her hands fisted in his hair, and he felt like a champion, like a victor, like a god among gods. He reached for the button of her jeans, but then she grabbed his hand. "What are you doing?" she whispered, lifting her head enough to look at him.

His answer was a grin as he continued unfastening her jeans. He sat up, pulled off her boots, then pulled off her jeans and panties. "Look at you," he murmured, as he raked his hands up and down her hips and thighs.

"I'm weak. And pathetic."

"You're strong. And not afraid to take what you deserve." He kissed her breasts again, and then trailed his lips down her abdomen, past her belly button.

She grabbed his hair and forced his head up.

"Don't," she said.

He grinned in answer.

"Jake, if you go down on me, I'll fall in love. I'll fall in love right here and now."

He chuckled as he pushed her legs further apart. "If that's all it takes, then I'm in." He spread her and kissed all around the sweet spot, teasing her.

"No, no, no, no...yes!" she cried as his tongue stroked her swollen nub. After that, her sounds were guttural. If she was speaking, he couldn't hear her. He licked her tentatively at first. Then kissed her deeper, sucking and teasing. He slipped two fingers inside of her, massaging her from inside until she was crying out and bucking...throbbing in release.

At last, she collapsed, her body limp. He smiled, kissed the insides of her thighs, crawled up, and collapsed next to her.

Their breathing evened and fell into sync. He reached down and laced his fingers with hers.

It was heaven.

Her shirt was shoved up under her chin. Her bra was pulled down. And Jake lay on his side, his head propped on his fist while he used his free hand to fondle her breasts. She couldn't help but giggle. It tickled. And with the sun soaking into her skin and the breeze moving sensually around her, this felt like the absolute peak of contentment.

Jake's hands were calloused, as was befitting a hardworking rancher, and the roughness of them stimulated her flesh. She knew he was simply basking in his own enjoyment, but she wondered whether he knew that he was turning her on again.

"You're like a kid with a new toy," she said.

"Mm-hmm." His smile was sleepy and blissful, his eyes following the path of his fingers. He hadn't asked for anything from her. Hadn't even hinted at it. She toyed with the idea of getting aggressive, pushing him back, and returning the favor. But there was something hypnotic in the way he was focused on her.

At last, she said, "I can't stay much longer—"

Just then, he rolled on top of her and covered her mouth with his own. She laughed against his lips and then moaned. He dipped down and sucked her left nipple into his mouth. For a moment, she was blinded by the sensation, her sight and hearing shutting down to make way for the overload of pleasure.

"You were saying?" he murmured as he moved over to give equal attention to the other breast.

"I…I have to…go visit…"

He pressed his thigh between her legs, and she stopped talking.

A few minutes later she lay trembling as he smirked down at her, clearly proud of himself. "Someday we should try doing this stuff in an actual bed," he said.

"Tonight," she said without hesitation. Because she wanted more from him, and she wanted to give him back some of the pleasure he'd given her. "My bed. But now I have to go. For real."

He rolled off of her and helped her to a sitting position. While she readjusted her bra and shirt, he gathered her pants and boots for her. It was hard not to stare at his hands. Something about those hands just made her weak all over. She dressed and stood and he pulled her into an embrace. "Where do you gotta go?" he murmured into her hair.

"I have to visit Richard. I've been putting it off all week, but I can't go to church tomorrow and face him without having paid my condolences in person."

"Were you and Molly close?"

She nuzzled her cheek against his shirt. "Yeah. It was a strange friendship. I mean, it was kind of one-sided, but I think I was all she had. And she was my only girlfriend."

Jake pulled back, frowned, and rubbed his thumb along her cheekbone. "I could go with you."

At first she laughed. But then she stopped and studied him. "You'd do that?"

"Ivy, you've been by my side all week. I wanna be by yours."

If it weren't so hard to breathe, just then, she might have told him it wasn't necessary. That she was capable of handling her own affairs. That she appreciated the gesture but didn't need him. Thankfully, though, she couldn't speak to say such stupid things to a man who only wanted to support her. So she simply nodded. Jake smiled, took her hand, and walked with her up toward her house.

"You know," he said, "I sometimes wonder if Molly wasn't having an affair."

Now, Ivy's breath was gone for a different reason. "Oh?" she squeaked.

"Yeah. I mean, I've seen her at the bar a time or two having way too much fun. She never drank or did anything where you could see it, but she flirted like crazy. Plus, that marriage never made much sense to me. The age difference, the interest difference...I don't know."

"Yeah. Who knows?"

"This must be really hard for you."

Her house was in sight, now, her truck parked on the far side of the driveway. "I cried a lot when I found out. It's all been so hectic, it feels like weeks have passed instead of days."

"I can't believe they haven't had the funeral yet."

"I hate funerals."

"Me, too. When I die, just plant me in the ground. None of these ridiculous frills and ceremonies."

"Me, too."

Jake got quiet as they approached Ivy's truck. She looked up at him. He was frowning in the direction of his home. "Dallas is going to be okay," she said.

He just nodded and held open the driver's side door for her. Her purse was in the front seat where she'd left it. She started to get in, but stopped, smiled, and said, "Do you want to drive?"

He grinned. "I don't have to drive to feel like a man, if that's what you mean. But I'd be happy to."

She climbed in and slid all the way across the bench, digging her keys out of her purse and handing them to Jake.

They turned down the gravel county road that would lead to the main highway. "After this, do you wanna go see Dallas?" she asked.

"We're sitting with him in shifts. I go in at nine, tonight."

"That's going to interfere with our bedtime plans, Jake."

He winced. "Damn it. I wasn't thinking…"

"Relax," she chuckled, "we can do it another night."

"Another night," he repeated quietly. "You might come to your senses by then."

"Mmm, true. I'm already starting to feel my senses waking up. Yep. I hear them. They're starting to tell me what a bad idea it is to let you into my bed. Wow. They're really making a lot of sense."

"You're a cruel woman."

She reached over and squeezed his thigh. "I'll come sit with you at the hospital for a while."

His smile seemed a little sad.

They arrived at the parsonage a few minutes later. Ivy wasn't sure what she'd expected. Maybe she thought the trees would be bare and the grass yellow, the house sinking in on itself, the whole environment in mourning. But it wasn't. The sun still shone through the fully-leafed trees. The grass was freshly mown, no doubt a kindness done by one of the pastor's flock—the people of Fair Grove could always be counted on to pitch in when tragedy struck. They might talk behind your back, but their actions spoke of good intentions.

Ivy and Jake held hands as they ascended the porch steps. Ivy knocked quietly, and a moment later the pastor opened the door. He wore a sweater over a button-down shirt and brown, twill slacks. His hair was thinning and he had on his reading glasses. All-in-all, he looked like a rather sad Mr. Rogers.

His smile widened a little at the sight of her. "Ivy, I was hoping you'd come by." He stepped aside and gestured for them to enter. Richard shook Jake's hand and then escorted them into the living room. "Can I get you something to drink? Tea? Water?"

"No, thank you," Ivy said. "I just wanted to come by and see how you were doing."

Richard leaned back in his chair across from the couch where Jake and Ivy were perched. He sighed heavily and nodded sadly. "I'm doing as well as can be expected. The worst part is the investigation. Of course they had to question me. In these sorts of things, the husband is always a suspect. I only wish I could have laid her to rest a few days ago. As it is, we'll be having the funeral on Monday. There was the autopsy and, because of how she was found, well, it will be a closed casket."

"I'm so sorry you've had to go through all that." Ivy swallowed down a burning sensation in her throat. She didn't want to think about her friend as a bloated corpse, gray and swollen from the creek water she'd been face-down in, but the image sprang to mind in spite of herself. The warmth of Jake's hand sliding around her waist gave her comfort. She resisted leaning against him, but she did scoot a little closer, her hip and thigh flush with his.

Richard smiled. "So the rumors are true?"

Ivy looked up at Jake. "This is still hush-hush," Ivy said. "But yes."

"I think it's wonderful. Best of luck to you both. Everyone deserves to be loved." He sighed and looked away.

Ivy's chest tightened as she thought about how little Molly had loved Richard, if at all. He must have known, on some level, that he'd married a very immature woman. By now, if he hadn't already thought of the possibility of her cheating, town gossip would have put the thought in his head. How horrible to lay your wife to rest while wondering if she'd been cheating on you. "If there's anything I can do...any way I can help..."

Richard's sad smile returned. "I thank you, Ivy. Your friendship meant a lot to Molly. She talked about you all the time."

"Is there anything I can do to help with the funeral arrangements?"

"Her mother has been handling that, I'm sure she could use some more food."

"I'd be happy to cook."

Richard leaned forward, opened his mouth, then closed it again. He glanced at Jake and then back to Ivy. "There is one thing. But...it's highly personal."

Jake cleared his throat. "I can wait outside."

Ivy smiled up at him. "Thank you."

He shot her a wink and left the room. When the front door clicked shut, Richard turned tear-filled eyes to Ivy. "You'd know if anyone would."

Oh, God. This was not what she wanted to do. Not how she wanted to do this.

"Who was it?" Richard asked.

Shit, he knew. He knew she was cheating, just not with whom. "Um," Ivy stuttered, "I don't...I'm not sure..."

"Ivy, girlfriends share with each other. She spent a lot of time at your house, though I'm suspecting she spent less time there than she said. I just can't stand not knowing who."

Ivy shook her head, her heart thundering, tears spilling from the sides of her eyes. "I don't...I can't..."

"At first I thought maybe she was in the habit of sleeping with random men. But the more I thought about it and remembered, I think it had to be one lover. See, her behavior changed a couple weeks ago. It was a distinct change, I can't believe I didn't see it happening. But that was when she spent so much time at your house...tell me, did she ever go to your house?"

Ivy lowered her eyes and nodded. "Yeah. She did."

"Ivy, honey, I need to know the truth. I need to know who Molly was sleeping with. I need to ask him why. And how. How could he do this? How could she? Did she think I wouldn't let her go if she wanted out? Did she think I was so...domineering...that I wouldn't let her out of the marriage if she wanted?"

Ivy wasn't sure she'd be able to speak; that if she opened her mouth, she wouldn't just collapse into blubbering tears. But she forced herself to try. "I don't think she wanted out of the marriage," she tried to say.

Then she shook her head and pinched the bridge of her nose.

"It wasn't your fault. I want you to know, I'm not angry with you. What could you do? It wasn't your place to tell me. You were just trying to be a good friend."

"I tried to talk her out of it," she squeaked. "And when I couldn't convince her, I tried to get her to just make it a one time thing. She got hooked on this guy and I couldn't do anything to stop her."

Richard fell to his knees in front of her and grabbed her by the shoulders, his fingertips digging deep. "Who was it? Ivy, talk to me. Who was it?"

She shook her head. "I don't know," she sobbed.

"Liar!" Richard shouted, standing and hauling her to her feet. He gave her a shake, rattling her brain, still sore from her concussion. There were so many emotions to sort through that fear and confusion were just two in the mix. "You know who it was and you're going to tell me!"

He kept shaking her. "I can't! I can't!" she shrieked.

And then the shaking stopped because Jake was there between her and Richard, one hand pressed to Richard's chest, the other extended behind him in a protective gesture in front of Ivy. "That's enough," Jake said calmly.

Slowly, through the blur of her tears, Ivy saw Richard's shoulders slump. The heat in his face faded and he sank back into his chair, pressing his palms into his eyes. "I'm so sorry," he said softly. "It's just driving me crazy. I'm sorry, Ivy. I hope I didn't hurt your head."

She only nodded, wanting to accept his apology, but unable to speak. Jake's hand was on her back, then, guiding her out of the house. As he drove them back to her house, Ivy looked at him. His jaw was tight, his expression stern. The hand that gripped the wheel was white-knuckled, but the one that held her hand only squeezed gently, his thumb rubbing back and forth over hers.

Dallas woke up that night.

Jake was sitting in the waiting room with Ivy standing behind him, massaging his shoulders. Since she wasn't family, she couldn't go in, so he'd decided to be with her for a few minutes before going to sit with Dallas.

Jake hadn't been able to speak after seeing Richard being so rough with Ivy. There was too much anger and violence in his state of mind at the time that he couldn't say anything. He'd wanted to beat the man to a bloody pulp for touching her like that, but it seemed wrong to harm a grieving man. Besides, as soon as he'd walked in, Richard had backed off.

Still, he'd driven Ivy home in silence, kissed her goodbye, and went back to the ranch to do some work. When she showed up at the hospital a little after nine, he was in a better frame of mind, at last able to smile at her and talk to her, though they didn't speak of what had happened at Pastor Allen's house. Jake had heard what Richard had been asking. So he knew it was true, then, that Molly had been cheating. What was worse, Ivy knew and hadn't shared. Even worse, she knew *who* Molly had been cheating with. Jake couldn't help wondering what other secrets Ivy kept, or how she'd found herself in the position of secret-keeper for so many people.

As she massaged a knot out of his left shoulder, a nurse came out, her smile bright. Jake had come to interpret the different smiles of the nurses. There was the tight, strained, "nothing's changed" smile. The weary, "I don't have time to talk to you" smile. But this one he had yet to see, and it gave him hope. He stood, taking Ivy's hand.

"He's awake," the nurse said.

Jake brushed away a tendril of guilt that said he should have been there and let himself experience the relief of knowing things were finally looking up.

"We're transferring him to a recovery room. Should be about an hour. But if you want to go ahead and call the rest of your family in, you can."

Jake let out a laugh and hugged the nurse. "Thank you."

"You're welcome," the nurse said, giggling and blushing as she walked away.

Jake turned to Ivy. She'd shed a couple of tears, but she was smiling. "Thank God," they said at the same time. And then laughed. And then hugged.

He kissed her a little longer than was appropriate, and then she left so that he could call in his family.

When the nurse returned, he followed her back to the recovery room. Dallas appeared to be asleep again, but when Jake touched his hand, his eyes fluttered open.

Dallas's eyes remained blank for a while, but when they focused on Jake, they widened. "I'm sorry," he croaked. "I'm sorry! I'm sorry!"

"Shh," Jake said. He had to push Dallas's shoulders back down onto the bed. He kept repeating 'I'm sorry' over and over until he was sobbing. "Jesus, Dallas, calm down. I'm so glad you're awake. Whatever you're sorry for, it's forgiven. Just relax. Just calm down."

Dallas's body went limp on the bed. Tears squeezed out his eyes and streaked down the sides of his face. "I'm so sorry," he whispered.

"You got nothing to be sorry for. Shit, I'm the one who should be apologizing. I almost killed you. God, I don't know how I could have lived with myself if..." He quit talking as a nurse walked in.

Jake stepped back as the nurse checked Dallas's vitals. By the time she was finished, Dallas was asleep again, but the spell was broken.

A few minutes later he stood in the doorway and watched his family file past him into Dallas's room. Cody passed by, and Jake suddenly realized how much he wanted to talk to his brother. Cody had always been the easiest to talk to. The least judgmental. He might even be able to talk to him about Ivy, though Jake himself couldn't understand this strange compulsion to confess his feelings to everyone.

As Boone filed past, Jake frowned, immediately forgetting about everything else. He grabbed his youngest brother by the arm and held him back in the corridor. As soon as everyone was in Dallas's room and out of earshot, Jake leaned down and looked into Boone's eyes.

Usually so bright and mischievous, the brown had dulled. There was no spark. No light. His normally healthy complexion was sallow. "Why are you losing weight?"

Jake asked, looking Boone up and down. The boy's clothes were clearly getting loose.

"I don't know." Boone rubbed his face up and down, a gesture from the old man who did the same thing whenever he was either tired or frustrated. "Been worried about Dallas, I guess. Haven't had much of an appetite."

Jake shook his head. "Let's get you looked at. The doctor's supposed to come in, maybe he can order some blood tests while he's here. See if you're sick like Dallas."

Boone shook his head and let out a breathy laugh. "It's not hemlock poisoning."

"There's no telling how much of the hay was affected—"

"Jake, you know damn well I don't do any work around there. I ride around on my horse and watch you all feed the cattle."

Jake shrugged. He couldn't argue.

"No, it's just stress. It's just…" The look in Boone's eyes turned suddenly pleading. Like he was desperate to tell Jake what was bothering him. Like he hoped Jake could just read his thoughts.

But Jake couldn't. "You can talk to me, Boone. What's bothering you?" Jake put his arm around Boone's shoulders and guided him down the corridor a ways.

Boone stopped and faced him. "I have this situation and…and I'm afraid."

Jake fully understood what it took for a man—particularly a Deathridge man—to admit that he was afraid. His heart sank for his brother. "Let me help. What's going on?"

Boone shook his head. His mouth turned downward as though he had a bad taste in his mouth. "I can't. I really can't tell you. It's just…"

"It's killing you, Boone. Don't let it eat at you like this. Whatever it is, I'm here. Talk to me and I'll help you figure it out."

Boone shook his head again. "It's unforgivable. You wouldn't help me if you knew what I've done."

Naturally Jake started positing scenarios in his mind. What had his brother done that was so unforgivable? The only thing that came to mind, the only thing that Jake probably couldn't forgive, was if Boone had somehow hurt Ivy, or took Ivy from him. But since asking that question would mean confessing that he had feelings for her, Jake bit his tongue.

"Boys! Boys, your brother is awake!" Clara shouted from the doorway.

Jake spared one last look for Boone before leading the way to Dallas's room. The nurse was helping him to a sip of water. Gideon stood behind Clara as they stared down at their son, weakened by days of unconsciousness.

Gideon caught Jake's eye and came toward him, taking him by the elbow and out into the corridor as Jake had just done to Boone. Only not for the same reason. "You're damn lucky he's okay, you know that?"

Jake just gritted his teeth.

"Speak up, boy. I didn't hear you." Gideon cupped his hand behind his ear, yet another gesture that reminded Jake of his childhood.

"I know," Jake said through his teeth.

"I expect you ought to go forward in church tomorrow and repent of this. God spared your brother, but it would have been just punishment for you if he hadn't."

Jake had the very admirable quality of being one of those people who think before they react, otherwise he'd have flown off the handle at this point. As it was, he had too many emotions burning through him. Relief, fear, confusion, anger, guilt…hatred. In that moment, with Gideon suggesting that Dallas's death would have been "just punishment" for Jake's negligence, he most definitely felt hatred. But he couldn't speak. If he did, everything would come out, and even he didn't fully know what that entailed.

Gideon must have seen something in Jake's eyes, during their little stare-down, because, for the second time in a week, he backed down. It was subtle, but Jake noticed the old man's frown turn from menacing to grumpy, his shoulders lower, and his gaze break away. Gideon turned back to the room, grumbling under his breath.

Jake watched him go and didn't feel pride. He didn't feel victory. He felt more guilt. Wasn't it unnatural for a man to cower to his son? Shouldn't a good son submit to his father until his father was no longer capable of ruling? Of course in his mind he knew these concepts were outdated if they were ever valid. But his heart ached at what was happening.

Jake left the hospital. He would visit Dallas another time. For now, he had some bedtime plans with a certain cowgirl.

It Took A Rumor

Ivy assumed she wouldn't be seeing her lover anytime soon, so she got into her pajamas and settled in to read. The pebbles hitting her window at eleven that night caught her by surprise. But then she smiled and went to her window.

Down in the shadows cast by the light from her bedroom lamp stood Jake, like a teenage boy, waiting for her to let him up. "How come you can't knock on the door like a gentleman?" she asked.

"Shh. I didn't want to wake up your old man," he whisper-yelled.

"He doesn't care. I'll wake him up myself, let him know I've got company."

"I can't do what I gotta do if I know your Pa knows I'm doing what I'm doing."

"Huh?"

"Never mind. Just let me in."

"Aren't you gonna climb up the drainpipe?"

"You serious?"

"Sure. As long as we're playing Romeo and Juliet, you may as well climb up here and take my virtue without my father's permission. Go the whole nine yards with this little charade."

He tipped his stetson up, put his hands on his hips, and leaned back on one foot. "You making fun of me?"

"Always."

"Listen, I can turn around and walk back home if you want. I mean, if you don't want what I'm offering."

"We both know that's a bluff. And a bad one. Go ahead and walk away, cowboy."

He shrugged, turned on his heel, and started walking. Ivy laughed until he vanished into the shadows. Then she stopped laughing and held her breath. *Come back,* she thought. *Come back, come back.* If it was a bluff, he won. "Jake? Jake! Get back here!" She heard his laugh from the darkness.

She ran downstairs and unlocked the front door, letting him inside. He grinned all the way upstairs and into her room. He stopped inside her door and looked around. "This is a lot more girly than I expected," he said, tossing his hat on her dresser and running a hand through his hair.

"I like pink. I'm not ashamed." She watched as he roamed the room, running a fingertip along the sheer pink window dressing, picking up a music box and putting it back down. He wore a hint of a smirk and seemed completely absorbed in his exploration. Ivy sat on the edge of her bed and waited. His back was to her at her dresser. He was fiddling with her top dresser drawer. He looked up, catching her eye in the mirror, and held up a finger—a pink, lacy bra dangling from it.

"I like pink, too," he said with a grin.

Ivy bounded off the bed. "I've got something way better. Go sit on the bed, I'll be right back." She dug around in her drawer for a cute garter set she'd had for ages and hardly ever wore. She grabbed a matching bra and some black stockings and headed for her bathroom. She left the door cracked just a bit so she could talk to him. "You should strip, cowboy. You're not going to wanna waste any time when you see me in this." Her voice echoed in the bathroom. The tile was cold beneath her bare feet.

"I like your confidence, Ivy, but I plan on taking it slow tonight." She heard the sounds of a boot hitting the floor.

"I don't want it slow. I want it fast and hard and thrilling."

"Well, you shouldn't have insulted me the other day at the diner, then. I got something to prove to you and I'm bound and determined to do it."

In spite of herself, she felt her cheeks flush. She stripped out of her pajamas, strapped herself into the underwear, reapplied deodorant, tossed her hair around a bit, and checked herself out in the mirror. Pleased with the effect, she opened the door and strutted into her room.

Jake paused in the middle of removing his second boot, his eyes and smile widening. Ivy fought like mad to keep her cool, but he'd already removed his shirt and there was nothing in the world sexier than Jake without a shirt.

"Wow," they murmured simultaneously.

Jake dropped his boot and padded over to her. He trailed a fingertip down her sternum between her breasts, sending goosebumps all over her skin, making her nipples tighten. "I'll never see another sight. For as long as I live, wherever I look, this is what I'll see. Burned into my retinas for all eternity."

She grinned. "I'm glad you like the look."

"I like you."

"I'm glad you like me." She pressed her hands to his chest and let them slide down his well-defined abs to the waistline of his jeans. "How's Dallas?"

"He's fine. Please don't say his name right now."

She started to unfasten his jeans, but he grabbed her hands and brought them around his neck, leaning down to kiss her. It was impossible not to melt against him, and so she did. His hands roamed her back and waist and ass, stopping to squeeze. She moaned against his mouth. He moved up her back, unclasping her bra and letting it fall to the floor.

He backed away far too soon, turning to pull down the covers on her bed. "Get in," he said.

More than willing to obey, she crawled in, making a production of it, on her hands and knees with her ass swaying.

Jake's hand pressed into the center of her back, pushing her down on the bed, her ass remaining in the air. He grabbed her hips and pressed himself against her. She felt his erection through his jeans. "Stay like this," he commanded in a husky voice.

It Took A Rumor

She stretched her arms across the bed, rested her cheek on the cool sheets, and smiled. A moment later she heard the tell-tale signs of a condom being ripped open and his pants hitting the floor. So much for taking his time. His hands came to her hips and before she could take a breath, he was inside her. The shock of it sent her passion into the stratosphere. He thrust into her, slow and deep, and slid his hand around front to massage her. She was coming, crying into her sheets, before they'd even reached the two minute mark.

While she was still trembling, he pulled out and rolled her to her back. He straddled her hips and grabbed her breasts, massaging them and moaning. His brown eyes were dark with lust and the grin he gave her as he met her gaze held a glint of wickedness she'd never seen in him before. As she watched his expression, she realized that she'd gotten too cocky too soon. Jake had just been nice, up until now. He'd just given her the power to direct their sexual encounters because he was a gentleman and didn't want to intimidate her. But Jake was a cowboy. And as she regarded the knowledge and greed and intense desire in his gaze, she finally fully realized that she was in for one hell of a ride.

The bed rocked, it's springs squeaking, and more than once Jake had to cover her mouth with his hand to stifle her cries. Well into the night, her body and sheets were drenched in sweat and her muscles trembled, weak from the power of his lovemaking. He'd penetrated her so many times she'd lost count. She was sore from it so much that when he finally lay on top of her and began to press into her, she cried, "I can't! I can't anymore, Jake."

He chuckled softly in her ear. "If you mean that, I'll back off. But I'd sure like to finish the job. I'm about at the end of my energy and you'd make my night if you'd let me have you like this."

Her legs shook from being held open so long, but she managed to wrap them around his waist. She met his smiling eyes and nodded. He smiled even wider, slid into her, and closed his eyes. "You fit me like you were made for me, Ivy."

She slid her hands into his hair and held on. His expression grew darker and more intense. He stared into her eyes as he made love to her steadily, faster and harder, his breathing quickening with hers. They rocked together into hot, blissful orgasms, groaning into each other's mouths, and trembling against each other's bodies.

At last he rolled off of her and pulled her against him, kissing her hair and stroking her back. Ivy wanted to talk. Wanted to tease him and then stroke his ego by praising his outstanding performance. But her body was satisfied, her mind exhausted, and her heart full. She fell asleep in his arms.

When she woke up, it was full daytime and Jake was gone, his hat on the pillow next to her head.

"The old man catches you smiling like that, he's gonna slap a knot on your head," Cody said.

He, Boone, and Jake were driving to church in Jake's truck. Gideon and Clara followed in the car. Dallas would be coming home tomorrow, so everyone's tensions had eased quite a bit. But Cody was right. If Jake didn't stop smiling, Gideon was gonna be pissed. Jake was supposed to be in a penitent mood. He was supposed to go forward after the sermon, hang his head, confess his sins, and ask forgiveness. What he'd rather do, however, was drag Ivy out the back door, into the woods, and have her out in the open underneath God's cathedral with the sun and wind on their sweat-dampened skin.

"Seriously," Cody said, "what's got you in such a good mood?"

Jake just shook his head.

"Must be a girl," Boone said, his voice uncharacteristically monotone. He'd tried to plead sick that morning, but Gideon would have none of it. "That's the smile of a man who hasn't been laid in forever finally getting some."

If the boy didn't look like he'd fall over with a light breeze, Jake would have slapped him. It wasn't a girl putting a smile on his face. It was *the* girl. Trouble was, he didn't quite know how to broach the subject with Gideon.

Boone suddenly jumped in his seat. He scrambled in his pocket, pulling out his cell phone. He stared at the screen and then laughed hysterically.

"Jesus Christ, Boone," Cody said.

"It's nothing," Boone said. "Just a notification from some game I haven't played in forever. Holy shit," Boone sighed, leaning back on the bench.

Jake pulled into a parking spot near the back of the lot to the side of the church. He looked at his younger brother. Boone's eyes were closed, his body visibly shaking. Jake met Cody's frown, both of them shrugging. Cody reached up and placed the front of his wrist against Boone's forehead, feeling for a fever. Naturally Boone slapped him away, but still, Jake waited for the verdict. Cody shrugged again, shaking his head. No fever, then.

They got out and met up with Gideon and Clara on the way to the front door of the church. People flowed in, a steady trickle of souls seeking salvation. Jake got in line behind Cody who was behind Boone who followed Clara and then Gideon. They strolled through the foyer, took a sharp turn to the left behind the back row of pews, and made their way up the side aisle to their favored pew. Except Jake stopped at the left turn while his family went on without him.

Because Ivy was across the aisle, a few rows up, about to take a seat. She slid her purse off her shoulder and sat it in the pew next to her Bible. When she looked up and caught his gaze, her cheeks flushed and she smiled—brightly and with an earnest joy. She was happy to see him. He was happy to see her. He'd left her late in the night collapsed in her bed, disheveled and satisfied. The blankets had been down around her waist and her arms had been flung to the sides. He'd gazed at her naked breasts and long throat and sweet, sleeping face before covering her up, kissing her, and leaving her his hat. It had been a silly, sentimental gesture, but he'd wanted her to wake up next to something besides an empty pillow. And now she was wearing his hat. She touched her fingertip to the brim, giving it a tip, and winked at him before taking her seat.

That was it. He was sitting by her. She was his girl and people ought to know it.

Except that as soon as he stepped toward her, Pastor Allen slid in next to her, taking her hand and leaning in. Probably apologizing for losing his temper yesterday. That's what it looked like, anyway, given the heartfelt expression on his face and the way Ivy nodded reassuringly. They hugged, the pastor stood, and Jake took yet another step toward her. This time his path was blocked by Myra Tidwell, looking prim and full of life in a turquoise jacket with matching earrings. She held her trusty iPhone and stylus at the ready.

"I see your hat on little Ivy Turner's head, I suppose I can take that as confirmation of a relationship?"

"It's none of your business, Myra." She had him blocked in. He couldn't squeeze past her without knocking her over.

"It's mighty big of you considering she was sleeping with Cody not a week ago."

"For God's sake!"

The people in the pews nearest turned and gave him a dirty look. Jake smiled apologetically and lowered his voice. "Can we do this later?"

"Did you poison your brother, Jake?" she asked as she wrote on the screen of her phone.

"Of course not. Not on purpose."

"You sure? Because it does tend to look like you were jealous and angry, what with Dallas having slept with Ivy, too. My, my, that girl has just worked her way through you boys, hasn't she."

"She never slept with any of them."

"Only you? You sure about that? Or is it wishful thinking?"

"Let me pass, Myra, I—" Just then a bony but powerful hand gripped the back of his collar.

"Get your ass in your seat right now," Gideon growled.

Jake didn't want to make more of a scene than he already had, so he allowed his father to shove him toward their pew. "You stay away from that woman. She's got the devil's tongue in her mouth." Gideon climbed over his sons and Clara and took his seat at the end of the pew closest to the center aisle, and then the choir began singing.

Jake stood with the rest of the congregation, and though he fought the urge, he couldn't help glancing over his shoulder at Ivy. He should go sit by her now. It would go a long way toward proving to her that he was man enough to stand up to his father. Trouble was, he'd actually have to stand up to his father, and he wasn't a hundred percent certain he was ready for that.

After the first two songs, Ellis Henry got up to read announcements followed by a prayer. Jake bowed his head and listened to all the people being prayed for. They included Dallas, Molly, Molly's husband and family, and even Jake and Eloise. Jake couldn't help smiling at that. How many churches were there that included a sick horse on their prayer list? All that mattered was that this one did. He wouldn't go anywhere else because of it.

After the prayer, they sang a few more songs, then sat and waited as Pastor Allen took the podium. There had been a lot of speculation as to whether he would actually preach that morning. Being a grieving man, no one would have blamed him a bit for taking off a few weeks. But there he was, tall and strong, if not a little dark under the eyes and wan in complexion.

"Let us all open our Bibles to second Corinthians chapter four:

"But we have this treasure in earthen vessels, that the excellency of the power may be of God, and not of us. We are troubled on every side, yet not distressed; we are perplexed, but not in despair; Persecuted, but not forsaken; cast down, but not destroyed; Always bearing about in the body the dying of the Lord Jesus that the life also of Jesus might be made manifest in our body."

Pastor Allen paused, his head hanging low, a solemn expression weighing down his brow. "Friends, here we see the purpose of our suffering. There has been a lot of suffering for a lot of people this week. We look to God and we ask why. Why would he place such burden on us? On mere earthen vessels? My friends, it is so that we may show the light of the glory of God to the world. It is so that Christ can arise. For how could he arise without first dying? We are that death. Through our suffering on this earth, we are the death of Christ put here so that he might save us and show his awesome power to the world.

"My friends, Christ does not want your suffering on this earth. He wants to deliver you from it. It is up to each of you to be worthy of that delivery. If you're burdened with sin this morning, come forward and hand it to Christ. Endure your suffering on this earth for the sake of the glory of God. Come forward and offer yourself a living sacrifice to the Lord. Confess your sins, accept His forgiveness, and walk again in the newness of life!"

The congregation stood and sang. This was the part where Jake was supposed to go to the front and confess to nearly killing his brother. He truly felt horrible for what had happened to Dallas, but he had a hard time accepting that it was totally his responsibility. It seemed like an accident more than anything. But Gideon was unwilling to absolve Jake, and so it would take God's forgiveness to convince his father that he was worthy to be called son again.

Jake glanced at his father and, sure enough, the man's steely glare was locked on him. If he didn't go forward and do this, he'd hear about it for sure. Might even have to take a beating for it. And he knew in his heart he wouldn't fight back. He'd give the old man the victory just to assuage his own guilt.

With a heavy sigh, Jake went up and sat on the front pew. As the congregation sang, the pastor sat next to him and leaned into him, their lowered heads nearly touching so that they could hear one another. "Would you like me to speak on your behalf?" Richard asked.

"No, thanks, preacher. I can manage."

Jake felt the warmth of another body to his left. He turned and found Ivy sitting next to him. She placed her hand on his back. The hat looked cute with her sundress and boots. She leaned in close to his ear. "Are you up here for fornicating with me? Because that's my sin, too, and I'm not quite ready for this level of confession."

He grinned at her. "I think in order to confess, you have to first feel guilty about it."

"You don't?"

"Not the least bit."

She linked her fingers with his as the song came to an end. Jake waited for the pastor to invite him to speak.

"Friends," Pastor Richard said, standing on the floor in front of the congregation, "I am always touched when God uses my voice to move the conscience of one of his people. Is there anyone else among us who wishes to unburden? Come, now, and give your sins to God."

There was silence. Jake frowned up at the pastor. Richard's face looked different. His eyes bright and a little out of control.

"Anyone?" Richard asked again, his voice cracking. "Any adulterers for instance?" Suddenly he laughed. "You can't tell me there's none here who've committed adultery."

Ivy left Jake's side and moved to take Richard's arm. At the same time there was a shuffling behind Jake. He turned to see Boone standing and stumbling out of the pew, clutching his cell phone, looking pale enough to pass out. Boone turned, tripped, recovered, and shuffled out the door.

"God is here, Boone!" Richard shouted. "God is up here! There's nothing but suffering for you out there!"

Boone made it to the door. That was when Pastor Allen broke from Ivy's grasp and gave chase. Jake was on his feet the next instant, joining Gideon and Cody as they ran to Boone's aid. By the time they got to the parking lot, Richard was on top of Boone, landing punch after punch. Boone had his arms up over his face screaming. It took Jake a moment to decipher what he was saying.

"You killed her!" Boone shouted over and over.

Cody plucked the wiry pastor off their brother. If Boone hadn't already been weak, there would have been no way the man could have knocked him over. Gideon helped Boone up, checking on his injuries. Jake knelt on his other side and caught a glimpse of Boone's phone. The text app was open.

-What do you want?

-Your suffering on this earth.

Jake recognized the phraseology from the sermon, but he still couldn't wrap his mind around what was going on. He stood to face the pastor even as Gideon brought Boone to his feet.

Jake didn't even look for Ivy. He knew where she would be…right at his side. Without thinking, he slid his arm over her shoulders and brought her closer. Cody stepped back from the now calm pastor. Richard would have to have a death wish to attack Boone, now, with all but one of the Deathridge men facing him.

"He killed her," Boone said, his voice cracking and weak.

About that time, Sheriff Rivera, who attended with his family faithfully, made his way to Pastor Allen's side.

"What's going on?" he asked. "Pastor? Why'd you attack Boone?"

Richard had regained his composure, or at least managed to cram it all behind tightly closed lips.

"Boone?" the sheriff asked. "You wanna explain?"

Ivy stepped out of Jake's grasp and touched Boone's face. She leaned in and whispered in his ear, but Boone just kept shaking his head harder and harder. "No!" he shouted, finally focusing his eyes on Ivy. "No!" He turned to the sheriff. "I didn't do anything. But you can be damn sure I'm pressing charges."

The sheriff hung his head for a moment. "Pastor, I don't want to arrest you in front of your congregation. Let's go into your office until everyone goes home. Then we'll head down to the station."

The pastor and the sheriff went inside. The crowd dispersed, except for Myra who was rapidly taking notes on her phone. Jake wanted to ask Ivy what had just happened, but he had another problem to deal with, namely that Gideon was already asking her the same question, and not in a nice manner.

"I'll be friends with anyone I want!" Ivy was shouting at him in response to whatever he'd shouted at her.

"Not with my boys, you won't. Turner, get this little s—"

"Pop!" Jake interrupted, before Jared Turner was forced to defend his daughter's honor again. "Let's just get Boone home, okay?" he asked. He looked to his mom for support, even though it was a foolish thing to do. She'd never stood up to Gideon and, as far as Jake could tell, she never would. Still, she took Boone's arm and started leading him to the truck.

The color in Ivy's cheeks faded. Jake's hat hung on the back of her neck by the tie underneath. She turned, smiled at Jake, and started walking toward him. Whereas a moment ago it had been the most natural thing in the world to take Ivy in his arms, now, with Gideon's glare centered straight on him, Jake instinctively took a step back. Now wasn't the time to add fuel to the fire, surely Ivy could see that.

She froze, her smile dying.

Jake gulped. He extended his hand. "Thank you for your help, Ivy," he said, hoping she'd take the hint and not be too angry at him.

She stepped forward, and for his ears only, said, "Screw you, Jake. I'm keeping this hat." She placed it on her head with a stubborn pout, turned, and walked past her father to their truck.

Gideon's glare was still burning through him. Jake could only imagine what he thought. "Is that your hat on her head, boy?" he snarled.

Jake studied his father for a moment. "Of course not," he said, just like Peter denying Jesus. And just like Peter, he found ways to justify his denial. It wasn't the right time. Gideon was in a fragile state. Clara was in a fragile state. There were any number of valid excuses.

On the ride home, his smile had vanished. He thought about her parting words and wondered what she'd meant. He did like his hat, but she was welcome to keep it. He was just as happy knowing she was wearing it.

Maybe he still had some time to win her over. He hoped to God he did, anyway. He no longer had a vision of his future that didn't feature her prominently front and center.

It Took A Rumor

In the past couple of weeks, Ivy had been visited either at work or at home by every single male Deathridge in the county, so it shouldn't have been surprising to her to open the front door to Clara. Clara's men would be relaxing, it being Sunday and all. They were probably all passed out for afternoon naps with their bellies full of of Clara's cooking and baseball games playing on their televisions.

The one exception would be Boone who was likely torturing himself over the same thing Ivy was…Pastor Allen.

Ivy had gone home not knowing where her responsibilities lie. Should she go to Boone and once more try to talk him into going to the police? Should she go to the police herself? Should she go to Richard and try to get a confession out of him?

Surely Boone's heated words during the fight would be enough to make the sheriff look a little harder at Richard as a suspect in Molly's murder. But the texts on Boone's phone, if they truly came from the pastor, would be vital evidence. Then there was Ivy's own experience the night she went to the house to check on Molly…surely she should tell someone. It terrified her to think of how close she'd been yesterday and today to the man who'd most likely given her a concussion last week.

There was so much on her mind, so much confusion roiling in her gut, that she was beginning to feel a persistent burning sensation in her stomach, and she couldn't bring herself to eat lunch.

When Clara knocked on the door, she was frenetically moving about the kitchen, trying to find something else to clean after having tidied up post-lunch. She still had Jake's hat hanging off the back of her neck and was ashamed to admit to herself that she had every intention of sleeping next to it in spite of the way he'd denied her that afternoon.

She went to the door and opened it.

"Mrs. Deathridge," Ivy said in surprise.

Clara smiled sadly. Her eyes were puffy and red-rimmed. "Is your father home?"

"Um, he's out in the garage. Come on in. I'll get him." She stepped aside, inviting Clara into the living room. "Can I get you something to drink? Ice water? Sweet tea?"

"Tea would be lovely. It's been a long time since someone served me tea."

Ivy wasn't sure what to make of the comment, but she went to the garage and alerted her father to Clara's presence before moving back to the kitchen to fill three glasses with ice and tea.

"Good afternoon, Clara," Jared said.

Ivy smiled at the sound of her father's voice. She put the glasses on a tray and took them into the living room where Jared and Clara were seated, both on the sofa angled toward each other. Ivy sat in a chair off to the side. Everyone took their tea before Clara sat hers back down and burst into tears. She fell into Jared's arms while Jared looked helplessly to his daughter. Ivy shrugged.

"Is it true?" Clara squeaked.

"Is what true?" Jared asked.

Clara pushed back and wiped her wrist over her eyes. "Was Gideon in love with Penny when he married me?"

Jared didn't hesitate. "Oh, Clara, no. No, honey. And Penny wasn't in love with him. They were two high school kids who dated for a couple of weeks. The fact is, Gideon hated me from the get-go and it was salt in the wound when the girl he was dating chose me. I doubt anything would have happened between them, it was just his pride is all."

"I don't think he's ever really loved me," Clara said. Ivy was surprised at how calmly she said it.

"I'm sure that's not true," Jared said, giving her shoulder a squeeze.

Clara shook her head. "He's driving us all away. My boys…they're scared to death of him. They have no respect for me, and why should they? I've never done a thing besides sit back and watch him terrorize them."

Jared met Ivy's gaze. They didn't know how to respond or what Clara wanted.

Clara took a breath and looked up at Ivy. She smiled sadly. "That's Jake's hat."

Tension drained out of Ivy's body, and she smiled back. "Yes."

"Is that why he hasn't had much appetite? He's in love with a girl?"

"I don't know about love, but we've been doing a lot of fighting and making up."

"Really?" Clara laughed. "Jake's my peacemaker. It's hard to imagine him fighting."

"He's certainly not very good at it. Mostly it's me yelling at him and him standing there looking confused."

"That sounds about right," Jared said with a chuckle.

Ivy shrugged. "Got momma's temper. Not my fault."

"Well, I do hope you'll give him another chance. I've never seen him quite like this," Clara said.

"He's pissed me off pretty good. We'll see if he cares to make it up to me."

"Oh, you must forgive him, you just have to," Clara said, suddenly very concerned. "It's not his fault, whatever he did. He's a good boy, and—"

"Mrs. Deathridge," Ivy said, laughing, "don't worry. Please? If it's meant to work out, it will. Jake's a good man, like you said. If he wants me, he knows how to get me."

Clara wrung her hands, distraught. "It's just, I feel as though my whole world is coming apart at the seams. Myra making such vicious attacks against my family, Dallas almost dying, Boone acting crazy. I just…I'm feeling very…mortal. I'm feeling very insecure. If I knew

Jake was safe, that he was taken care of, well, then at least one of my sons would be okay."

Jared leaned forward and took her hands in his. "I hope I'm not speaking out of turn. But Clara, any one of your boys…hell, all four of them, would always be welcome on my ranch. If anything happened with Gideon and he were to push them away, I've got more than enough work, here. I'll be honest, I lost those two farm hands last week and I've been putting off hiring more because, well, it looks like the prospect of a son-in-law is becoming more likely."

"Dad!" Ivy reprimanded.

He shrugged. "You're obviously a woman in love, honey. And I think the world of Jake. It's just a bonus that you've fallen for a rancher."

"A rancher who doesn't want to leave his ranch."

"If his family will have you, then go with him," Jared said. "Or build a house on the property borders and keep working for your respective families. There's any number of ways you could work it out. The main thing is that you treat each other with respect and love each other."

Ivy winced, a little, at the "respect" part of it. Perhaps she could do a little better toward Jake in that department. "None of it matters if he's unwilling to acknowledge me in public. That's a deal breaker."

"Being a little impatient with the boy, aren't you?"

"Maybe. But he's being a coward, so it evens out."

Jared laughed and rolled his eyes. "Anyway, Clara, you needn't worry. If there's anything we can do to help you and your family, just say the word."

"Gideon would have a fit if he knew I came here. But I just don't care. I'm so tired of working and working and nobody caring. I think if I vanished off the face of the earth, the only thought that would cross those boys' minds is, 'Where's dinner?'"

"That's not true," Ivy said, leaning forward and squeezing Clara's hands.

"It is, though, dear. And I don't blame my boys, I've done this to myself as far as they're concerned. But Gideon…I just don't think he cares. He's so entrenched in his view of things, the rest of us are just pawns."

Ivy shared another look with her father, neither of them certain what to say. Hopefully it wasn't true. Hopefully Clara was just going through a time of doubt and Gideon would offer her the affirmation she needed. But Ivy doubted it. What she knew of the man…Clara was dead-on right with her assessment. He'd built himself a tiny empire and was ruling with an iron fist.

Suddenly, Clara gave herself a little shake. She fished a handkerchief out of her handbag and dabbed at her eyes. When she looked up, it was with a smile for Ivy. "Come over for tea tomorrow afternoon, won't you? I think we should get to know each other. Your momma and I were good friends for a while, you know?"

"I'd love to have tea with you."

It Took A Rumor

"Good. We'll get Dallas settled in his house in the morning, then after I feed the boys lunch and send them back out to work, you can come over. Maybe we'll invite Myra and give her something else to gossip about."

Ivy laughed at this sudden evidence of humor.

After she walked Clara back out to her car, she went inside and gave her father a hug,

There was no leaving Dallas alone in his house. Clara couldn't bear it. She set up the guest bedroom for him, insisting, even against Gideon's objections, that her son be close at hand so that she could care for him.

After his father and brothers left, Clara perched on the edge of the bed next to Dallas and brushed the hair off his forehead. His face was turned away, staring out the window with no expression. She could only guess what he was thinking.

"It must be hard for a working man like you to be in bed during the day," she said, thinking of Gideon and how much he'd fussed that summer he broke his arm.

Dallas let out a humorless laugh. "Actually, it's pretty comfortable. Kind of glad for the excuse to do nothing."

Not sure what to make of it, Clara kissed him on the cheek, and went back into the kitchen. Her men had left crumbs from their sandwiches everywhere and dirty dishes in the sink. She'd never resented it before, but suddenly she was wondering why she hadn't taught four grown men how to wash a plate.

As soon as she finished cleaning up, she put on some water for tea and got out her prettiest set, an English teapot with pink flowers and matching cups and saucers. On the coffee table in the living room, she laid out a tray of fruit and cheese. She'd initially intended to put out cookies, but Ivy was a modern, healthy girl, and probably wouldn't eat them. Almost as soon as she'd set the tea on the table next to the fruit, Ivy's arrival was heralded by the sound of hoof-clods.

Clara smiled to herself. Jake was getting himself a good, solid country girl. Only a couple of weeks ago, Clara had had a different impression of the girl—always in her business clothes, the country drawl sanitized from her speech. But lately she seemed to have lapsed back into her rancher's-daughter persona.

Ivy knocked on the screen door and came in. Such an adorable thing in a pretty sundress over leggings, cowboy boots, and Jake's hat which she swept off her head and hung on the pegs next to the door—as though she was already at home.

"So glad you came, dear. Have a seat."

Ivy sat with her ankles crossed. Clara was pleased to see she knew how to conduct herself like a lady. Ivy accepted her tea, squeezing in a drizzle of honey from the honey bear on the tray next to the pot.

"No Myra?" Ivy asked.

"Absolutely not. I abhor that woman. Between you and me, she still smokes pot, did you know that?"

Ivy nearly spat her tea. "Uh, no…how…?"

"I saw her make an exchange with that Kinsley boy in the alley beside the diner one day. She didn't see me and I've kept it to myself, but I'm thinking of starting my own blog. It's about time she had some competition."

"Mrs. Deathridge, you'd be my everlasting hero if you did that. It's time she had a taste of her own medicine. I'll even help you set up the website."

"Excellent. It'll be a healthy pursuit for both of us."

Ivy nodded agreement, and Clara took a moment to appreciate how well she was getting along with her future daughter-in-law. It was a shame the moment couldn't last any longer.

There were no sirens, only the sound of tires on gravel and a cloud of dust passing by the windows. Clara sat her cup on the coffee table and rose to look out the screen door. "Why, it's Sheriff Rivera. I wonder what he wants." She opened the screen door as the sheriff approached. He was in full uniform, a somber expression on his face. "Good afternoon, Sheriff. Won't you come in?"

He stepped inside, nodded politely to Ivy, and said, "I'm afraid I need to borrow Boone for a few minutes. I've got some questions to ask him."

"Oh," Clara said, feeling confused. "Well, he's out on the ranch somewhere. I think they were headed to the corral to weigh the calves and check on the sick ones."

"Do they have phones?"

"I'm texting him," Ivy said, her head bowed over a cell phone, thumbs working. Clara was grateful her future daughter-in-law knew how to work those insufferable contraptions.

"Why don't you have some tea while you wait," Clara said.

The sheriff obliged and sat on the sofa opposite Ivy. They drank in relative silence for a moment. "He's on his way," Ivy said at last. "I texted Jake, too."

The sheriff merely nodded. He looked pretty funny in his uniform with his big strong hands holding a dainty, feminine teacup.

A few minutes later, the back door opened. Apparently Gideon wouldn't let his boys vanish on him, because he'd come with them, an angry glower on his face. Of course, that might have just been his natural expression. Clara could hardly tell anymore.

"What's this about, Sheriff?" Gideon asked. "We got work to do. Don't much appreciate having the day interrupted like this."

"All I needed was Boone," the sheriff said.

Boone was right behind Gideon, followed by Jake and Cody. Jake's eyes went wide at the sight of Ivy. "Ivy!" he exclaimed. "What the hell are you doing here?"

"Having tea with your mother," she spat, though if her tone was any indication, she wanted to say something much harsher. Clara couldn't blame her. The boy hadn't exactly offered the warmest of greetings. Then again, he wouldn't…not in front of Gideon.

"Boone, this conversation might be best just the two of us," Sheriff Rivera said as he stood.

Clara sat in a chair across the coffee table from where Ivy was perched, teacup in hand, ankles crossed. To Clara's right stood the Sheriff, back to the wall. To her left stood Gideon, blocking any exit from the sitting room. Behind him the boys were fanned out. Clara looked up and saw Dallas appear at the edge of the hallway in his pajamas.

"You got something to say to my boy, you'll say it in front of me," Gideon said.

"Gideon, your boy ain't a boy anymore. Frankly, I don't need your permission to talk to him. I just need his." He cocked his head to make eye contact with Boone.

Boone shifted on his feet. "It's…it's about her?"

The sheriff nodded. "Richard Allen says you did it."

Boone turned his horror-filled eyes to Gideon who was now glaring over his shoulder at Boone. "What did you do, boy?" Gideon snarled.

"Nothing. I didn't do nothing, I swear!"

Gideon turned on Boone. "Don't lie to me, you little hellion. What did you do?"

"I swear, Pop—"

Gideon smacked him on the ear.

"Hey, Pop, come on," Jake said, stepping in between them.

Now Ivy was on her feet, tea spilled on her dress. "Come on, Boone, I'll go with you. Let's step outside and talk to the sheriff."

It Took A Rumor

Gideon turned to face her, eyes bright with rage. "I'll thank you to mind your own business. What the hell are you doing in my house anyway?"

Clara didn't know Ivy terribly well, but she recognized the flush as one of rage. Some instinctive reflex deep in the most primitive part of her brain made her sink back into the chair and make herself smaller.

"I'm here as a friend to your wife, and now your son, which is perfectly within my rights," she said, keeping her tone shockingly civil.

"You ain't welcome here. I don't want any Turner blood in my house, especially not you!"

The cup and saucer landed on the carpet unharmed as Ivy shouted, "You ridiculous old bastard, I'll go wherever the hell I want and talk to whomever the hell I want. You can act like you own this place and the people in it, but you don't own me. Fuck you, Gideon!"

"Fuck you, you little brat. Sheriff, this girl's trespassing and I want her out."

Ivy laughed. "You are absolutely out of your mind!"

Jake stepped forward, faced Ivy, and in a low voice said, "Maybe you should go. We can talk later."

For some reason, his words made Ivy go pale, like the calm before a storm, and then redder in the face than ever. She sucked in a breath and shoved him in the chest. "I'm not here for you. I was here for Clara. And now I'm here for Boone, so if you don't have the balls to stand up for me, at least have the balls to keep your damn mouth shut! Boone, let's go outside with the sheriff."

"He ain't going anywhere," Gideon snarled.

"Ivy, please," Jake said.

"I want you out, girl! Sheriff, get her out."

"Ivy, I'll walk you. Come on," Jake said.

Her head turned back and forth between them until finally her hands curled into fists at her side, she threw her head back, and screamed. "Enough! Oh, my God, I hate this! I've hated this for so long and I'm so fucking sick of it! Fine, Gideon, you've obviously got your boys fully in your service. Every last one of them cowers to you—"

"My boys know the meaning of respect."

"That's what you call it? Respect?" She spun to face the sheriff. "Boone and Molly were having an affair, okay? Richard found out she was having an affair, but he didn't know who with. All he had was Boone's phone number. Since Molly had him programmed in her phone as 'sex god' Richard didn't have a name, but he's been harassing Boone with threatening texts. We'll be happy to go with you to the station and give statements."

Ivy spun to face Gideon. "Jake and I have been fucking. That's right. The dirty little Turner slut's got her hooks all up in your oldest son." She pivoted, pointed her finger at Dallas, and said, "He hates you so much that he'd do anything to get off this ranch, Gideon. Anything. Jake didn't poison Dallas. It wasn't Jake's negligence that lost you your cattle. It was Dallas pulling the dumbest sabotage ever. And Cody—"

"Ivy, please," Cody said, stepping forward and shaking his head. "Please don't."

With tears streaming down her cheeks and her face screwed up in pain, Ivy sucked in a breath. "Cody's gay. He's having an affair with one of my ranch hands. And I do believe he'd have took that secret to his grave to keep you, Gideon, from ever finding out. Is that respect? Or is it fucking fear?"

The room fell utterly silent except for the little chokes and sobs coming from Ivy whose face was buried in her hands. Clara looked down at her own hands and saw that they were shaking. Dallas had collapsed and was now sitting on the floor with his back to the wall staring straight ahead. Cody's face was pale and expressionless. Boone looked about to throw up. And Jake was…angry. Jake was fire-ant mad. In all of Clara's memory, she couldn't conjure up a time when Jake had stared at someone with such pure and heated anger as he was staring at Ivy.

But it was Gideon who broke the silence. "You vile little bitch," he snarled.

Suddenly, Jake turned, and Clara saw clearly for the first time. His anger wasn't meant for Ivy, it was meant for Gideon. And it had been there, simmering away, for years. "You ever talk to my girl like that again I'll deck you, you understand?" Jake shouted.

Gideon's rage amped up even more. "Watch your mouth, boy."

"No, sir, I'm done watching my mouth. You did this. All of this. Shit," he said, shoving his hands through his hair. He paced a few steps before seeming to remember Ivy. He closed the distance and brought her into his arms. "All right," he said, looking around. His eyes landed on Boone. "Boone, go on with the sheriff. Tell him everything you know, everything you've been hiding. We'll get you a lawyer if we need to."

Ivy pushed back and dried her eyes with her palms. She sucked in a breath. "Um, yeah. I need to go with them."

"We'll just step outside," the sheriff said. "Depending on their answers, we may not have to go anywhere."

The sheriff, Boone, and Ivy filed toward the front door. Ivy stopped in front of Cody. "I'm so sorry," she said softly. "I didn't mean to…"

Cody turned away from her, his jaw ticking.

She followed Boone out to the front porch. Jake was still pacing the living room while Gideon seethed where he stood. Clara couldn't be certain where his rage would land. By all rights, it belonged on Dallas who had betrayed the family in a way that shocked Clara to her core. The second choice would have been Jake who had never so blatantly disrespected Gideon before, let alone in front of strangers. But apparently what rent Gideon's soul more than everything else was Cody, because he turned and backhanded the boy across the cheek.

Cody just took it, his head snapping to the side, and then slowly turning back to meet Gideon's gaze. "You're dead to me," Gideon said.

Cody simply nodded and walked out the back door.

"You want off this ranch so bad," Gideon shouted to Dallas, "congratulations. You got your wish. You got one week to get the hell off my property."

Dallas didn't move. He just stared straight ahead.

"And you," Gideon said.

Jake stopped his pacing and faced him. "You ought to be real careful about what you're fixing to say. Because you just threw away half of your work force, and I'm your best hand."

"I can hire more," Gideon said belligerently.

"Not at what I work for. You're not hiring anyone who does the work I do for what I get paid."

"This ain't about money or jobs. It's about family. And you ain't family. Not after you betrayed me with that—"

"Call her a whore one more time, Pop, and we'll see if you can can take as good as you give."

Gideon clamped his mouth shut, glaring at Jake for a moment.

For the first time ever, Clara saw just how old Gideon was. How worn and tired. Jake towered over him, young and strong and no longer willing to submit. "Get out of my house. You're no son of mine," Gideon said.

Jake didn't react any more than Cody had. Instead, he went to Dallas and knelt in front of him. "You wanna stay with us while you get better?" he asked.

Dallas nodded listlessly.

"Good. I'll come get you in the truck later. We'll get you back on your feet. Then I'm gonna beat the shit out of you."

Dallas gave a hint of a grin. "I'll look forward to it."

Jake stood and left out the back door.

No one had spared Clara a glance. A thought. She was a part of the background, woven in to the tapestry of their environment. Not a real person with feelings, but a nameless, faceless, soulless servant.

Clara buried her face in her hands and wept.

There were so many things that needed his attention. Dallas needed moving. Ivy and Boone needed support. But it was Cody that Jake went after first. He found him in the field.

It appeared Cody had walked just far enough to lose sight of the house before falling to his knees and crying. Jake knelt beside him, rubbed his back, and said, "This is a good thing. For both of us."

Cody shook his head, his face covered by his hands. It was quiet on the pasture, the grass tall, now—up to their shoulders when they were sitting in it. Not much breeze, but the heat of the sun wasn't overwhelming.

"Yeah," Jake said. "It is. Now we can love who we want to love. No more hiding."

Cody turned and threw his arms around Jake's neck. Jake laughed at first, the first tendrils of the excitement of freedom reaching into his soul. He pounded Cody on the back even as Cody clung to him. "It's all right, little brother. You're gonna be okay."

This was what made it possible for Jake to stand up to Gideon. His brothers all, in the moment that Ivy spilled their secrets, needed support. They needed their father to counsel them and comfort them. Instead, they'd gotten slaps in the face and disownment. Gideon was the only father Jake had ever had, yet he somehow knew that he would never treat his own son like that. It wasn't enough to eliminate the sense of guilt he found at rejecting

Gideon's authority, but it was enough for him to decide that the guilt was worth the action.

Cody let out one sob that might have been a laugh, muffled against Jake's shoulder. "I didn't want anyone to know. Not ever. How could she do that?"

Jake was certain had she not been in the throes of passionate rage, she would have kept Cody's secret. His wasn't like the others, and he didn't deserve to be outed like that. "All that matters is that she did. It's out, now. We do know. So you may as well make the best of it."

"I thought she was my friend."

"She is, man. She screwed up and you can tell her all about it when you pull yourself together. Right now, let's just get our bearings, okay?"

Cody fell back, sitting with his legs splayed in front of him, squinting at the horizon. "You're sleeping with her?"

Jake sat next to him, hugging his knees to his chest. "Hopefully."

"How long has that been going on?"

"A few weeks."

"That's how the rumors got started?"

Jake frowned. "You know, I still don't know how that happened. She and I did…that…a week before the rumors began. And then when Myra started gossiping, it wasn't about that particular…incident…which no one could have known about. So I really don't know."

"Are you in love with her?"

Jake took a moment to inhale and exhale and roll the thought around in his mind. "Yeah," he said at last.

Cody laughed. "Wow. Well, she's lived next door forever. What took you so long?"

"Never had occasion to talk to her until after her mom passed and she took over the business. She had that city boyfriend for years, I just never gave her much thought. Plus, she was a kid for most of the time I've known her. Hell, I think I even changed a diaper or two back when our moms were friends."

"That is really fucked up."

Jake smiled. Not fucked up. Just…interesting. "What about you? Are you in love with the guy? Jordan, right?"

Cody was silent for a long time. When he spoke, his voice was back to its usual low and quiet. "I don't know if it's love. But I've never felt this way about anyone."

"How did Ivy find out?"

Cody snorted. "She caught us after the fact in an old abandoned barn on her property."

Jake winced. "Bummer."

"You should have seen her," he said, laughing. "She closed her eyes before she turned to run, had to feel her way out of the barn and back to her horse. Pretty cute."

Jake smiled to himself, glad that Cody had already begun forgiving her. He could justifiably refuse to forgive her forever. Spilling Cody's secret was the worst thing she'd done that day. No one else, not even Jake, had had the right to ask her to bear the burdens of their secrets.

Still, maybe it was because he had such a soft spot for her, maybe it was because he knew she regretted it the instant it happened—but he wanted Cody to forgive her. She deserved a second chance.

As if reading his mind, Cody said, "She was a good friend to me. She blew her top, is all. Who wouldn't? Can't believe Dad talked to her like that."

"I can't believe she's been juggling all this. And I don't know how many times I've accused her of sleeping with one of you guys. She ought to turn around and never look back. But I hope she doesn't. I hope she can forgive me."

"She will. She's a good person."

Jake nodded. A breeze kicked up. The smells in the pasture weren't always pleasant, but this breeze carried a hint of lilac from where it grew on the fence bordering the Turner property. "What are we gonna do?" he mused quietly.

"I guess we're gonna apply for jobs with Mr. Turner."

"Gideon will come around. He'll have to."

Cody shook his head. "I'd hate to abandon you, Jake. But my father just looked me in the eye and told me I was dead to him. He almost lost a son for real last week and he turned and said that to me, Dallas barely home from the hospital. I don't think I could ever work for him again."

"He just needs time—"

"Yeah? Well, he can't have it." Cody got to his feet and started walking in the direction of their house. Jake followed. "You think this isn't hard enough for me? You think I wanted this for myself?"

Jake sighed. He was right. Gideon's behavior was unforgivable. Still, this ranch was family property, and he couldn't help but hope they could all stay together in the end. But right now, this was about Cody's struggle. "When did you first know?" Jake asked.

"That I was gay? I've been denying it all my life. I can't remember a time I didn't prefer guys. Couldn't even get it up for a woman without thinking about..." he trailed off.

"About who?"

Cody shook his head. "Never mind."

"No, no. You have to tell me. Who?"

Cody stopped and rolled his eyes, looking at Jake in exasperation. "Brad Pitt's character in Thelma and Louise."

Jake burst into laughter.

"Shut up, asshole. I don't care how straight you are, he was hot in that movie."

Jake shook his head and fell back into step beside Cody. "No way. I've never thought a dude was hot."

"Never? Really?"

"Well...I mean, I can acknowledge that a guy's good looking or in good shape or whatever, but it's never turned me on."

"If you say so."

"Stop trying to make me question my sexuality."

"Why shouldn't you? Why shouldn't we all? Maybe we wouldn't have so many problems if we didn't draw so many hard lines about it."

They finished the walk home confessing to embarrassing crushes. Inside the house they found Ivy sitting on the end of the sofa. Boone was laying down, his head in her lap as she stroked his hair like a puppy.

The jealousy surged through him, but Jake didn't allow himself to react to it. He took a seat in one of the armchairs. Cody took the recliner. Ivy would only meet Cody's gaze, tentatively. She kept her head, low, in an uncharacteristic posture of humility. "We got Dallas put back in his room," she said. "He's sleeping."

"Thank you," Jake said.

Ivy gulped, her attention focused on stroking Boone's hair. After a long moment of silence, she looked up at Cody. "I feel like any apology will be completely inadequate. I don't deserve your friendship after that," she said. "Even as I was saying it, this voice in my head was screaming for me to stop."

Cody's head was bowed, too. He nodded in acknowledgment, but took some time to process. At last he leaned back in the recliner. "Honestly, I think it's for the best. I like to think I'd have had the guts to come out eventually, but this way I just have to face up to it. Don't get me wrong, that was a really shitty thing to do. But I forgive you."

Ivy's eyes welled with tears. "Thank you," she said, her voice faltering.

Now she turned to face Jake, and he almost couldn't breathe looking at her. He doubted he would see this side of her very often. This penitent, humble side. This vulnerable, shaken side. In fact, he hoped not to, but he was glad of it all the same. The barriers that keep two people from truly seeing each other always seem thinner in moments of vulnerability. For now, he felt he could see straight into her soul.

"Jake, I want you to know," she said, "I didn't know what Dallas was going to do. I knew he wanted out. He told me he'd get me an angle I could work to get you guys to sell. But I had no idea he'd do something this stupid and horrible."

"What's done is done, Ivy. I'm sorry you had to carry all that for so long."

"You don't seem angry at him."

"Oh, I'm angry. I'll deal with him when he's well. It's just, he almost died. At this point, my relief outweighs my anger."

Ivy smiled sadly and sweetly at him.

Jake looked at Boone whose eyes were open, staring at the ceiling. "So it's your turn. Talk."

Boone sighed. With apparent great effort, he sat up and swung his legs off the sofa. "I already told the sheriff everything. Right now they're investigating Richard for Molly's murder. But he told me not to leave town."

"We gave him our cell phones," Ivy said. "We can get them back tomorrow. He's getting all the texting history off of them. There may be an alibi for Boone on there and plenty of incriminating texts from Richard."

Jake nodded, taking in her meek, folded hands and downcast eyes. He turned back to Boone. "You were sleeping with the preacher's wife," he said, halfway hoping Boone would deny it.

"Yeah, man, I fucked up, okay? It was a thrill. Shit's so boring around here and I got a little high on the idea of being with a married woman."

Ivy looked away, her jaw setting.

"God damn you, Boone! Show some remorse!" Jake didn't make the conscious effort to stand—just one minute he was sitting, the next he was on his feet towering over his youngest brother.

Boone shocked him by jumping up, meeting him eye-to-eye. "Remorse? You've got no clue how this has felt! It's my fault she's dead. Mine. I didn't kill her, but I may as well have. And I've had her psycho husband scaring the shit out of me via cell phone all week, I can't even catch my breath long enough to grieve. I didn't love Molly, okay? But she meant something to me. I'd have defended her if I'd known she was in trouble. I'd never have wished this on her, and I do miss her, and I do feel so much guilt over this it makes me sick. This whole thing has been a nightmare."

Jake stepped back, sitting again. Boone collapsed onto the sofa and pressed the pads of his fingers against his eyes. "Why don't you go to bed," Jake said. "Get some rest."

"I need a drink." He climbed back up and stumbled into the kitchen.

Jake dropped his head back. After a few breaths, he realized all he wanted to do was wrap his arms around Ivy and spend a lazy afternoon in bed. He leaned forward and scrubbed his hands through his hair. "So what do you wanna do, Ivy? Stay here, or go back to your house?"

Her eyebrows shot up in surprise, though why she should be surprised was a mystery to Jake. All he knew was that that soft moment of a few minutes ago was over. The ire was coming back to her. "Tell you what, hoss. I'll go back to my house. And you stay here and think about what you've done."

"What *I've* done? What do you mean what I've done?"

"You stood there while your father yelled at me and you didn't do a damn thing. You still haven't taken me on a proper date or acknowledged me in public. You've provided no romance whatsoever. And you sit there and nonchalantly assume that I'm going to go to bed with you. There's no relationship, here, Jake. You gotta build that, and so far we've got two solid hookups and a little fooling around under our belts. Do better." With that, she stood and headed for the front door.

As it slammed behind her, Jake decided he wasn't going after her. Not right then. He was too exhausted. Too burned. "I suck," he moaned, leaning back into the sofa cushions again.

"At least," Cody replied.

"I don't know where she gets off saying I didn't give her romance, though. We spent Friday night together and I devoted my entire being to making her happy. I thought that was pretty romantic."

"I really don't want to know about that."

Jake sighed. "I guess it's right she makes me work for it. I'm just exhausted right now."

"I think we all need a little time to recover."

Jake found the prospect of going to bed alone too depressing, even though he'd never had Ivy in his bed. He crashed on the couch, Cody in his recliner, and the other two in their rooms. When they woke up, there would be a whole new world to adjust to.

Part 6: Everyone's Endings

Myra's Blog

There's nothing I hate worse than a domineering man. Many of you know about my second marriage. Theodore was an abusive drunk, and I'm ashamed to say I fell victim to his violence for more years than I care to admit.

Now I'm not saying Gideon Deathridge is abusive or a drunk, but I will say...you reap what you sow. It appears the Deathridges have endured a major falling out, and who should be at the center of it all, but little Ivy Turner. I have to say, I'm not shocked to find out that Ivy has been sleeping with Jake all this time. It was obvious from the start, if you ask me.

And I'm not too terribly shocked to find out Boone was having an affair with the pastor's wife. The boy was always a wolf in sheep's clothing.

Dallas's treachery, however, is not only shocking, but deeply disturbing. You need mental help, Dallas. I hope you get it.

The most entertaining bit to me, however, is the news that Cody plays for the other team. I hope you'll all join me in welcoming Cody to life outside the closet. We wish you the best. I'm sure many a female heart is grieving today.

Thursday afternoon, Cody drove into town, dropped by the bakery for some pastries, then by the country store for a couple decks of cards and some board games. After that, he went, uninvited and unannounced to the Turner house.

Jake was working his ass off on the ranch even as Gideon ignored his existence like a pouting child. Jake had managed to drag Boone out to work, claiming that it would keep his mind occupied, but when he'd tried to get Cody to go with him, Cody had gently, but firmly, told him to fuck off. He had a life to live and he was damn sure not going to live it under the auspice of a man like Gideon who ruled with an iron fist and withheld love for no good reason at all.

He pulled into the Turner's driveway around nine in the morning. When he knocked, he was surprised to see the door swing open and reveal a shirtless and bruised Jordan.

Jordan smiled sadly. "Hey, man. The Turners are out. Ivy's at work. Mr. Turner's with the cattle."

"Perfect," Cody said, smiling for the first time since before the Big Revelation, which is what they'd all taken to calling Ivy's outburst on Monday.

Jordan stepped aside, looking a little confused. "I heard what happened."

Cody ignored him as he kicked off his boots. He had a bag full of games in one hand and a box of pastries in the other. "Where are you hanging out?"

"Uh, upstairs. I just came down for coffee. I didn't think they'd want me roaming around."

"Psh. They're responsible for the condition you're in—"

"I don't think that's necessarily true—"

"—And I'm sure they mean for you to make yourself at home. Here, let's take the living room."

"I don't know if we should…"

Cody ignored him again as he moved into the living room. He sat the box and bag on the coffee table and pulled it closer to the sofa. Then he grabbed Jordan's hand and led him to the sofa, making sure there were enough cushions around him. "I should put on a shirt," Jordan murmured.

Cody snorted. He wasn't going to get lucky with the kid, not in the condition he was in, but more clothes was definitely not the direction he wanted to go. He headed to the kitchen. "Did you already get your coffee?" he shouted over his shoulder.

"I was microwaving some."

"Screw that. I'll make a fresh pot." It took him a moment to figure out the Turner's coffee pot, but once he did, he flipped it on and headed back to the living room, hopping over the back of the couch and landing next to Jordan.

"You seem…chipper," Jordan said.

Cody laughed. "Yeah, well, I'm temporarily without the weight of the world. No job, no judgmental asshole of a father, and a cute guy I'm hoping will be my friend. What do you say?"

Jordan's look was skeptical. "Are you okay?"

"Better than ever."

Jordan sighed, closing his eyes. "No, Cody. Are you okay?" When he opened his eyes again, Cody's bullshit euphoria vanished and he sank back into the neutral place he'd been the past few days. It was a sort of numbness as his anger fell away and he began to reassess his life and think about the possibilities for his future.

He met Jordan's gaze and nodded. "I am okay. I really am. I think Jake's right. Once the old man sees how much he's lost, he'll come around. But I don't think I can ever work for him again."

Jordan grinned. "The Turners are hiring."

"So I hear. Not sure I'd get much work done, though." He let his gaze wander down and back up again, enjoying the blush high on Jordan's cheekbones. "Right now I just came to play with you."

"Huh?"

Cody laughed. "Games." He pulled the cards out of his bag, as well as a Scrabble board and a Monopoly game. "Take your pick. I figure you must be bored. We can hang out while you get better. Get to know each other a little."

"That sounds really nice," Jordan said with a hesitant smile.

"Good. You get all better, I'll take you on a date. If you'll have me."

His smile widened. "I'll have you."

Cody leaned in and kissed him on his scratchy jaw. He lingered, nuzzling gently into Jordan's neck, aching for more, longing for so much more. And suddenly, he wasn't numb anymore. Suddenly, all the feelings surfaced at once. Cody left his face buried in Jordan's neck even as he squeezed his eyes shut and forced back the tears.

"Hey," Jordan whispered. "You can let go with me. I won't tell anyone."

Cody inhaled slowly, determined not to break down a second time this week. "You just smell so good," he said, trying not to choke on the words.

"So do you. Come on, talk to me."

Cody sat up and looked deeply into Jordan's eyes. And then they talked. They spent the rest of the afternoon sharing their stories, learning each other's challenges with being gay and dealing with friends and family. In between, they touched and kissed and cuddled. Talking to Jordan helped Cody get his feet back on the ground. He'd been off balance, floating around confused. But connecting with this boy who was so much more secure than him truly gave Cody the grounding he needed.

Late in the afternoon, Cody cleaned up the mess from the food and drink they took. He put the games away and helped Jordan up to his bedroom before saying goodbye.

It Took A Rumor

The real victim, as far as Ivy was concerned, was Clara. Maybe it was because she was a woman and therefore related to the woman in the story more than the men. But all poor Clara had ever done was love and serve, and what did she get in return? A bunch of ungrateful men walking all over her and completely disregarding her feelings. In fact, Ivy was so emotionally overextended about the situation that running into Myra was the last straw.

It was Friday morning and Ivy was in town running errands. She decided to drop by the flower shop and save the florist a trip. Mrs. Engle was behind the counter arranging a bouquet when Ivy walked in. "Are those for me?" she asked, exasperation in every syllable.

"As a matter of fact, they are. From…" Mrs. Engle made a show of looking at the card.

"I know who they're from," Ivy said with a sigh. "I don't suppose he wrote anything besides his name this time?"

"To Ivy. From Jake."

"He's a real charmer."

Mrs. Engle gave her a tight smile and handed her her flower arrangement. Ivy was unimpressed as she'd been receiving flowers from Jake all week. No words. Just flowers. What was she supposed to do with that?

When she turned to leave was when she ran into Myra who was on her rounds, gathering more gossip for her blog. Ivy stuck her nose in the air and proceeded to walk past the nosy old lady, but alas, it wasn't to be.

"Good morning, Ivy," Myra said, way too cheerfully. "I hear there's soon to be some important news regarding your future nuptials?"

"You would know better than me, I'm sure," Ivy answered blandly. "Excuse me." Once again she tried to leave.

"Ivy, dear, why are you being so rude? It's very unladylike."

Ivy spun on Myra. "Unladylike? Unladylike! You've spent the last three weeks slandering my name all over the internet making me out to be the whore of Fair Grove, Oklahoma, and you think calling me unladylike is going to make me want to talk to you? God you're such a bitch, Myra!"

Myra's jaw dropped and she fell back a step, her hand over her chest. "I have never been spoken to in such a manner. I swear, I don't know what this generation's coming to—"

"Oh, shove it up your ass!"

"Um, Ivy," said Mrs. Engle's meek voice, "would you mind watching your language in my store?"

"Fuck off, Caroline. You too, Myra." She started to walk away.

"I hope you know, this is going on my blog."

She spun back again. "What the hell difference does it make? If I don't do something worth talking about, you're just going to make something up, right?"

Myra smirked.

"Seriously, do you not care at all who you hurt? There are innocent people on the sidelines of this thing who just got shit all over because of you."

For a brief second, Myra's smirk faltered. "Gossip is a harmless enterprise with a longstanding tradition that goes back—"

"Whispering about how Mabel Hale uses a store-bought pie crust is harmless gossip. Telling a woman that her husband has been in love with someone else for their entire marriage…that's dirty and mean, Myra."

Her smirk at last vanished. "I never said that. I only insinuated it. I wasn't claiming it was true."

"Well it *was* true. Turns out, Gideon's been feuding with my father all this time over it."

Myra's heels clicked on the floor as she closed the distance between herself and Ivy. "Is Clara all right?"

"No, Clara isn't all right. Who the hell do you think you are asking that question?"

"Listen, I've got no love for Gideon Deathridge. I think he's a beast. But I never meant to hurt Clara. It was all meant in fun and if it ended up having some truth in it, well, I don't see how that's my fault."

Ivy rolled her eyes and turned toward the door.

"Wait!" Myra met her at the door. "I'd like to talk to her. Clear the air."

"So talk to her."

"Perhaps you could arrange a tea? After all, she's your future mother-in-law."

"Oh, for God's...listen, I am far, far away from being engaged to Jake Deathridge. He still hasn't even asked me on a date."

Myra's smirk returned. "We see the signs, dear," she said, taking a step back.

Ivy wanted to scream.

"So what about that tea? Perhaps at your house, this afternoon?"

"I don't see why you can't just go talk to her."

"I won't step foot on Gideon Deathridge's property. Besides, I doubt Clara would take my calls."

"Then why should I help you? I don't know if you've picked up on this, but I'm on Clara's side, not yours."

"You'll help for two reasons. First, because I want to make things right with Clara, and I think you believe me. Second, because if you don't, when you do start your wedding plans with Jake Deathridge, I will make up the most outlandish story possible as to why Jake is being forced to marry you. Maybe I'll say that the Deathridge ranch is bankrupt and he's marrying you for your money. Or maybe I'll say you're knocked up with one of his brother's babies and he's trying to salvage your honor. Or maybe—"

It Took A Rumor

"That's enough. Jesus, how come you couldn't just ask nicely. Three o'clock." With that, she left to finish her chores and call Clara.

She didn't tell Clara about Myra, which made it feel a little like an ambush. But Ivy promised herself that at the first sign of any bad behavior from Myra, she would jump up and carry the old lady out on her shoulder.

Ivy walked into her house to find two cowboys making out on the couch. It was a gentle make-out session, since one of them was healing from some cracked ribs and bruising, but it was enough to make her blush to her ears.

They both looked up when the door slammed. Jordan's eyes went wide. Cody simply grinned. Ivy let out her breath and laughed. "This what's been happening during the day while I'm at work?"

Cody nodded while Jordan shook his head. "I'm sorry, Ms. Turner," Jordan said.

Cody slapped him on the arm and stood. "Relax. She's gonna be my sister-in-law soon, at least according to the rumor mill. Ain't that right, Ivy?"

"It most certainly is not." Ivy dropped her purse next to the door and stormed into the kitchen. "And if one more person says that to me today, I'm going to hurt them. I'm going to hurt them bad." She slammed a kettle of water onto the stove. "You boys are going to have to do your canoodling someplace else, I'm fixing to have company over for tea."

"You want us out of the room, or out of the house?" Cody asked.

"Jordan can stay, but one of my guests is your momma, so you might not be in a very sexy mood knowing she's down here chatting with me."

The brief glance at Cody revealed a mildly disgusted expression. "Hey, J, you wanna go for a ride?" he said, making his way back to the living room.

They were gone by the time Ivy was setting cookies on a platter on the coffee table. Store bought cookies. Not the best way to make a good first impression on one's future mother-in-law.

"Damn it!" she shouted at her thoughts. Not a future mother-in-law. Not even close.

She had a half-dozen flower arrangements in her bedroom, so she retrieved a couple of them and set them in the living room. A pitcher of iced tea and a tray of fruit completed the impromptu layout.

Clara arrived five minutes past the arranged time. She wore a smile, but the emotional toll of the past week was apparent on her drawn, pale features. "Come on in," Ivy said, opening the screen door. She left the main door open to let a breeze blow through. It was August, but unseasonably cool.

"I'm so happy you called," Clara said. "I've been going stir-crazy. There's not much to do to keep my mind off…everything."

Ivy perched on the love seat which sat directly across the coffee table from the main sofa. Clara took the middle cushion and accepted a glass of iced tea. "Oohh, Lorna Doones, my favorite," Clara said, taking a cookie.

Ivy did a mental cheer even as her body sank with relief.

She immediately tensed up again, however, at the sound of tires on gravel.

"Is someone else coming?" Clara asked.

Ivy was spared answering as she rose to open the door. She made it about halfway before Myra swept in, not bothering to knock. "Ivy, dear, what a lovely spread," she said as she took the chair at the far end of the coffee table. "I don't suppose modern young women know how to bake a proper cookie these days. So sad. Another lost art." She took a cookie anyway and turned to Clara. "How are you, dear."

Ivy plopped down on the love seat, fighting the urge to curse at her second guest. She could make a damn cookie, it was hardly an art. She could make all kinds of cookies. It was unreasonable to expect someone to bake fresh pastries for a tea party arranged only the morning of...

Ivy forced herself to shut down her thoughts. They were fruitless, and besides, the focus had moved away from her inadequacy as a hostess and onto Clara's tension with Myra.

"I don't think you really care how I am," Clara said with uncharacteristic boldness.

"Of course I care. You must believe I never intended to hurt anyone. Well...I never intended to hurt you, at least."

"But you did, Myra. You go about spewing your poison without a care as to who gets hit by it. It's shameful, what you do."

Myra didn't exactly look penitent, but she did lean back in her chair and sigh. "In this case, perhaps you're right. In this case, I might have gone too far. Tell me, what is the status of your marriage?"

Ivy's jaw dropped at the boldness and audacity of the question. But then, this was Myra. Pretty silly to be surprised at anything that came out of Myra's mouth.

The true shocker was Clara's answer. "Same as ever," she said, sipping her tea. "Loveless and unfulfilling." She turned to Ivy. "I know you and Jake are having fun together, but I don't recommend the institution."

Ivy gaped at her, and then turned to gape at Myra who was laughing cheerfully. "I have three experiences with marriage, Clara, and for the most part, you're right on the money. Ed was a good man. Ed was good. Maybe if he'd lived longer things would have gone bad, but as it is, I have to write that marriage off as a success. The others, though..." she shivered and finished her cookie.

"I'm a rancher's wife," Clara said. "There's lots of work. I like the work, it keeps me from dwelling on the deficiencies. I feel I've failed with my boys, but then, how can I demand respect from them when I don't demand it from my husband. No, I see the failure of my marriage as my own failure. I love my boys, but I've done them a great disservice, and I fear I haven't prepared them properly for how to treat women of their own."

Ivy would spend time pondering this statement and eventually come to the conclusion that Jake and Cody, at least, were far more emotionally evolved than their father.

But for now, her head swung back and forth between Clara and Myra, as though watching an intense tennis match.

"Have you considered moving to town? Taking a job?" Myra asked.

Clara shook her head and chuckled. "That's ridiculous. A woman my age? I have no money of my own. No job experience."

"Bullshit," Myra said, the curse word sounding a bit like out of place on Myra's refined lips. "You've run a ranch for forty years, haven't you? You can type, do basic accounting, manage calendars, plan events."

"Well, yes, but that's hardly a resumé."

"It's precisely a resumé. Ethel at the paper is getting married in two weeks. They're looking for a new office manager right now."

Clara stared at her for a moment, her cheeks brightening a little. "No," she said, shaking her head at last. "They'll want someone younger."

"They might. But they'll hire you."

"Why?"

"Why? Because I have photo evidence of something Mr. Gladden will definitely not want his wife to see. He owns the newspaper, he'll make sure you get hired. If you're interested."

Clara was silent for another moment. "I…I'd have to think about it."

"Take the weekend. Have an answer for me on Monday."

Clara nodded. "It would be a tiresome commute in and out of town every day."

"So move to town. I've had the upstairs of my house closed up for years, it's just too much for me. Time to time I think about renting it out. You could have it, free of rent for the first month, then we'd negotiate something reasonable after you get a couple paychecks under your belt. What do you say, Clara? It's only life, but it's the only life you've got. And there's enough of it left to live it the way you want."

Clara sat her tea glass on the table, the ice rattling inside. She lifted a shaking hand to her lips, tears welling in her eyes. Slowly she curled into herself and sobbed. Myra was right there at her side, rubbing her back and hushing her. "There, there," she said, among other consoling nothings.

Ivy, probably a minute or two later than she should have, rose to go to the kitchen, giving the two older women some space. She washed a few dishes, brewed some more tea, and when she ran out of things to keep herself occupied, returned to the living room. Myra was back in her chair and the two women were laughing about something.

"Old times," Clara explained, offering Ivy an apologetic smile.

Ivy smiled in return, clearly the outsider in this little threesome.

But then, Clara grew more serious. "Ivy, I wonder if you and Jared have talked about the possibility of hiring my boys on?"

Ivy quickly switched into business mode. "Of course we have. Jake, Cody, and Boone would be welcome. My father is infinitely forgiving, but I don't see how I could find my way around to hiring Dallas. He crossed a line that, to me, is a deal breaker. Besides, he's been very clear about not wanting to work on a ranch anymore."

Clara nodded sadly. "Gideon's age is getting to him. He can't do the things he used to. I think the time will come, soon, that he'll have to sell. Perhaps we could give Dallas his share and he can go where he wants."

"That seems wise. He could easily be in prison for what he's done. But I don't suppose you want to go that direction?"

"Of course not. He didn't mean it to go as far as it did, he was just…ignorant."

"Then maybe you can help him find a direction that would give him more fulfillment. Like Myra's done for you today."

Clara smiled and nodded. "But you would hire Boone? He's lazy, you know."

"Is he?" Ivy said, laughing. "That's not a very good reference from his former employer."

"Well, he works when he's supervised. He just doesn't have any drive in him. No work ethic."

"We'll see how he feels, if he even wants to work with us. There's plenty of supervision around."

"And Cody? You don't have a problem with him being…being…?"

"Gay? Of course not. It's not a factor. How much time he spends during work hours making out with Jordan might be, but I'm sure if he wants to work with us, he'll save his social life for after work hours."

Clara squirmed. "This…Jordan…he's a good man?"

"I believe he is. He's a young man. Just turned twenty. Very sweet and hard working. I think you'll like him."

"I'd like to meet him," she said softly. "I'd like to talk to my boy and ask him how this came to be. What we did. What we could have done."

Ivy resisted the urge to preach at her. To inform her that this was simply who Cody was. To tell her the only thing she could have done differently was have different DNA. But she kept it to herself. "I think if you approach him, he'll talk to you. It's Gideon he's avoiding at the moment."

Clara nodded again. "And Jake. You'll marry him if he asks?"

Ivy's sense of decorum vanished, she slammed her glass on the table, and leapt to her feet. "The man hasn't so much as asked me on a date! How can we talk about marriage when I don't even know if he loves me. I haven't even had a chance to figure out if I love him. There's been no conversation…none…about a future like this! I have no idea what he even wants in a wife, let alone whether I want to agree to it."

"Ivy, dear, calm down," Myra said, blandly.

Ivy was pacing at this point. She closed her eyes and inhaled deeply, letting out the air, and repeating the process several more times before taking her seat again. Clara's eyes were wide, but her expression suggested amusement. "I'm sorry," Ivy said calmly at last. "I've been asked this question several times today and I'm clearly at my wit's end."

"I won't say another word," Clara said, and damned if the woman didn't look like she was suppressing laughter.

Ivy slumped in defeat as the two older women shared knowing looks. As though her destiny were already written in stone and the fact of her fighting it was the funniest thing on earth.

After they left, Ivy cleaned up and went to the office to finish out the work day.

It Took A Rumor

Clara sat down with Gideon and Jake at the kitchen table Saturday evening. The other boys hadn't come up for dinner that evening, which was just as well, because Clara hadn't cooked and the men had been forced to make themselves sandwiches. The kitchen was shiny and clean. No pots and pans on the stove. The only evidence of life, the two plates in the sink that Jake and Gideon had used for their meager dinner. Of course they hadn't washed them. Why would they? That's what Clara was for. Only she'd done her very last dishes in that house earlier that morning. They would just have to figure some things out on their own.

As Clara had moved about the house that day, she could hear the echo of her heels on the wood floors in the silence. It was just as well she'd made her decision. She'd die of heartbreak at the lack of noise—no boys bickering at the table, laughing at each other, talking about the ranch. Why would they ever come back after the way Gideon had treated them.

Of course, Jake had come back. Clara couldn't fully understand her oldest boy, except that he'd always been forgiving where Gideon was concerned. Always willing to submit to his father's authority. Still, it didn't seem like that was what was happening lately. The dynamic between father and son had shifted.

Gideon hadn't wanted to sit down with her. He claimed he didn't have time to deal with any female problems, if she wanted to buy new fabric for a quilt, she would just have to wait until they sold some cattle at auction next week. His easy dismissal of her made it that much easier to say what she wanted to say. Having Jake there made it harder.

"Something wrong, Mom?" Jake asked. He had brewed a pot of coffee and now sat across the table from her, next to Gideon, both of them freshly showered after a hard day's work. Jake's hair was still damp and tousled. His skin was bronzed from life outdoors, and he looked strong and content. Ivy was a lucky girl.

"I've got some things to say."

Gideon grunted and glanced at his watch. Clara figured there must be a baseball game on or something, and he was in a hurry to get to it. Too bad for him.

"I'm moving out."

Her words didn't immediately register. Jake was sipping his coffee, smiling at her, still waiting. Gideon was barely listening. But then Jake's smile faded. "Wait, what?"

"I'm moving out of this house and into town." The decision had cost her one night's sleep. Thirty-nine years of marriage sold down the river for the price of one night's sleep. She'd wept, fought, justified…but in the end, her eyes had been opened too far to go back. There would still be some grieving to do. Some accepting. But there was no doubt she was making the best decision for herself.

Jake was still frowning, his coffee cup caught in limbo between the table and his mouth. "For, like…how long?"

"Forever, baby."

Jake looked at his father, whose attention was now solely focused on Clara. His gaze was angry and annoyed. "What's gotten in your head, woman?" Gideon asked.

"I've lived in service to you most of my life, Gideon. I haven't asked anything in return because that's what love is. It's unconditional. No expectations. But you still had a responsibility. You can only walk on someone so long before they break or leave. I'm leaving before I break."

Gideon slammed his fists on the table. "What the hell is going on with you? You stop fixing dinner. Start dressing in those ridiculous shoes. What are you doing?"

"I'm leaving."

"Like hell you are! I done nothing but be a good husband and provider. Gave you four boys, didn't I? A roof over your head?"

"Pop, stop," Jake said quietly.

Gideon turned on his son. "I'll thank you to keep your nose in your own business."

"That's enough."

Gideon raised a hand to slap him, but Jake caught it in his powerful, young grip. Gideon's eyes went wide with rage while Jake's stayed cool, his grip on Gideon's wrist unrelenting.

Clara watched in awe, the silent power struggle. She watched as Jake came into his own and Gideon crumpled in defeat, pulling his arm back and rubbing his wrist. Jake said, "Maybe if you'd raised your voice and hand a little less and listened a little more, your wife wouldn't be walking out on you right now."

Gideon grumbled at him under his breath but didn't yell.

Jake turned back to Clara. "Is there anything I can do to get you to stay, Mom? You've been a rancher's wife all your life, I'd hate to see you give that up."

Clara laughed and then smiled adoringly at Jake. "You are such a sweet boy. You always loved this life and you'll likely love it until you die. But I was here for my family, nothing more. You boys are all grown up, you don't need me anymore—"

"That's not true."

"It is. You don't need me here all day every day wasting away and cooking your food. You can hire someone for that. And I won't be going far. I'll still be your momma who loves you. I just can't finish out my remaining years this way. You understand?"

Jake was clearly doing his best. His brow was furrowed with the effort to understand. He even nodded. "Yeah, I just…I wish I'd known you were unhappy."

It Took A Rumor

"I'm not sure how long I've been unhappy. It's snuck up on me. The self-pity, the feeling of being walked over…it's been gradual. But now that I see it, I can't live with it anymore. Gideon?"

Her husband frowned up at her, ten years added to his face. He grunted.

"Do you have any questions? Anything you want to say?"

His arms folded over his chest, he looked away. She was dead to him same as Cody and Dallas. And she didn't have Jake's strength or the will to do like Jake and dominate the situation. She didn't want to.

"Do you have a plan?" Jake asked at last.

"I do, in fact. I'll be working as an office manager at the newspaper. And I'm going to rent Myra's guest room."

"Myra? As in Myra the Mouth?" Jake asked, all composure lost. "How could…why would…?"

"She offered. I think she understands where I am and what I'm going through. You'll see someday, when you get to a certain age, age alone can be enough of a common factor to unite two people. Plus, she's been married three times. She can help me through this."

Jake sat back and shoved his hands through his hair, clearly baffled by the whole thing. "Okay," he said slowly, almost as a question.

"It's the right thing for me," Clara assured him.

He nodded blankly. Gideon got up and left out the back door. She'd try to talk to him again later, once he'd had time to process everything. There would be things to say to each other. Goodbyes that wouldn't be as easy as she wished. But for now, she let him go.

Jake sat in silence, clearly stunned.

"Son?"

His eyes focused on hers. "Yeah?"

"I want you to take this ranch from him."

Instead of surprise, what she got was a hardening of the lines in his face. He nodded. Clara had expected him to react in surprise or question her, but her boy was wiser than she'd given him credit for. "He'll lose it if I don't," Jake said. "Cody ain't coming back. I wouldn't want Dallas to come back. Boone will work, he's got nothing else going. But still, the workload's gotten heavier and without you, someone's going to have to manage the money."

"Your future wife perhaps?" Clara couldn't help asking.

Jake's lips started to turn up. "My future business partner. Not sure she's gonna wanna marry me. Not sure I want her to end up like…" he stopped.

Clara sighed. "Oh, honey, she won't. She's nothing like me. She's like her mother who would never have let herself be used up like this. It's why I like her so much. She's good for you."

Jake got a faraway look in his eye as he nodded. "She is good for me. I hope I'll be good for her."

"You will be, I have no doubt. Perhaps you've learned something here? Perhaps seeing what you've seen the past few weeks will help you in the future?"

He met her gaze again and nodded. "Yeah. I think so."

They ended on a hug and with Jake taking charge of the plans for packing and moving her things.

Jake found his father at the woodpile splitting logs. It was where Jake would have gone if he'd just found out his wife of forty years was leaving him. Hard work helped you sweat out the bad feelings.

Gideon didn't acknowledge Jake's arrival. He just hefted the ax, swung it over his shoulder, and slammed it into a split log. He was old, older than his years, and his body was weakening, but there was still power in his muscles.

Jake leaned against a nearby fence post and folded his arms over his chest. The afternoon was balmy with a warm breeze and a sky full of cumulus clouds floating by. "Did you see it coming?" Jake asked.

Gideon didn't answer. He leveraged the ax out of the log, swung again, and split it completely this time.

There wasn't any point trying to get Gideon to talk about his feelings. Hell, he probably didn't even have feelings. So Jake went straight to business. "We're gonna need a cook. I don't know the first thing about cooking, and neither do you. The Gleasons got that daughter, Angie, she's seventeen. She might work for the summer until we find someone more permanent."

Gideon placed another hunk of wood on the stand and swung his ax again.

"And we're gonna need someone to manage the bookkeeping. Might have to hire someone from the accounting firm where Joann Richie works. It'll be an extra expense, though. Then we've got Cody leaving, so there's pros and cons to that. Reduces our expenses. But increases our work load. I'd like to try and see if we can do without him before we go hiring another hand."

Gideon slammed his ax into the dirt and spun around, his face twisted in rage and pain. "My wife just left me!"

Jake's teeth tightened together.

Gideon's mouth shifted, his eyes softened, and his shoulders dropped. "My wife just left me," he said, more softly this time.

Jake looked down at the ground. There was any number of ways he could respond. He could offer condolence. He could explain to the old man that this was his own doing. He could even go ahead and abandon ship right along with his momma, and don't think it wasn't a temptation.

But instead, he remained silent and waited.

Gideon sank onto the chopping block, his forearms resting on his knees. "I just don't understand it. She ain't never complained."

Jake thought about Ivy and her big mouth. He'd never have to read her mind. He had no doubt she'd be making her needs clear up until the very end.

"I don't know what I'm gonna do," Gideon continued. "You lie next to a woman every night for forty years, you kind of count on her being there."

Jake smiled sadly. "Maybe you can win her back."

"With what? If all this wasn't enough for her, I'm not sure I got anything left to give."

"You're looking at it the wrong way, Pop. You didn't give all this to her. She gave all this to you. Your ranch, your boys, your life…she did that. You owe her, and you didn't pay. Now she's going to take care of herself."

Gideon didn't lash out. He didn't say anything for a long time. The crickets started piping up, preparing for the arrival of night. Jake needed to get home and address his brothers. He was ashamed to admit it to himself, but he kind of couldn't wait to see their faces when he told them their mom was leaving their dad.

"Son?"

Jake looked up. "Yeah?"

"You love the ranch, right?"

"Yes, sir," Jake said.

Gideon didn't smile, exactly, but he softened a little. "I'd hate to think I worked so hard for nothing. I always took pride in being able to leave something valuable to you boys."

"You should take pride in it. You'll see your grandchildren run around on this land one day. You've earned that."

"Have I? I'm not so sure."

Jake sighed. He stepped forward and gave Gideon's shoulder a squeeze. "It's never too late to make amends, Pop. Never too late to change."

Gideon sighed. "These grandchildren...they ain't gonna have Turner blood in them, are they?"

"Almost certainly. I don't see me and Ivy dating very long. I already know she's the girl I wanna marry, and I'm pretty sure it won't take much convincing for her."

Gideon lowered his head. "I don't like it."

"You'll get used to it."

"She ain't a proper rancher's wife."

"Maybe not by your standards, but I like her just fine. You think you can be polite to her from now on? For me?"

Gideon nodded grudgingly.

"I'd appreciate that, Pop."

With that, he turned and headed home.

Jake waited all week for Dallas to get back on his feet. When he got home that evening, he met him in the hallway, Dallas on the way to the fridge for a beer Saturday night.

"Feeling better?" Jake asked.

"Yeah," Dallas said, shuffling first to the right, then the left, looking for a way around Jake. "Lots. I appreciate you all taking care of—"

Jake punched him in the face, hard. He shook his hand, wincing at the pain in his jarred knuckles. Dallas stumbled backwards. Jake caught him by the front of his shirt and slammed him against the wall.

"You almost killed yourself," Jake growled. "You almost killed my horse. You did kill eight of our cows and made another two dozen sick. You're lucky we don't put you down, son."

Dallas had tears pooling in his eyes from the hit, his cheek bright red. "I'm so sorry," he said weakly. "I thought I'd maybe make the cattle sick enough to slow down production, cost Dad enough money that he'd have to think about selling to the Turners."

"You just about did it. That vet bill's like a second mortgage."

"I'm so sorry. I didn't mean to hurt Eloise. Or you, Jake. I was just thinking about getting out. I hate this place. I hate this work. And I hate…"

He didn't have to say it. Jake knew who he hated. He released his brother and stepped back. "Come on into the living room. I gotta talk to you guys about some things. I'll grab you a beer." Jake headed to the kitchen and took a six-pack out of the fridge. His brothers all sat in various postures in the living room—Cody in his recliner, Boone and Dallas on the couch. Jake handed them all beers, muted the television, and took the other recliner.

"Mom's leaving Dad," Jake said.

"What?" all three of his brother's said in unison.

He explained to them the situation and then waited as they all sat in shock. He could certainly relate to the feeling. It was his own fault for not crediting her with any depth of feeling. Just because he never saw her cry didn't mean she didn't do it in private. Just because she served them quietly and diligently didn't mean she liked it. And the more he looked back on his relationship with her, the more he realized how much he'd taken her for granted, how little gratitude he'd shown, and just how poorly he understood who she was as a person. Jake wouldn't make that mistake again. Not with anyone.

Cody was the first to speak. "Well," he said slowly, "good for her."

Boone and Dallas nodded and murmured their agreement. It was about like Jake had expected. Their mom had always been a fixture in their lives rather than a dynamic actor in her own story. This decision of hers opened all their eyes to the fact that she was a person with needs and wants.

"So I want to ask you guys what your plans are," Jake said. "I don't expect any of you to stay on—"

"We couldn't if we wanted to," Cody said. "We've been disowned."

"Yeah, well, I'm in charge now. He's not going to disown you. He's going to do what I tell him. So I want to talk about your futures and the future of this ranch. I need to know what you all want and where you're going before I can make any decisions."

He waited, watching his brother's expressions. Boone spoke up. "I've thought a lot about what I want this week," Boone said. "Honestly, I've just been screwing off, not really thinking about the future. But…now that I think about it, I realize there's really nowhere I wanna go. Nothing I wanna do."

"You ready to get your ass in gear and work like a man?" Jake asked.

Boone nodded. "Yeah. I am. If I can stay on, I'd like to. Assuming the sheriff don't decide to arrest me for murder."

Jake leaned back, not amused. Still, one down. He looked at Dallas whose head hung low. "All I know is I want out," Dallas said.

"Okay. What's your plan?"

Dallas looked up in despair. "I don't have one. I just know I'm not cut out for this."

"I can't work with that. You need to figure out what it is you do want, then we'll see if we can help you get started. Give you a financial boost. But I don't know what that looks like until you tell me what you want."

"I know, Jake, but...but I just don't...I don't know what I want."

Jake blew out a breath. "Take some time. Figure it out. But don't think you can sit around here forever feeling sorry for yourself. Next week you'll come back out and work with us. You'll work here until you decide where you wanna go and what you wanna do."

Dallas nodded. "Okay. Thanks, Jake."

Now it was Cody's turn. "What about you?" Jake asked.

Cody chuckled. "I'm going to work for the Turners. Talked to Ivy about it this morning. But I was hoping I could keep living here?"

"Absolutely," Jake said.

"If things get serious with Jordan, he and I might get an apartment together or something. But that's a little ways off."

Jake relaxed. "Okay. So you've for sure got work?"

Cody nodded.

"Then you'll get your share of the profits, if there are any, from this year. But after that you're out. Right?"

"Right," Cody said, smiling. "I'll even start paying rent if you want."

"No, way. This place is just a bunkhouse, basically. You can even move the boyfriend in here for all I care. I'm gonna build a house for me and Ivy over on that hill that looks out over the big pond…you know the one?"

Cody laughed. "You're going to build a house for you and Ivy? Is she aware of this?"

Jake shrugged, trying to show more confidence and nonchalance than he felt.

"Man, you'd better have a conversation with her. She's not happy with the flowers."

Jake frowned. "What? She said be romantic. Flowers are romantic."

"She doesn't know what they mean."

"They mean I like her. What the hell else would they mean?"

"Yeah, Jake, I don't think it's enough."

Boone laughed suddenly. "You're so pathetic. Girls like to talk. Whatever you think you're feeling for her, when you say it, you gotta exaggerate it by a factor of ten."

"I'm not taking advice from you, Boone, no offense," Jake said. "I was just trying to butter her up before I made my move. Draw out the anticipation. But if it's just pissing her off, then I'll accelerate my plans." Truth be told, he was a little resentful of the things she'd said to him. He knew in his head that the most successful way to maintain a relationship was to assume that the woman was right and he was wrong. But her words rang in his ears: *There's no relationship, here, Jake. You gotta build that, and so far we've got two solid hookups and a little fooling around under our belts.*

That simply wasn't true. Shouldn't he call her on that? Shouldn't he demand that she acknowledge that what they had was more than a couple of hookups?

He went to bed that night thinking of her. Thinking of how he wanted to approach her. Analyzing the parts of her speech that were righteous and the parts that were flawed. In the end, it all boiled down to the fact that he wanted to be with her, no matter what. He'd have thrown pebbles at her window again if he thought he'd get a good reception. But Ivy was ready to quit screwing around and get serious. So he would have to wait until morning.

It felt so strange, getting dressed for church. Going through the same routine as always even though the world around her had experienced some drastic changes. Still, Ivy prepared coffee. She sliced a grapefruit and toasted some bread, setting two places at the table. When her father came down, he was dressed in his Sunday best the same as always. They sat across from each other and smiled stiffly.

"Who do you think will preach?" Ivy asked.

Jared shrugged, giving his austere breakfast a woeful look before digging in. "I suppose Lyle, since he was assistant pastor. Maybe they'll just start paying him, save the stress of going through a hiring process."

Ivy hoped not. Lyle had a bland personality and a monotone voice. "It feels weird. I mean, just last week Richard was our pastor. Now he's the man who might have murdered his wife. Biggest thing that's happened in Fair Grove in ages."

Jared nodded.

Ivy ate, not tasting her food. She'd spent a lot of time that week crying. A lot of time being angry. A lot of time wishing and hoping for things that didn't seem likely to happen. Today would be a day to rest.

There was a knock at the front door, and Ivy rose to answer it. Jake stood there, dressed in jeans and a blue button-down, no hat. Of course, she could give him his hat, but she didn't want to. "What are you doing here?" she asked.

"Ma'am, I came to ask your Pa if I can escort you to Sunday service," he said, deepening the drawl in his voice.

Ivy found herself ready with a smile. She pushed the screen door open, and stepped aside, letting Jake continue with his act.

Jake led the way into the kitchen and took a seat at the table.

"Jake," Jared said in greeting.

"Mr. Turner," Jake replied. "Mind if I take Ivy to church this morning?"

"Do you intend to sit by her?" Jared asked.

"Yes, sir."

"Do you intend to stand up for her in the face of your father's disapproval?"

"Yes, sir, but that won't be a problem anymore. I've taken care of it."

Jared's eyebrows went up. "Oh?"

"Yes. Gideon will be polite to my…to Ivy. He won't cause any more trouble."

Jared met Ivy's gaze, eyes wide with approval. "Well, son, in that case, you may take her to church if she wants to go with you."

Ivy was still standing at the foot of the table behind her chair when Jake turned his questioning gaze her way. "May I take you to church, Ivy? In public for the whole world to see?"

She couldn't stop the gleeful grin and the swell of girlish excitement. She dashed upstairs to her room, grabbing Jake's hat off the pillow on her bed. She picked some flowers from the arrangements that matched the yellow sundress she was wearing. After arranging them, she tied them with a yellow ribbon around the band and positioned the hat on her head.

Jake met her at the front door, smiling and holding out his hand, which she took. He helped her into his truck, and as they bounced down the gravel road, Jake kept looking at her. "That dress, Ivy," he said.

"What about it?"

"You wore that on purpose."

"I did not. I didn't know you were coming to pick me up."

"You knew you'd see me at church."

She laughed. "I swear. It's just a dress I wear a lot. I wasn't thinking…"

"You were thinking in the diner that day, though, weren't you?"

Ivy felt herself blush. "That was a business meeting."

"Come on. Give me that much. Admit you wore it on purpose."

Ivy smiled at him, finding it simultaneously fun to string him along and impossible to refuse him what he wanted. "Fine. I wore it on purpose."

He laughed. "Knew it. You're trouble."

They pulled off the gravel county road and onto pavement, the ride becoming much smoother. Jake was quiet, but a few glances at his face revealed contentment. It was easy to relax next to him.

"Mom's leaving Dad," he said abruptly.

Ivy took in a breath. "How do you feel about that?"

He shrugged. "A little sad. But mostly happy for her. Kind of makes me question everything I believed about marriage."

Ivy realized she was twisting the seatbelt in her hands. She forced herself to let go and smooth her hands over her skirt. "Like what?"

"Like…I always thought I'd find me a woman who could cook and clean and garden and manage books. I'd make sure she was tall, like at least five-ten, and had a lot of brothers so there'd be more chance of her giving me sons. And while she was bearing my sons, I could hire her brothers to help me with the ranch. That's kind of the plan I had in my head. Never really occurred to me to think about whether a woman would want to do all that for me. At this point, I don't think *I* want a woman doing that for me."

Ivy was suppressing a smile. At five-four and an only child, she definitely didn't fit the bill. "What do you think, now?" she asked.

"I think you're trying not to laugh at me."

A laugh escaped, then. Jake reached over and brushed the backs of his knuckles down her neck.

"I think that's the wrong way to go about finding a wife," Jake said. "I think when you fall in love, you don't start looking for if she can fit your expectations. You spend time getting to know who she is and what she wants and how your two lives might be able to fit together. What do you think about that?"

She thought that there wasn't enough time left on this short drive and her heart was pounding too hard for her to speak. "I think that's...wise."

"Wanna pull over and work off some of this nervous energy?"

The abrupt change of subject had her laughing again. "God, Jake. I would love to, but I can't show up in church looking like what I'd look like."

"I won't mess you up too much."

She looked at him, seriously considering his proposition. He was grinning, watching the road, his head bobbing with the dips and bumps in the highway. What would he say if she told him to pull over?

Unfortunately—or maybe fortunately—they reached the parking lot of the church before she could make her decision. Jake's expression turned to a frown. "Damn. Record attendance today."

Ivy temporarily forgot her feelings in the wake of a surge of disgust. "This is why Myra's stupid blog is so successful. People eat up the drama."

It Took A Rumor

Jake had to park on the side of the road since the parking lot was full. But before he got out, he turned and took her hand. "Now I wanna say something to you."

She gazed into his dark eyes, trying not to smile. "Okay."

"You and I didn't get off on the right foot, and I acted like a jerk several times, I fully understand that. But you told me there was no relationship here. You said all we had were hookups. Now, you can't possibly have meant that. Did you?"

She gulped, a wad of emotions stopping up her throat, and shook her head.

"Good. Because last week, you and I were partners through some tough situations. We were at each other's sides. We had good conversation, good cooperation, and good lovemaking. That's a hell of a lot more than hookups. That's the beginning of something that can last forever. Don't you think?"

She nodded, tried to breathe, ended up gasping, and threw her arms around his neck. "I'm sorry," she squeaked. "I didn't mean it. I was just angry."

"Well, I was stupid. You had a right to be angry."

She shook her head to disagree, but before she could, he took her mouth with his own, kissing her deeply and calming her in the process. His hands trailed up her arms and neck and cupped her jaw. She gripped his forearms, feeling their strength and gentility. When their lips finally parted, she opened her eyes. His were still shut, his brow furrowed as if in pain.

"What's wrong?" she whispered.

He opened his eyes. "Nothing. Everything's right. It's just a lot. I feel a lot for you right now."

"Oh, Jake."

He smiled, kissed her again, more lightly this time, and hopped out of the truck. Ivy got out on his side, and they held hands as they walked toward the church building.

Boone met them outside, just a few steps from the door. "Sheriff called me in this morning. They're charging the pastor with murder. Found a baseball bat with your blood on it, Ivy. Found other evidence, too."

Ivy closed her eyes, pity warring with relief. "It's so horrible, but I'm really relieved for you, Boone."

"Yeah. Me, too. I feel guilty about it, but relieved. I know for a fact I'm going to hell for what I did to Molly and her husband, but I'm sure glad not to be going to jail."

Ivy and Jake followed Boone into the church building. He veered left to sit with his mom and Dallas.

The atmosphere had changed from prior weeks. It was partially due to all the nosy nellies crammed in the church hoping for more drama. That would pass. The people would fade back into their lives, not to be heard from again until the next big drama. But after they left,

Ivy knew that some changes remained permanent. Like the fact that Jake's dad wasn't there.

Clara sat in their regular pew with Boone and Dallas. No sign of Cody, even though Jordan was with the other ranch hands, songbook in his lap at the ready.

"Where do you want to sit?" Ivy asked.

"I'll sit with you. Wouldn't want to make your old man sit all by himself."

So with a big smile, she slid in next to her father, sandwiched between what was quickly becoming her new understanding of family. Jake slid his arm around her shoulders, something her father would likely never do again at church, having handed that particular torch to his future son-in-law.

Because that was what Jake was. Ivy knew that whether they married or not, however they chose to manage their respective businesses, whether merging them or keeping them separate, for all intents and purposes, Jake was her man. Forever.

The choir director started the song service and everyone who was able stood to sing. Ivy felt dwarfed by the heights of the two men on either side of her, but she felt oddly powerful, too. Being loved so fully by two such strong men...it was very empowering.

After the singing, everyone sat and Lyle, the assistant pastor, stood to give a sermon. He thanked everyone for coming and said absolutely nothing about the pastor's scandal, much to the disappointment of eager ears in the audience, Ivy was sure.

After the sermon and another song, Lyle invited announcements and prayer requests. Ivy jumped at the movement to her right as Jake stood and moved to the front, standing on the floor in front of the podium. He ducked his head and started to reach up, almost as if to remove the hat he wasn't wearing. He flashed Ivy a quick grin before saying,

"My family and I wanna thank all of you for the cards and flowers when Dallas was in the hospital. He's here this morning, doing much better."

There were murmurs of "amen" and "praise God."

Jake cleared his throat. "I also want to ask prayers for my mom. She's starting a new life for herself, one she deserves very much."

Ivy saw Clara dab at her eyes with a handkerchief.

Jake frowned at the floor for a moment, apparently thinking about what he would say next. When he looked up, he said, "I don't wanna pretend like we don't all know why we're here today. I ain't gonna pretend like you don't know all about my family's business…the lovely Myra Tidwell sees to it on a regular basis that we all know everything that goes on in each other's lives, even some things that aren't going on." He nodded with a mischievous smile to Myra who returned his looking with a wave of her hand and a bow of her head, queen of her domain.

"So…I ain't a preacher," Jake said glancing back at Lyle, "but I hope we'll all think about how our decisions affect others. My baby brother made some choices that had dire consequences and he's gotta live with that for the rest of his life. A woman's dead and a man's in jail…that's what you all came here for isn't it? You wanna see what will happen next?

"Here's what's gonna happen. We're gonna go back to our jobs tomorrow. We're gonna talk and speculate about Molly Allen's murder and Richard Allen's guilt until we get tired of the subject. We're gonna internalize it and make it personal. We're gonna write ourselves into the story, giving ourselves the biggest role we can realistically manage. Then we're gonna get sick of hearing each other talk about it and it's gonna fade into the background.

"But the fact is, for some people, this will never fade away. For some people, Molly's murder was real. Richard will be living with it forever. Boone will. Dallas, he's gonna have to live with the consequences of his actions…for the rest of us it's just a story. For Myra, these are just stories. Just entertainment. So, I guess I just ask, for just this one moment, that we all take a second to understand that our entertainment is someone else's personal tragedy."

The room was quiet. Some heads lowered in shame. Others raised in defiance. Everyone was guilty of what Jake was describing.

He let out a breath. "Anyway, I know in this community that when push comes to shove, we step up and help each other out. And I also know it's somehow built into us to get a thrill out of learning other people's secrets. Who didn't get a kick out of learning that Miss Louisa used to be a cabaret dancer?"

There was low laughter. Louisa, a spunky woman older than dirt, grinned and blushed.

"Or that Mr. Andrew Philbert's magical secret barbecue sauce is really just the off-brand he buys in bulk at Costco."

"Now that's a flat-out lie!" Andrew shouted, eliciting laughter from the crowd.

Jake grinned and shook his head. "I guess, overall, this past couple of weeks the gossip's hit too close to home. It's gotten a little dark. A little too harmful. And I hope we'll all keep that in mind in the future."

He started to walk away when Myra stood, phone in hand, camera on. "I notice you're willing to address everyone else's business, yet you conveniently avoid anything to do with you."

Jake looked at her. "I think you kind of missed the point, Ms. Tidwell."

"Oh, I got your point just fine, young man. But I've been on this earth a good deal longer than you. I'll make right my wrongs, but don't think your little speech is going to stop me doing what I do best. Now, do you care to clear the air about you and Ivy Turner?"

Ivy's face flushed. God, Myra was ruthless. Right in front of the whole church, too. Surely Jake would put her in her place.

He hung his head, but when he looked up, instead of an angry frown, he was fighting back a smile. "Ivy Turner and I will be mixing business with pleasure. A lot. In the near future. So any rumors you hear on that front are probably true." With that, he winked at Myra, and came back to his seat, sliding his arm over Ivy's shoulders and bringing her against him.

She stared at him in shock until she started laughing. She had to bury her face in his chest to keep quiet as the final prayer was said.

Epilogue

Myra's Blog

Far be it from me to speculate on anyone's motivations. But it seems to me the engagement of Jake Deathridge and Ivy Turner happened fairly suddenly. And then to run off for a weekend and show up married the following Monday? Something doesn't sit quite right. I'm sure you all will agree with me that there are only a few reasons to logically explain an elopement of this sort. Please vote in the poll below. I'm sure you know where I land on the subject. Ivy was no bride in white, after all, and she has been wearing a lot of loose-fitting tops lately. If you know what I mean.

Jake stood on the hill overlooking the lake as the last of the framework was erected for his house. But he wasn't watching the house, he was watching his phone. Ivy had indeed been wearing looser clothes, lately. In fact, though she still looked hot as hell, if he was being honest, she was becoming slightly squishy around the middle.

"Oh, shit," he said.

"What is it?" Cody asked, sauntering toward him.

Jake showed him Myra's video. Cody watched, then rolled his eyes and handed Jake back his phone. "Are you kidding? She's just making shit up."

"Yeah, sure. But, Ivy did complain about some nausea the other day."

Cody's eyes went wide. "Oh, my God. Are you serious? Well, that confirms it. Congrats, Pops."

Jake punched him in the chest. "Don't let these guys knock off before five," he said, "I'm going to talk to her."

"Sure, boss," Cody said, rubbing his chest.

Jake climbed on Eloise, situated the hat he was still breaking in on his head, and rode to Ivy's office. The trailer was situated about as far as it could get from where Jake was building his and Ivy's new house. The ride seemed to take forever.

But at last he arrived at the trailer, hoping Edna was gone for the day. She wasn't. She was at the front desk, smiling sweetly at him.

"She's on the phone," Edna said, which was silly, because Jake could clearly see off to his left that Ivy was at her desk on the phone. But he thanked Edna anyway.

He mouthed, *I need to talk to you,* to Ivy. She nodded and held up a finger. He turned and stepped outside, stroking Eloise as he waited for Ivy to join him in the gravel lot outside the trailer.

She stepped out, threw her arms around his neck, and nipped at his ear, making him almost giggle. "I want you," she whispered. "Right. Now."

For a split second, he was turned all the way on. But it vanished when he remembered hearing some women talk about increased libido being a symptom of pregnancy.

He stepped back and held her at arm's length. "Did you see Myra's blog today?"

"No. I swore off it, you know that. What'd she say to get you so upset?"

Jake swallowed and looked her body over. She hadn't worn the prissy business clothes he'd first met her in, not since they'd started dating. She'd taken to dressing more like a cowgirl, no longer fighting herself and her environment. Jake took in her jeans and the loose-fitting blouse that hung mid-thigh on her. "She commented on your clothing."

Ivy looked down. "Mine? What's wrong with my clothes?"

"She just mentioned that you've been wearing a lot of stuff that fits kind of...loose. Since we got married." He looked at her, hoping she'd figure it out without him having to say it outright.

Instead, she just frowned at him. "So? What's that got to do with anything?"

Jake cleared his throat, sensing he was moving out to where the ice was much thinner. "She commented on how quickly and quietly we got married. She's got people voting on why that is."

Ivy's expression went cold, and she dropped her arms to her sides. "Are you asking what I think you're asking? Based on gossip?"

Jake shrugged, helpless. He needed to know. "I mean, there have been changes."

Her arms folded over her chest and an eyebrow cocked up. Not a good sign. "Changes? Do tell."

"I mean, you were feeling kind of sick the other day."

She nodded, gesturing for him to continue.

"You've been really," he lowered his voice and glanced around, "horny, lately."

Her jaw dropped at this.

For some reason he couldn't comprehend, he opened his mouth and said, "And your jeans have been fitting a little tighter."

"Oh, my God! You are an idiot, you know that?"

He slumped. "Yeah, I know," he muttered.

"I'm getting fat? Is that what you're telling me?"

"No, not at all. You're not getting fat, you look great. Amazing even. It's just, I've noticed the change—"

"You think you haven't put on weight, Jake?" she grabbed his shirt, lifting it before he could stop her. "Where's that six-pack, huh? I used to could trace the ridges every time you exhaled. Where is it now?"

He grabbed his shirt and shoved it back down. "It's hidden under all those cookies you make for me, that's where."

"And?"

"And all the big breakfasts and lunches and dinners. The pancakes and the chicken and dumplings and the turkey sandwiches, and…you're an amazing cook, Ivy!" he shouted at her accusingly.

"Thank you!" she shouted back. "But surprise, I eat, too. We got married, we spend a lot of time in bed, and we've packed on a few pounds. So sue me. And I was sick the other night because you made me eat that very questionable Mexican food leftover in your fridge. And as for my being…horny…I'm sorry if I can't get enough of you, okay? I love you, you stupid ass. I love your body, I love being with you."

"I love you, too! I wish we could stay naked together all the time!"

"Me, too!"

They ran out of words and breath. And then he looked up at the sky and laughed. "Shit."

After a long moment, she finally exhaled. "I'm not pregnant. I'm just chubby."

"You're not chubby. You look incredible."

"Shut up. The damage is done and I'm going on a diet as of right now."

He swooped his arm around her waist and pulled her in, looking down into her eyes. "I'm sorry. I saw Myra's video and I just freaked. It was stupid. You're right, I'm an idiot."

She nodded in agreement. "Can I ask you something?"

"Anything." He pushed her hair back and brushed his lips along her cheekbone.

Her breath grew a little airy. "Were you excited or disappointed at the prospect of a baby?"

He kissed beneath her ear. "Neither. Just shocked."

"Because we talked about it."

He pulled back and looked into her eyes. "Just you and me for two years. Then we can talk about it. I remember. No worries, Ivy."

She smiled sweetly, and he kissed her.

"Now," he said, pulling her toward Eloise, "let's go down by the creek and take care of your needs. Can't have a wife of mine left unsatisfied."

It Took A Rumor

He climbed up and pulled her on behind him. She wrapped her arms around his waist, and they rode toward the sunset.

The End

Acknowledgments

I've always felt like inspiration for creativity comes from somewhere outside myself. Like there's some kind of pool of stories that we all have access to if we'll only tap into it. So first and foremost, thanks to whatever higher power or muse I'm feeding off of to enjoy this creative life.

Writing is an evolving skill. When I started out, it was a very solitary pursuit. As I grow, I'm finding it to be more and more social. Thanks to my local critique group, Amy D., Amy E., Debra, Rexanna, and Robin for your support and your practical, insightful criticisms. You've all opened new avenues of information and inspiration to me, as well. Plus you're just a hoot to be around.

Thanks to everyone who beta read for me: Becky, LB Dunbar, Alexis Noelle, Jessica Hawkins, and the aforementioned critique group. You've each left your marks on this book, so I hope it's something you can be proud of.

Thank you, Cassy Roop, for being a badass cover designer and a really cool person.

Thanks to the ladies in Author BFF's and to Lia Fairchild for founding that group. I honestly can't envision my existence as an author without you all.

Thank you, Joe, for your financial support and for believing in me relentlessly and seemingly without reason.

And most importantly, thank you to my three kids for putting up with my scatterbrained behavior and the occasional cereal-for-dinner night. You're the best part of my life and I hope you'll one day be proud of me, just as I am of you.

About The Author

Carter Ashby is a city girl at heart, but a country girl by birth. Her two great passions are motherhood and writing. When not involved in these things, you might find her reading, baking bread, meditating over a pot of tea. Connecting with readers is one of the primary joys of authorship. You can find Carter at www.carterashby.com, or on Facebook, Twitter, Pinterest, or Instagram.

Did you like this story? Here are more books by Carter:

Not A Chance
Without You Here

<u>The Big Girl Panties Trilogy</u>
Zoey and the Nice Guy
Maya and the Tough Guy
Addy and the Smart Guy

<u>The Fidelity Series</u>
The Closer You Get
Play It Again (coming soon)

<<<◇>>>